HOW TO SAY
GOODBYE
IN ROBOT

NATALIE STANDIFORD

SCHOLASTIC PRESS
NEW YORK

HOW TO SAY

GOODBYE

IN ROBOT

Library of Congress Cataloging-in-Publication Data available

ISBN-13: 978-0-545-10708-2
ISBN-10: 0-545-10708-3

10 9 8 7 6 5 4 3 2 1   09 10 11 12 13 14

Printed in the U.S.A.   23
First edition, October 2009

The display type was set in Stillness.
The text type was set in Frutiger.
Book design by Phil Falco

FOR MY SISTER, KATHLEEN

You can love somebody without it being like tha

ou keep them a stranger, a stranger who's a friend.

TRUMAN CAPOTE, *BREAKFAST AT TIFFANY'S*

HOW TO SAY
GOODBYE
IN ROBOT

CH APRIL MAY JUNE JULY AUGUST

CHAPTER 1

Goebbels materialized on the back patio, right before we moved to Baltimore, and started chewing through the wicker love seat. We figured he was an escapee from one of the neighbors' houses, probably the Flanagans two doors down. The Flanagans had a lot of pets, and the parents looked the other way while their sons, Pat and Paul, fed them various foods that animals shouldn't eat, like Twinkies and Pop Rocks, and then raced them to see how the food affected their performance.

"Can't blame the little guy for making a break for it," Mom said. She picked up the gerbil and stroked his tiny head. He pooped in her hand.

"Here." Mom passed him to me. "He's yours."

"Gee. Thanks." I'm not exactly a rodent person. But we couldn't send him back to the Flanagan Torture Chamber, so I put the gerbil in a fishbowl until we had a chance to go to the pet store and buy a cage. He tried to scamper out, but the sides of the bowl were too slippery and steep. I fed him some sunflower seeds.

"What are you going to name him?" Mom asked.

"You can name him," I said.

"No, he's yours," Mom said, hurt creeping into her voice. "You name him."

"Okay," I said. "I'll call him Goebbels."

We had just studied World War II in school and I was reading *The Rise and Fall of the Third Reich* that summer. Joseph Goebbels was a Nazi propaganda guy, very diabolical. I didn't know any German, but I was fascinated by the way the names were pronounced — *GOEbbels* sounded like *GERbil*. That was the only reason I thought of the name.

"You can't call him Goebbels," Mom said. "That's a terrible name."

"You said I could name him."

"What about Peaches?"

"He's not a Peaches," I said, looking at his gnawing little front teeth. "I'd never saddle any living creature with a name like Peaches."

"Oh, and I suppose it's better to be named after a *Nazi*." Mom's face pinched up, hurt, as if I'd just mashed her finger in the door. The Pinch was a new look for her.

After lunch we drove to the pet shop. Mom waved to Motorbike Mike, the mustached biker dude who ran the costume shop in the same strip mall. Mom and I were frequent costume renters. We liked to dress up and create scenes from old movies, which I then photographed. It was just this thing I did. I didn't enjoy official extracurricular activities, like the Social Committee or the school newspaper, but I had to do something, so I took pictures of myself posing as, say, Barbara Stanwyck in *Double Indemnity* or Elizabeth Taylor in *BUtterfield 8*. When I looked at the pictures, I could almost believe I lived in that shadowy, glamorous, black-and-white world. Mike's shop had wigs, dresses, makeup, fake guns — everything we needed. But we didn't stop for costumes that day. We were on a gerbil mission. We bought a little gerbil cage with an exercise wheel, a bag of cedar chips, and some gerbil food.

When we got home, Goebbels was lying at the bottom of the fishbowl, dead.

"Oh," Mom said with a catch in her throat that meant tears were only seconds away. "Oh *no*. Why? Why-y-y-y?"

I poked at Goebbels's stiff little legs with a straw. "Maybe the Flanagans poisoned him before he escaped," I said. "They probably fed him Sweet'N Low to see if it would cause cancer — and it worked."

"We'll have to bury him," Mom said. "We'll have a funeral." She picked him up and cupped him in her hand. Then she started to cry. "We're moving next week. We'll have to leave him behind. Who will tend his tiny grave?"

If other people had been around, I would have been mortified. Actually, no one else was around, and I was still mortified.

"Mom, please," I said. "We knew him for two or three hours, tops."

"Poor Peaches!" she sobbed. "Poor little Peaches."

I once had a cat named Iggy, who died when I was twelve. The night after he died, a huge water bug skittered across the kitchen floor of our old house in Austin. The bug's zigzaggy gallop looked like Iggy's, and my grief-numbed body flushed with hope and grati- tude. He was back! For a split second I was sure that bug was Iggy reincarnated, come back to live with me again. I didn't care that he was a water bug, as long as I could have my Iggy, whatever form he took. Then Dad squashed him — the water bug, I mean — and that hope turned acid and dissolved. I felt I'd lost Iggy yet again.

But I was wrong. The water bug wasn't Iggy. Iggy wasn't coming back, not in any form. I repeated those words to myself over and over until I stopped seeing him in every fly, every moth, every mouse, and accepted it. I learned my lesson. By now, Mom should have learned this lesson too. No amount of wishing will bring back the dead.

"His name wasn't Peaches," I said. "He was probably old. How long do gerbils live, anyway? A few weeks? A year?"

"Oh!" Mom cried. "You're heartless." She put the gerbil's body back in the fishbowl and stared at me hard. "You're not a girl," she told me. "You're a robot!"

The sobs returned then, the kind that shake your whole body. She melted onto the kitchen floor in a puddle of tears and lilac cologne.

Maybe I am a robot, I thought. *Am I?* I knocked on my belly. It didn't clang, the way a robot's belly should. Far from it. But that assumed a robot was always made of tin, or steel, or some other clangy metal. By now, it seemed to me, scientists should have invented a robot material that felt and sounded more like human flesh. Or at least that wouldn't clang.

Meanwhile, there was Mom, still crouched in her pool of lilac-scented tears. *What is she so upset about?* I wondered. It couldn't be the gerbil. She'd been crying a lot even before we found him. It had to be the Move. But we'd already moved a thousand times — it felt like a thousand times, anyway — and it had never seemed to bother her before. I was the one who hated moving, until I finally got used to it. I learned not to get too attached to anything. I stopped thinking of the houses we lived in as *my* house, or the street we lived on as *our* street. Or my friends as my friends. Not that I had so many.

We moved for Dad. Most professors stay at one university, but Dad was always looking for more grant money or smarter students or more kowtowing from his colleagues. So we moved from Iowa City to Madison to Austin to Ithaca. . . . Up next, Baltimore. Johns Hopkins, the holy grail of pre-med students and biology professors like Dad.

I'd have to start my senior year of high school in a new city at a small private school where all the other kids had known each other since they were three. And you didn't see *me* crying. So what was Mom's problem? Ithaca was freezing in the winter, and the town was pocked with deep gorges that Cornell students threw themselves into when they got depressed, and no one blamed them. Baltimore had to be better than that. At least it couldn't be worse.

"I don't understand," I said. "Why are you so upset?"

She sat up, sniffed, and wiped her eyes. "I don't know. The poor little thing! I can't leave him behind. . . ."

"You mean it *is* the gerbil?" I said. "You're really upset about the gerbil?"

She gave me a piercing, angry stare then that scared me. Her eyes seemed to say, "Where did my sweet little daughter go? And who is this hard-hearted robot?"

I looked at the dead Goebbels. The moment seemed to call for a bit of ceremony, a gesture of some sort. So I stiffened my limbs and held my hands flat and straight, like a mime. With an expressionless face I jerked my hands over the gerbil's little body and squeaked, "Ee er oo. Ee er ee. Eh-eh."

Mom lifted her head. "Oh my God," she said. "What are you doing?"

"I'm giving the gerbil a final benediction," I said. "In Robot."

JULY AUGUST SEPTEMBER

CHAPTER 2

My first morning in Baltimore, I woke up in my box-filled room, got dressed, and took an exploratory walk down our new street. It was a mid-morning Tuesday after the off-to-work rush, so the neighborhood was quiet. The brick and stone houses were medium-old, from the 1920s or so, with tall elms guarding patchy little yards, and here and there a sprinkler whirring over the grass.

I turned a corner and came to a small church. There was a headstone near the path leading to the church's wooden doors. I stepped closer to read the headstone. It said FOR THE UNICORN CHILD.

That is so cool, I thought. What a funky town this was. I imagined a neighborhood Legend of the Unicorn Child, about a one-horned little boy who'd died tragically, hit by a car or shot by a mugger or maybe poisoned by lawn pesticides. The story of the Unicorn Child was so real to these people they'd erected a stone in his memory.

Then I read it again. The stone didn't say FOR THE UNICORN CHILD. It said FOR THE UNBORN CHILD.

That night I lay in bed, staring at the leafy shadow mice skittering across my bedroom wall. Our new house was muggy and airless and made strange groaning noises. Dad wasn't home from work yet, even though it was almost midnight. And the next day I'd start at Canton, my new school. I knocked on my stomach again, wishing that metallic clang would answer back. Even Robot Girls get nervous sometimes.

I'd been the new girl before; I didn't care what the Canton kids would think of me. One year and I was out of there forever. *I don't care what they think*, I chanted to myself. *I don't care, I don't care, I don't care what they think.* I repeated those words until they felt truer than true. By then it was two in the morning. Dad had come home and he and Mom were in their room. I wasn't sleepy.

In Ithaca I'd listened to the radio to fall asleep — the Bob Decker Show out of Albany, full of late-night conspiracy talk about the pyramids, alien invasions, shadow people, 9/11, clairvoyant spies, the Kennedy assassination, and on and on. Somehow the paranoia in the callers' voices soothed me. I guess I found it reassuring to know I wasn't the only one who felt a vague, hard-to-define anxiety and was looking for something to pin it on. But I couldn't pick up the show down here in the Land of the Unborn Unicorn Child.

So I began my alternate insomniac bedtime routine: imagining myself dead. I used lots of different death scenarios. There was the classic funeral scene: lying in my open coffin, dead but more beautiful than I ever looked in life, like Snow White in her crystal bier. Everyone I knew would pass by to gaze at me and cry. They should have appreciated me while I was alive. The world as they knew it will never be the same.

The last mourner was always a boy, whatever boy I had a crush on at the time. He'd be a wreck, totally destroyed by my death. When he saw me in my coffin, he'd suddenly realize that he'd loved me all along. The other kids in school, the fools who had ignored me all year, were wrong, so very wrong. The injustice of it would overwhelm Crush Boy, who'd run into the street and throw himself in front of a truck.

It was all very satisfying.

Then there was Slow Hospital Death, where I touched the heart of a handsome doctor, and Death in My Sleep, where Mom came in to wake me up for school but . . . oh no . . . she just . . . couldn't . . . wake me. . . . My spirit would float over the bed, laughing, *Ha-ha! I won't be going to school today.*

Those were just the Greatest Hits, but there were many, many more.

I'd never told anyone about this nightly habit. I was sure my parents would send me to a shrink if they knew, and the shrink would institutionalize me or drug me or give me shock therapy or at least make me visit him five days a week. They wouldn't understand. I didn't want to die. I just found death soothing to think about.

The next morning Mom burned her hand on the waffle iron. No one had asked for waffles; no one wanted waffles. She just got it into her head to make them for the first day of school, even though it was 95 degrees out with 95 percent humidity. She'd been accident-prone all summer — tripping over sprinklers, catching her hair in the fan, numerous cooking mishaps — so no one made a fuss over the burned hand. We were used to Mom hurting herself. I tossed her an ice pack and gulped down a banana and some orange juice.

Dad came downstairs, knotting his tie. "Hurt your hand?" He took the ice from Mom and peered at the burn. "I think you'll live." He kissed the spot, replaced the ice, grabbed the last banana, and kissed my forehead. "Good luck today, kiddo." Then he left for work, buzzing through our morning like a fly.

I pushed away from the kitchen table. "I'd better go too."

I looked at Mom, trying to decide whether to kiss her or not. She pressed the dripping ice pack on her hand and blinked at nothing. I waited for her to reach for me and ask for a kiss, but she didn't look up.

Missed your chance, I thought. *No kiss.* I knocked on my stomach. *Clang clang.* I was starting to hear it now.

On my way out I looked back at her, sitting at the table alone in her bathrobe. She caught me staring. Her hollow eyes said, *Please leave. Please just hurry up and leave.*

So I left.

The Canton campus — a cluster of Gothic stone buildings buffered from the city by playgrounds, athletic fields, and a thin strip of woods — was only half a mile from my house, so I walked to school in the soggy heat.

Each day began with an assembly in the Upper School auditorium, where the Canton students arranged themselves alphabetically, by class. I found myself on a metal folding chair in the fifth row next to a girl with curly black hair. Like me, she was wearing a plaid kilt and a white shirt, the girls' uniform. But somehow I looked dorky and she looked cute.

She smiled at me. "All right. Finally."

"Finally?" I didn't know what to do with this strange greeting. Was this girl expecting me?

"I mean, finally I have a buffer between me and Ghost Boy." She nodded at the empty seat to my right. "I've had to sit next to him in Assembly for the past eleven years. It's nice to get a break."

I swiped my hand through the air over the empty seat. Was this girl saying there was a ghost sitting next to me? Maybe she was crazy. I decided to fold my hands in my lap and stare straight ahead, in case she was.

But the girl wouldn't leave me alone. "What's your name?"

"Beatrice Szabo."

"I'm Anne Sweeney," she said.

I patted the empty seat beside me. "And who is your ghost friend?"

"Jonah Tate," she said. "He's not really a ghost . . . I don't think. He just looks kind of like Casper, without the sugary smile. You know, pale and shapeless and . . . white. You'll see when he gets here."

"Sounds more like the Pillsbury Doughboy," I said.

"If you poke Jonah in the tummy, he definitely will not giggle," Anne said. "He's more of a Death person than a Dinner Roll person, know what I mean?"

"Not really," I said.

"We had a funeral for him once," Anne went on. "In seventh grade. Someone spread a rumor that Jonah was dead, and then when he showed up for school, we all pretended we couldn't see him or hear him, to try to make him think he was a ghost. Then we held a mock funeral for him behind the gym. This one boy gave a hilarious eulogy about how much we would have missed Jonah, if only he'd ever said or done anything memorable. For a while, any time we saw Jonah, we'd scream 'Aaahhh! A g-g-g-ghost!'"

"That's . . . pretty mean," I said.

"Yeah, I know," Anne said. "But we were just kids. Shhh! Here he comes now."

A pale-haired boy slid down the row into the seat next to me. His skin was flour-white and his eyes were gray as pond ice. He did look kind of like a ghost. He smelled of menthol, Vicks VapoRub. I couldn't decide if that made him seem more ghostly or more earthbound. Anne Sweeney elbowed me and rolled her eyes, as if to say, *See what I mean? Total Casper.* Then — just for kicks, I guess — she said, "Aaahh! A g-g-g-ghost!"

Jonah squeezed his eyes shut and shook his head.

"Sorry, Jonah," Anne said. "I had to do it. For old times' sake."

The principal, Mr. Lockwood, took the podium and officially opened the new school year. "Welcome, Canton shtudentsh new and old," he said through clenched teeth. "Before we begin, let'sh refresh our shpirits with a few vershes of good old Hymn Number Shixhty-Sheven, 'For Losht Shouls Come Home.'"

Mr. Lockwood was lanky and fiftyish, with short brown hair and a rectangular head that, from my seat in the auditorium, looked like a block of wood with a face on the front. We rose to our feet. I glanced around for a hymnal, but there weren't any. No one except for me seemed to need one. All around me the students of Canton began to sing.

For lambs without a shepherd
For fish who rivers roam
For ships without a compass
We pray Thee bring them home.

For all of us are wanderers
Our hearts are full of holes
We pray Thee lead us homeward
Embrace Thy poor lost souls.

At least, that's what I thought they sang.
"Be sheated." We sat.
I half listened while Mr. Lockjaw — in my mind, he'd become Mr. Lockjaw — spoke about sheasons and beginningsh and shpiritual refreshment, then introduced the new faculty members. I felt keenly aware of the Ghost Boy's presence beside me. I sensed he was sneaking secret peeks at me, but whenever I looked, he sat stiff-necked, eyes forward.

After about twenty minutes, my first Canton Assembly was over. A boy with long greasy hair and smudged glasses played a recessional on the baby grand while we filed out row by row.

"What's your first class?" Anne Sweeney asked me.
I looked at my schedule. "French."
"Me too! Come on. *Allons y!*"
I went with her to be polite, but the whole time I was secretly thinking this girl was a little too perky for eight-thirty in the morning.

I didn't say goodbye to Ghost Boy. Which made sense, since I hadn't said hello.

At Canton, as at most schools, everything possible was alphabetized. My locker, therefore, sat between Anne's and Ghost Boy's, just like my Assembly seat. At ten o'clock I found myself with a free period and no idea what to do with it. I stood in front of my open locker, staring into its tinny darkness. The halls were quiet. No one else seemed to have a free period but me. I decided to pass the time by giving my locker some personality.

I taped two photos to the back wall of the locker: Mom as Gloria Wandrous in *BUtterfield 8*, wearing a black Liz Taylor wig and a fur coat over her slip, defiling a mirror with lipstick: *No Sale*. The look on Mom's face was furious and indignant. She made a great Liz Taylor. That shot was one of my favorites.

The other picture was me in the same getup, same pose, playing the same character from the same movie. The main difference between Mom's Gloria and mine was the facial expression. Mom's was better. She looked tragically pissed, and I looked like my wig itched.

At the bottom of my backpack I found an old Bob Decker bumper sticker.

THE BOB DECKER SHOW
WLTN AM 1350 ALBANY
LATE NIGHT TALK — CAN YOU HANDLE THE TRUTH?

I slapped the sticker on the inside of my locker door.
There. Locker decorated.
Ghost Boy shambled along and opened his locker without a word. I saw him peek at me very quickly while he spun the dial on his lock. ´

A couple of boys loped by, backpacks dangling from their shoulders. "Help! A g-g-g-ghost!" one of them said. They both cracked up. Jonah glowered under pale eyebrows. Apparently Anne Sweeney had restarted this old joke, and I felt partly responsible. To make up for it, I said, "I think ghostliness is a good quality. I pretend I'm dead all the time."

"What?" He stopped rummaging through his locker to look at me full in the face at last.

"It helps me go to sleep," I said.

"That just shows you don't know anything about death," Jonah said.

"Do you?" I asked.

He hesitated before saying, "I'm a g-g-g-ghost, aren't I?"

"I think being dead might be nice. Restful."

"Death is not restful. It's just nothing."

"That's what seems restful to me," I said. "The nothing. Not being here. Not being anywhere."

"But what about the pain?" Jonah said.

"There might be a tiny nanosecond of pain," I said. "But after that I imagine it goes away."

"Maybe for the dead person," Jonah said. "But the people left behind —"

"I don't mind if *they* feel pain," I said. "That's sort of the point."

"The point of what?" He blinked at me.

"Of imagining myself dead," I said.

"Oh." He paused. "What a waste of time." He eyed the inside of my locker, taking in the pictures and the bumper sticker. Then he left, walking quickly down the hall toward the library. The sound of his footsteps was real enough, not ghostly at all.

*   *   *

"Garber sat next to Beatrice in French class today," Anne Sweeney said at lunch. She'd invited me to sit with her. At first I thought she was being friendly, but I was beginning to suspect she had an ulterior motive, something to do with this Garber guy.

When they heard *Garber*, the other girls at our lunch table looked at me with sudden interest. Anne introduced them: Tiza Rahman, Carter Blessing, and Ann Cavendish, or AWAE, which was short for Ann-Without-An-E. Since Anne Sweeney had come to Canton first, in pre-K (versus AWAE's first grade), she retained the rights to the name Ann/e in any and all versions throughout the universe. Poor AWAE was stuck with an acronym, pronounced *ay-way*.

"Garber." AWAE sighed. "He sat next to you."

When I'd gotten to French class, Anne had slipped into a spot in the back between two of her friends, ditching me. There were only two seats left, both in the front row. I took one. "Sorry!" Anne whispered across the room. "I don't do the front row."

As the bell rang, a guy had strolled in and grabbed the last seat, next to me. He was long-haired and pretty, the kind of boy who hovers on the verge of androgyny but never quite crosses the line. He hid his sly, symmetrical features behind a pair of heavy, black-framed glasses, which only emphasized how cute he was. Before he sat down, my internal heat-seekers sensed what was coming my way: deep blue eyes that melted girls like Velveeta in a microwave. I tried to resist those microwave eyes, but sometimes there's no defense against them. I had a feeling I'd be seeing him weeping over my coffin later that night.

This was Tom Garber.

"He likes fresh meat," Carter said, stirring her yogurt. "Remember when he went after Lucy Moran? She lost it, totally in love, one week into the school year. Tom told me he was only being friendly because she was new."

"A week later he started going with Katie Greenberg," AWAE chimed in. "Lucy went catatonic. She sat around chewing her split ends like a zombie."

"Then she started wearing that veil, remember?" Tiza said. "As a sign of mourning. Lockjaw finally told her the veil had to go since it wasn't part of the uniform." (Clearly I wasn't the only one who thought of the principal as Lockjaw.)

"He let her keep the black armband, though," AWAE said.

"She lodged a protest," Carter told me. "She said the school was infringing on her religious freedom. The Tolerance Committee actually had meetings about it. She'd made up a new religion — the Church of Heartbreak. The CH. We called it 'the Chuh.'"

"If she'd been Muslim, they'd have to let her wear the veil," Tiza said.

"No, they wouldn't," Carter said. "This is a private school. They can do whatever they want."

"Lucy's family was Episcopalian," Anne said. "The whole thing was ridiculous."

Jonah Tate sat down at the next table, alone. He opened his lunch bag and unwrapped his sandwich. I immediately felt conscious of the snarky tone of our conversation.

"Eek!" Anne whispered. "A g-g-g-ghost!"

"Shh!" Tiza said. "That's really juvenile, Anne. And so over."

"I've been hearing it all morning," AWAE said. "Takes me back to seventh grade. The good old days, before everything counted."

"Before SATs," Anne said. "And college —"

"Please," Tiza said. "I hated seventh grade. Everybody was so mean then. Ty Travers was always snapping my bra strap."

"Whatever happened to Lucy Moran?" I asked. "And the Church of Heartbreak?" I hoped Lucy was still around, with her veil and black armband. She sounded nervous and weird enough to be friends with me.

"After Christmas, Lucy didn't come back to school," Carter said.

"No one ever heard from her again. She barely lasted one semester — *all because of Tom Garber.*"

"Wow," I said. That was one powerful boy.

"I saw her downtown once," AWAE said. "She goes to the School for the Arts now."

"He ruined her," Carter said.

"Don't listen to them, Bea," Anne said. "Lucy Moran was seventh grade."

"Garber hasn't changed," Carter warned. "He still likes the newbies. And we haven't had one in so long."

They all stared at me. "Well," I said, "new or not, I'm sure I'm not his type."

Experience told me that not that many guys were into flat-chested sticks with big round lollipop heads and stringy hair, unless by some miracle that was the regional definition of cute. If so, I hadn't come across that particular region. Mom kept telling me I had to grow into my face, but I knew a euphemism when I heard one.

"How do you know you're not his type?" Anne said.

Tiza scanned me with the laser accuracy of the socially astute and, I assumed, found me wanting. "Don't push her, Anne. She knows what she's talking about."

At the next table over, Jonah cut his ham sandwich into bite-size pieces and arranged them in geometric patterns in front of him. I felt sure he was eavesdropping on us.

"We'll see whether she's Tom's type or not," Anne said. "Like, right now."

A mysterious force vacuumed the air out of the lunchroom.

"Hey, girls," Tom Garber said. He flashed his teeth and microwaved the entire table as he slo-mo'd by. The light glinting off his glasses temporarily blinded me. "*Bonjour,* Beatrice."

He settled at a table in the back with his friends, a tangle of shaggy, noisy boys. Normal air pressure was restored.

"He singled you out, Bea," Anne said.

"He pronounced your name the French way," AWAE said.

"He's got Newbie Fever," Carter said.

A paper jet violated our airspace and landed on top of my turkey sandwich. Written on the wings, in red calligraphy, were the words

TO: BEATRICE
FROM: FUTURE BEATRICE

All our eyes darted in Jonah's direction.

"Jonah is a synonym for weird," Anne said.

I unfolded the plane.

"What does it say?" AWAE asked.

I read the message to myself. There were no explicit instructions to keep the note private, but some instinct kept me from sharing it.

"Nothing," I said.

"Come on, what's it say?" Carter prodded.

"Really. Nothing." I balled up the airplane and dropped it into my backpack.

"Jonah has a crush on you," Tiza said.

"Jonah doesn't have crushes on people," Anne said.

"He could," AWAE said. "Why not?"

Anne shook her head. "He just doesn't."

"He walks among the living," Carter said. "But he can't have ghost-human relations."

"Who cares, anyway," AWAE said. "Like it's a tough decision: Jonah or Tom? How will Beatrice ever choose?" The other girls laughed.

"Neither of them has a crush on me," I said.

"Tom does," Anne said. *"Newbie."*

When lunch was over, I pressed the wrinkles out of Jonah's note and reread it.

TO: BEATRICE
FROM: FUTURE BEATRICE
1120 AM. MIDNIGHT TONIGHT. BEATRICE
OF THE FUTURE WILL THANK YOU.

1120 AM. It had to be a radio show. Could be anything. Conservative ranters, sports talk, swing music, advice from the local rabbi . . . anything.

I sometimes wonder whether radio geeks have some kind of symbol tattooed on their foreheads, or antennae growing out of their skulls, invisible to everyone except other radio geeks. They seem to find one another with shocking ease. Of course, all Jonah had to do was notice the Bob Decker bumper sticker on my locker.

1120 AM, midnight.

Maybe Anne and her friends were right. G-g-g-ghost Boy was a lost cause, beyond the reach of the human world. But what about the Robot World? Robot World had room for misfits of all stripes. We would see.

CHAPTER 3

At three-thirty, I slogged home from school through the sticky September air. It was like swimming through Jell-O. I went into the kitchen for a snack. Mom was bumping around upstairs. Dad walked in through the front door, his briefcase overflowing.

"Hey, kiddo." He sat down at the kitchen table. "Thought I'd stop in for a couple of hours before my lab tonight. How was school?"

"Fine." I paused to wash my hands at the kitchen sink and noticed Mom had hung a new set of curtains in the window: white with red chickens printed on them. She'd had a crazy thing about chickens lately. I turned around, and there was Mom in the doorway in a red-and-white polka-dot bikini. Talk about crazy.

"You're home," she said to Dad. "I thought you had lab tonight."

"I do. I just stopped in to see how Bea's day went. What's with the suit? You going running in the sprinkler?"

"I . . . it's hot out. This was the coolest thing I could find to wear."

She opened the refrigerator. Her ribs made me think of a stray dog. Ribsy. That was the name of a dog in a book I'd loved as a child: *Ribsy*, by Beverly Cleary. Ribsy and his boy owner, Henry, were friends with Beezus, whose real name was Beatrice, like mine.

Mom pulled out a plate of cold chicken. "Drumstick, anyone? It's good luck to eat chicken on the first day of school."

"I thought it was good luck to eat chicken the first night in a new house," I said.

"That too," Mom said. "Chicken's an all-around good-luck food."

Dad looked at me like we had a secret together. "Really? Who says?"

"My grandmother used to say so," Mom said. "Down in Florida." She looked funny in her bikini, waving that drumstick around. Like a deranged spokesmodel.

Dad loosened his tie. "Bea and I manage to wear actual clothes, even in this godforsaken heat."

Mom read something on Dad's face she didn't like. She dropped the plate of chicken on the counter and her face puckered into the Pinch.

"I'll go change." She ran upstairs.

"Seems a little funny, wearing a bathing suit in a house where there's no pool," Dad said. "And no beach. In the middle of the city. Like walking around in your underwear." He sat down at the kitchen table. "Have you noticed we've been eating a lot of chicken lately? Fix me a cracker or two, will you?"

I put the chicken away, got crackers and peanut butter, and brought them to the table. Dad and I took turns dipping our knives into the peanut butter jar and smearing our crackers.

"She's tired a lot," I said. "And she cries. Over dumb things."

"Moving is stressful," Dad said. "Second only to death."

"I'd think death would be a whole lot worse than moving." I didn't really know, since I'd experienced a lot of moving but not much actual death. Just cat death, great-uncle death, gerbil death, and imaginary death.

"She'll be all right," Dad said. "We'll stay put for a while now."

I wondered if staying put was what she needed. No matter how much we moved or where we lived, Dad had his students and his

research and the book he was working on and his fascinating colleagues. Mom and I had each other. Or we used to, until I became
a robot and she became crazy.

Something changed in Ithaca. Mom disappeared some nights —
she said she was taking self-improvement classes in things like
psychology and creative writing — and left me alone with the TV.
"Your dad should be home any minute," she'd say on her way out
the door, but she usually got home first, no matter how late it was.

If Dad noticed the changes in Mom, they didn't seem to
bother him.

"So tell me all about school," Dad said, licking peanut butter off
his knife. "One of my colleagues has a daughter in your class.
Caroline Sweeney. In the Neuro-Chem Department. I think her
daughter's name is Anne?"

"She sits next to me in Assembly," I said.

"Nice girl?" Dad bit a cracker.

"I guess." As Ghost Boy would probably say, n-n-n-not really.

The floorboards creaked. Dad turned around. Mom lurked in the
hallway, listening. Caught, she stepped into the kitchen, swinging
the skirt of a red-and-white polka-dot sundress.

"Is this decent enough for you?" she said.

"How long were you standing there?" Dad said.

"I wasn't standing anywhere," Mom said. She looked like a kid
who'd just been tagged in hide-and-seek and didn't want to be It.

"Hey," I said. "That dress looks just like your bikini."

"Polka dots are good luck," Mom said.

Dad went back to work at five. For dinner that night, Mom and I
ate cottage cheese and watermelon in the kitchen under the beady,
watchful eyes of the curtain chickens.

We didn't talk much. She didn't ask me how school went.
She glanced at the phone every once in a while, as if expecting

it to save her from some discomfort or awkwardness. But it didn't ring.

She stared into our new backyard, which was crabgrassy and needed mowing. "Remember Peaches?" she asked.

Not the gerbil again. "Goebbels," I said. "I wonder if the Flanagans ever noticed he was missing." The funeral had been painful. Mom read three poems — Keats, Shakespeare, and Auden — over his Kleenex-box coffin before settling him into his backyard grave. She wept while I covered the box with dirt. I resented being designated gravedigger. I resented having to go through the ritual at all.

Mom set down the gravestone — a rock she'd painted gold. On it was written HERE LIES A KING OF GERBILS. RIP PEACHES.

"Yeah," Mom said. "Goebbels. I wonder if he knows how much we cared about him."

The cottage cheese curds stuck in my throat. "But we *didn't* care about him."

"Speak for yourself, you heartless child," Mom said. "I cared. There's a gold headstone in our former yard to prove it."

"Okay, okay," I said. "You cared. You care about all living things, no matter how insignificant. You're Jesus. You're Buddha. You're frigging Gandhi in polka dots." Somehow I wasn't included in her love of all the world's creatures . . . but I was afraid to say this out loud. I didn't want to trigger another meltdown. And as much as I liked to think of myself as a girl robot, being called heartless by my own mother didn't feel great in my tinny stopwatch of a heart.

Just before midnight, I lay in the dark, spinning the AM dial on my clock radio until I found 1120. *All right, Ghost Boy,* I thought. *Let's see what you've got for me.* I planned to listen for a little while, and then put myself to sleep by imagining Tom Garber weeping over my virginal corpse.

An announcer's voice said, "WBAM, Baltimore 1120. News, talk, and golden oldies. It's midnight. Stay tuned for the Night Light Show with your host, Herb Horvath." After a long *beep* to mark the hour and a dorky jingle — "WBAM in Baltimore!" — an old swing tune played, and Billie Holiday's smoky voice purred, "Talk to me, baby, tell me what's the matter now . . ."

A voice spoke over the music, a voice so mellow it had a smell: brandy, pipe tobacco, aftershave, and a touch of Bengay. "Good night and good morning to you, all my Night People. This is the Night Light Show, your Light in the Night, and I'm your host, Herb Horvath. It's early on a Tuesday morning, and Baltimore is steaming. Will autumn ever come? Doesn't feel like it, does it? You know the number: 410-555-7777. Call in, tell me what's on your mind. Let's keep each other company, shall we? While we're waiting for the first calls to pour in, let's listen to this beautiful number by John Coltrane and Johnny Hartman called 'Autumn Serenade.' Here's hoping it brings some cool weather along with it."

The song played — tenor sax, piano, and another smooth, mellow man's voice crooning.

I turned up the radio, lay back in the dark, and let the voices wash over me.

Herb:
Okay, here comes our first caller. WBAM, you're on the air. Welcome to the Night Light Show.

Old lady:
Hello, Herb. It's Dottie calling from Essex.

Herb:
Hello, Dottie. What's on your mind tonight?

Dottie:
Remember sweet old Brutus, my kittycat?

[Sniffs] I don't know if I mentioned this, but Brutus went to Kittycat Heaven a couple of months ago.

Herb:
Oh, I'm very sorry to hear that, Dottie.

Dottie:
I miss him so much. And I think he's trying to contact me — from the other side.

Herb:
What do you mean, he's trying to contact you?

Dottie:
He's been appearing in my dreams every few nights. I'm lying in bed and he walks right over my stomach and stands on my rib cage, staring at me. He moves his mouth like he's talking. Not meowing, but talking.

Herb:
What does he say?

Dottie:
He says, "Bistro. Bistro. Bistro."

Herb:
Bistro?

Dottie:
That's what I don't understand. Why is he talking about restaurants? What is he trying to tell me?

[A tinkly little bit of music plays, the sound of fairy dust being sprinkled.]

Herb:
That's a stumper, Dottie. Let's toss that out to our listeners and see what they come up with.

Dottie:
Thank you, Herb. I appreciate it. Nighty-night all!

Herb:
Nighty-night. You're listening to the Night Light Show with Herb Horvath. WBAM, AM 1120. Next caller, you're on the air.

Myrna:
Herb, this is Myrna from Highlandtown.

Herb:
Hello there, Myrna. Nice to hear from you again.

Myrna:
I tried to call on the anniversary of Elvis's death, but I couldn't get through.

Herb:
Yes, the lines are always jammed on Elvis nights.

Myrna:
Dang, that man looks good on velvet. Notice I didn't say "Damn"? I'm doing my darnedest to keep my language clean for you, Herb.

Herb:

I appreciate it, Myrna. I've still got the Elvis portrait you sent me, up on the wall in my office.

Myrna:

I did that myself. Paint-by-numbers.

Herb:

It's a beaut.

Myrna:

I can't believe he's dead. I know it's been a
while now, but . . . I still wear my hair the way
Priscilla wore hers on their wedding day, in case
he comes back.

Herb:

From the dead?

Myrna:

Who's more likely to come back from
the dead than Elvis? If anybody can do it,
he can.

Herb:

Maybe you're right. I bet he's looking down at
you from Heaven right now, Myrna. He's thinking,
My, that's a fine-looking woman in that black
beehive hairdo.

Myrna:

Why, thank you, Herb.

It was just a bunch of lonely old people, but I could kind of relate to them — especially Dottie, haunted by her dead cat. And Myrna haunted by Elvis. Everybody was haunted by somebody. I couldn't turn it off.

Herb:
We've got to move on to our next caller. Night Light, you're on the air.

Ghost Boy:
Good evening, Herb. This is Ghost Boy.

I sat up. This had to be Jonah. The voice sounded like his. So this was why he wanted me to listen — he was a regular caller.

Herb:
Hello, Ghost Boy. What's cooking tonight?

Ghost Boy:
Not much. Summer's over. I'm just feeling sad about it.

Herb:
Did you have a good summer?

Ghost Boy:
No. But it's still better than the rest of the year. No school, for one thing.

Herb:
What year are you in school, Ghost Boy?

Ghost Boy:

Senior. Almost free. Once I graduate, there will be nothing to hold me in place. No schedule or responsibility or expectations to fulfill. I'll be light as a helium balloon, drifting up into the sky with no direction. Just carried by the wind.

Herb:

What about college, Ghost Boy? You seem like a smart kid.

Ghost Boy:

Most colleges won't take dead people. Ha-ha. Well, I just wanted to check in. I haven't called in a while, but I'm still here listening. Lurking. Just wanted you all to know. I'll keep my eye out for Elvis. Oh, and a special hello to Burt. I hope he checks in.

Herb:

Chances are he will. You know Burt. Nighty-night, Ghost Boy.

Ghost Boy:

Nighty-night.

Jonah had wanted me to hear that call. Why? Was this just a connection between two radio insomniacs, or was he trying to send me some kind of message?

Herb:

Next caller, you're on the air.

Caller:
Meow meow meow meow. Hi, Herb, this is
Dottie's cat calling from Kittycat Heaven. Meow!

Herb:
Don Berman, this is not nice.

Don Berman:
I'm not Don Berman! I'm Dottie's kittycat with a
message from the Great Beyond. You're an ugly
old biddy, Dottie! I always hated you and I'm coming to get you! Meow! Meow! Me —

Herb:
Sorry, Don, but I had to hang up on you. We
don't allow that kind of thing here on the Night
Light Show. Dottie, dear, if you heard that, you
know better than to take Don Berman seriously.
We all know how he is. Next caller, welcome to
the Night Lights.

Judy:
Herb, this is Judy from Pikesville. I just want to
say: Dottie, honey, don't you listen to that awful
Don Berman. I don't know why he does these
things. We all love you and I'm sure Brutus is very
happy up there in Cat Heaven.

Herb:
Thank you, Judy. I'm sure you're right.

Judy:
Herb, that Ghost Boy should be asleep. He has

school tomorrow, and it's almost one o'clock in the morning! Don't you have a minimum age for callers? They should be at least twenty-one.

Herb:
Well, I guess it's up to his parents to set his bed-time, if he has parents. . . . Perhaps he doesn't. What if he really is a ghost?

Judy:
Oh, Herb, don't be ridiculous. He says he goes to school. Where do you think he goes, the School for Ghouls?

Herb:
Judy, I think you just made a joke.

Judy:
What? Oh no, Herb, I don't joke. I'm deadly serious. . . .

I let my mind drift along the airwaves, where all these listeners and callers had found a secret world. Jonah had given me the key to that world, even though he barely knew me.

I had to prove myself worthy.

CHAPTER 4

The next morning, I felt spacy and tired but strangely alert too. The Night Lights still babbled in my head like a vivid dream that wouldn't turn off even after I woke up.

Jonah was already in his seat when I got to the auditorium for Assembly. He looked different now that I'd heard him on the radio. More real, less ghost.

I went to my seat. "Hey — thanks, Ghost Boy."

No answer.

"I heard you on the radio last night," I explained.

"Okay, but don't call me Ghost Boy."

I stiffened. He'd sounded so likable on the radio, I'd forgotten how prickly he was in real life. "Sorry."

He sighed, slouched, and stared at the stage as if impatient for Assembly to begin.

"How often do you call in?" I asked.

He shrugged. "Once in a while. Did you like it?" Something new in his voice when he asked the question — nervousness? warmth? — spurred me on.

"It's great!" I said. "I used to listen to the Bob Decker Show out of Albany — do you get that here?"

"I don't know. I never looked for it."

"Doesn't matter," I said. "The Night Light Show is much better.

How long have you been listening? Have you ever met any of the other callers? That Don Berman guy?"

"No," Jonah said, finally looking at me, but giving no hint about how he felt about what he saw. "I'm a little bit afraid of them."

"I have these pictures in my head, you know, of what they look like, but I'm sure I'm totally wrong —"

"I just thought you'd like the show," Jonah said, looking over my shoulder. "I wasn't trying to be your best friend or anything."

"Oh." Now I felt weird. Why did he turn me on to the show if he didn't want to talk about it? I couldn't ask, because Anne Sweeney suddenly arrived on a breeze of honeysuckle shampoo.

"Hey there!" As soon as Anne sat down, Jonah started studying something in his backpack. I got the message: *End of conversation.* "Wow, Bea, you look tired."

"I do?"

"Yeah, you've got circles." She traced the dark hollows under my eyes. "Want some concealer? Mine's probably too light for you, but it's better than looking like one of those football players . . . what's that black stuff they put under their eyes to block out the sun? Eye something?"

"Eye black?" I said. Just a guess.

"Yeah, that's it." She dug through her monogrammed canvas tote bag until she found a tube of concealer and passed it to me.

"That's okay," I said. "I like looking tired."

"You do not." She laughed. "You're so funny." She reached across me to tap Jonah's arm. "Isn't she funny, Jonah?"

He didn't move, didn't make a sound, like he was pretending he wasn't there, or that we weren't there, that he couldn't hear or see us. Anne wasn't having it. She tapped him again. "Jonah! Answer me! You rude thing."

His mouth twitched. "Anne Sweeney, stop talking. Please."

"Oh, that's what you always say." Anne turned to me. "See why I don't even try? It's not worth the effort *at all*."

Mr. Lockjaw took the podium and the students quieted down. "Glad to shee the firsht day didn't shcare you all off. Sho many of you came back for more. Har har har."

The students sighed restlessly. No one laughed except one of the teachers sitting up on the stage, a heavyset woman with a white skunk streak running through her teased black hair.

"Har har," Lockjaw finished. "Mosht of you know Mizh Jacobshon, Dean of Shtudent Life. She'sh going to read a few announchementsh thish morning about ekshtracurricular activitiesh. Mizh Jacobshon?"

The woman with the skunk streak replaced Lockjaw at the podium. Ms. Jacobson, I presumed.

"You're all required to take at least one extracurricular a year, including sports," Ms. Jacobson said. "These must be school-approved activities, no independent study, no exceptions. Here are the group leaders for the following student activities. Drama Club Chair: Olga Ulianov. Social Committee Co-Chairs: Anne Sweeney and Michael Morse . . ."

I listened to the list halfheartedly, sure I'd find nothing that interested me. Then, as Ms. Jacobson droned on, I heard a combination of words that surprised me. "Yearbook Committee: Editor, Nina Fogel. Art Director, Jonah Tate."

I looked at Jonah. "You're the art director of the yearbook?"

"I know, isn't that peculiar?" Anne said. "The person with just about the least school spirit ever in the whole world, and he's in charge of the freaking *yearbook*! He *volunteered* for it!"

"Why?" I said. "I would have thought the Philosophy Club was more your speed. Or Chess Club, or Future Chemists. Not that I really know you or anything, but —"

"Beatrice Szabo," Jonah said through clenched teeth, sounding almost like Lockjaw. "And Anne Sweeney. I'm going to say it one more time, and you had better listen. Stop. Talking."

"Okay, okay," Anne said. "Touch*y*."

I was afraid to say another word. But I thought maybe *I'd* join the yearbook. It seemed, counterintuitively, to be the place for people with no school spirit. And it was impossible to have less school spirit than I had. Even Ghost Boy couldn't top me in that department.

"Who needs this dump?" Anne said, surveying the limp cafeteria scene. She wrinkled her nose as the smell of boiled broccoli assaulted us. "Let's hit the Morgue." She and AWAE marched out of the lunchroom. I stood on the threshold, not sure what to do.

Anne stopped and waved her hand in front of my face. "Yo, Beatrice. You coming?"

I blinked. When I'm in a new situation, sometimes my response times are slow. Like, if I don't know what to do automatically, out of habit, my engine stalls.

"Come on, Beatrice," AWAE said. "We're leaving."

My brain gears warmed up and began to whirr. "I didn't know we were allowed to leave."

"Of course we are," Anne said. "Senior privileges." She grabbed me by the wrist and shook my arm. "You're so stiff. Relax." She headed for the door, pulling me along.

"So . . . is the Morgue what it sounds like?"

"Does it sound like something?" AWAE said. "We're having French fries."

We climbed into Anne's Mini and drove half a mile off campus. To my disappointment, the Morgue was short for Morgan & Millard, a drugstore and coffee shop nestled among a row of storefronts on Roland Avenue. First Strip Shopping Center in America, an iron plaque announced. Built in 1896. It wasn't much of a shopping center, just an ice-cream shop, a florist, a bank, a real estate agent, and the Morgue.

The Morgue was bustling. We pushed our way through a small

front area selling candy and magazines, past a long counter crowded with old ladies and kids from the local private schools, to a table near the back. A bunch of boys from Canton had colonized the corner booth. I spotted Tom Garber and a few others from our class.

"How's it going?" the waitress muttered.

"Just French fries for me," Anne said. "And a Diet Coke."

"Me too," AWAE said.

I quickly scanned the menu. "I'll have a grilled cheese and a Coke."

The waitress nodded and left. Anne and AWAE took out their cell phones and started poking at them. I'd left my cell at home. We weren't allowed to use them at school, and I wasn't expecting to hear from anyone, anyway. I ran my fingers over the old wooden table scarred with names and initials carved over the years. "How long has this place been here?"

"Forever," Anne said, still staring at her phone's tiny screen. "My parents used to come here when they went to Canton."

"My dad did too," AWAE said.

I touched one of the fresher carvings: *TG & AS*. "AS," I said to Anne. "Is that you?"

She leaned across the table to peer at it. "Yeah. Somebody carved it in middle school."

"Who's TG?" I said. "Anyone I know?"

Anne and AWAE exchanged a glance. "Maybe, maybe not," Anne said.

"Tom Garber?"

"It was middle school," Anne said. "It was nothing."

"Tom was totally in love with her," AWAE said.

"He was not," Anne said.

"What's this one?" I rubbed a scratched-out MTMTMTMTMTMT. "Someone was obsessed with the initials MT."

AWAE shrugged. Anne glanced at the mark. "Maybe Jonah did that."

"Jonah?" I was surprised. "You mean Ghost Boy? Who did he have a crush on?"

The waitress brought our plates. The fries came with a dish of brown gravy. Anne and AWAE swiped their fries through the glop. I ate my grilled cheese.

"Nobody," Anne said. "MT was his brother."

"MT could stand for Mandy Torelli," AWAE said. "Remember when Jack Harper liked her?"

"It doesn't, though," Anne said. "If Jack Harper scratched initials into a table, it wouldn't look like a crazy person did it."

I swiped a finger over the initials. There was a touch of crazy about the way they were scrawled into the wood, a desperate edge. "What happened to MT?"

"He died," AWAE said. "In third grade."

"They were twins," Anne said.

Twins. Jonah had a twin. "How did he die?"

"In a car accident," Anne said. "With their mother. They both died."

I stopped eating.

"Jonah used to be sort of normal, before it happened," Anne went on. "I live down the street from him, and we played together when we were little. He was, you know, okay. Approaching human."

"His brother was retarded," AWAE whispered.

"He wasn't retarded," Anne said. "Well, not *just* retarded. Brain damaged. His brain didn't get enough oxygen when he was born. He was basically a vegetable. He couldn't talk or walk or anything. He couldn't feed himself. Jonah's mother took care of him all the time."

"My father told us it was merciful that he died young," AWAE said. "But it was really sad about Mrs. Tate. Remember those skeleton cookies she used to bring to school on Halloween?"

"What was his name?" I asked. "Jonah's brother."

"Matthew," Anne said.

"Were they identical twins?" I said.

"I don't know," Anne said. "It was hard to tell, because Matthew was always slumped over and drooling. But they both had blond hair and that sickly pale skin."

"Can we talk about something less morbid now?" AWAE said. "Like, when did St. Mary's girls start wearing their knee socks that way? Have you noticed how they *all* bunch them up around their ankles? It can't be a coincidence."

I tried to imagine a twin of Jonah's, disabled, now dead. Jonah called himself Ghost Boy, but he was alive; Matthew was the real ghost. I wondered if he haunted Jonah at night, in his sleep, like Dottie's cat or Myrna's Elvis. Maybe that was why Jonah listened to the Night Lights, to keep the ghosts away.

"She's doing it again," AWAE said.

"Beatrice." Anne tapped my plate with her fork. "Beatrice. You're doing that thing again."

"What thing?"

"This thing you do sometimes. I've noticed it in Assembly. You get this blank look on your face. Kind of like you hear what we're saying but you don't care."

"It's so weird," AWAE said.

She was right: I didn't care about how the St. Mary's girls wore their socks. But maybe I should have. Everyone else seemed to care about those things. Even if it was only as an observer, a sociologist of high school mores, I should have cared more than I did.

Why didn't I? Maybe Mom was right after all. She'd given birth to a mutant. My heart was cold and steely. It was so obvious even AWAE could tell.

Dad made dinner that night: lasagna, his specialty. "The chickens spoke to me," he said, tugging on the kitchen curtains. "They said if we don't ease up on eating their fellow fowl, they're going to come alive at night and jump off the curtains and peck out our eyes. I hear and I obey, O Great Kitchen Chickens." He bowed to the curtains, hands clasped in prayer.

I couldn't help laughing, even though it was stupid. Mom flashed me an angry look. She was wearing big, dangling chicken earrings she'd made out of cardboard that day. "Don't encourage him," she said. "He's teasing us."

"I think he's teasing *you*," I said.

"It isn't nice," Mom said. "Why can't we be nice to each other in this family?"

"We are nice," Dad said.

"I don't mean fake-nice," Mom said. "I mean real-nice."

I could see Dad checking out then, his eyes glazing over. "Have some lasagna."

"Nobody's nice all the time," I pointed out.

"That's for sure," Mom said.

I cut a bite of lasagna with my fork and ate it. "Good lasagna, Dad."

"Thanks."

"Why are you always on his side?" Mom said.

"I'm not. I just like his lasagna. Jeez."

I was afraid to say anything after that. I didn't need her jumping on every innocent little comment I made. Dad and I ate, and Mom deconstructed her lasagna, separating the parts into categories: noodles on one side, bits of meat next to that, vegetables circling the plate, a pile of gooey cheese in the middle.

"Making an art project?" Dad said.

"I'm just trying to understand how it's put together," Mom said.

After I finished my homework, I got into bed to read *To the Lighthouse* for English. I found myself restless, glancing at the clock, waiting for midnight to come. I wondered if Dottie's cat had visited her in her dreams. I wondered if Ghost Boy would call in.

At last it was time to turn on the radio.

Burt:
Herb, it's Burt from Glen Burnout.

Herb:
How's the Amoco station tonight? Busy?

Burt:
You better believe it. How's Peggy?

Herb:
[clears his throat] Doing well, doing well.

Burt:
Getting a lot of face time with her, Herb?

Herb:
Burt, you know the rules. Nighty-night. *[Herb hangs up on Burt.]* Next caller. You're on the air.

Morgan:
I'm glad you hung up on that pervert. *[Tinkle of piano keys in background]*

Herb:
Hello, Morgan.

Morgan:
You all haven't been out to visit me in a while,

Herb. The Mermaid Lounge is open year-round for your dining and drinking pleasure. We serve the finest in steaks, seafood, and cocktails. Tequila Sunrises a specialty. Come on down and visit our lovely waitresses: Linda, Donna, Dawnielle, and Betty Ann. Say hello and give them a wink. Oysters are in season! With yours truly on the keys five nights a week, Wednesday through Sunday. *[Emphatic trill on piano]*

Herb:
I was thinking of firing up the Flying Carpet. Have you got room for a few visitors at the Mermaid this evening?

Morgan:
Come on out. It's quiet tonight. The season's over, and I could use the company.

Herb:
How about a little taste to tempt the listeners?

Morgan:
Happy to oblige. *[Morgan plays "Feelings" full of flourishes, Liberace-style.]* How'd you like that?

Herb:
Lovely, Morgan. Nighty-night.

Morgan:
Nighty-night, y'all. Come down to the ocean and see me soon.

Herb:

Next caller, you're on the air.

Weird high-pitched voice:

Hello? Herb? This is Irene from Fell's Point. First-time caller!

Herb:

Welcome, Irene. How are things down in Fell's Point?

Irene:

Good, good. I'm just a little old lady, living alone with my cats. My children never call me. . . .

Herb:

You know how kids can be. They get busy, but I'm sure they're thinking of you.

Irene:

They are not, the little brats. I'll take cats over children any day. One of my cats is about to have kittens. Her first litter.

Herb:

That's great. What's your cat's name?

Irene:

[voice suddenly drops from a falsetto to a baritone] Don Berman! Don Berman! Don Berman! Don Berman! Ha ha ha ha ha! *[Hangs up]*

Herb:
[chuckling insincerely] What would we do without our regular calls from Don Berman? Heh heh heh. Next caller, you're on the air.

Ghost Boy:
Hi, Herb, it's Ghost Boy.

Herb:
What do you know, Ghost Boy?

Ghost Boy:
I'm feeling restless tonight. Warm night, can't sleep. . . . I sure could use a trip on the carpet. I bet the ocean's nice and calm tonight.

Herb:
All right, you talked me into it. Anybody want to take a ride to Ocean City with Ghost Boy and me, the carpet's warming up. I can take three more callers.

Ghost Boy:
If you've never taken a ride on the carpet, don't be shy. Call in. It's worth it.

Herb:
The number is 410-555-7777.

Jonah knew I was listening — he was inviting me to call in. I wasn't sure what this Flying Carpet thing was, but I picked up the phone and dialed. If Don Berman wasn't afraid to talk on the radio, why should I be? Herb Horvath was Mom's ideal: real nice to everyone.

Herb:
Who've we got here? Caller Two?

Louanne:
It's me, Herb. Louanne from Mount Washington.

Herb:
Welcome aboard, Louanne. Caller Three?

Robot Girl:
Hi, I'm Robot Girl from Homeland.

Herb:
Robot Girl, eh? First-time caller?

Robot Girl:
Yes.

Herb:
Welcome. Caller Four?

Burt:
Burt here. Why do we always have to go to Ocean City on the stupid carpet? Can't we go somewhere cool once in a while? Like Vegas?

Herb:
Burt, you're not supposed to call in more than once a night.

Burt:
I know, but you hung up on me, Herb. I didn't

get my five minutes. And I've got to get to
Ocean City tonight. That weasel Morgan owes me
twelve bucks.

Herb:
Sorry, Burt. Another time. Have we got another
Caller Four?

Myrna:
Me! Myrna! I'll go if Morgan promises to play
"Delilah" when we get there.

Herb:
I can't make any promises for Morgan, but I
think we can talk him into it. Everybody on? All
buckled up?

Ghost Boy, Louanne, Robot Girl, Myrna:
Yes.

[Funny little sound effects: ding-ding! whoosh!]

Herb:
Off we go! *[Sound of wind rushing by]* Isn't it a
beautiful night? Look at the lights of the city
below us.

Myrna:
I see my house.

Louanne:
I see the cars on the Beltway.

Ghost Boy:

I can see Horribleplace. The tourists look like bugs.
The tourists ARE bugs.

Herb:

We're flying over Annapolis. Here comes the Bay
Bridge.

Ghost Boy:

Slow down. Robot Girl is new in town. She hasn't
seen all this before.

Robot Girl:

How did you know I'm new?

Ghost Boy:

You said so.

Robot Girl:

No, I didn't.

Louanne:

See the lights on the bridge, Robot Girl? All white
like a diamond necklace.

Myrna:

The bay is full of boats tonight. Anchored in the
little coves. Big ships chugging toward the ocean.

Herb:

Over the bridge . . . Now we're on the Eastern
Shore. It's dark over here.

Louanne:
Nothing but cornfields.

Myrna:
And melons, and tomatoes.

Louanne:
Peaches.

Ghost Boy:
And rivers winding through the muck.

Robot Girl:
It's beautiful.

Herb:
I see it up ahead. The tall buildings —

Myrna:
Ocean City! I can smell the salt air.

Louanne:
And the French fries.

Herb:
Let's ride down the boardwalk.
Any of you ever stay in the old
Commodore Hotel? They just painted it
aqua blue.

Myrna:
I liked it better white.

[The tinkling of piano keys and glasses, murmur of voices.]

Herb:
Here we are! The Mermaid Lounge. Well, Morgan, we made it.

Morgan:
[Breaks into "Happy Days Are Here Again"] Table for five? Have a seat everybody. What'll you have? Just tell Johnny the bartender here.

Myrna:
I'll have a sidecar.

Louanne:
Just coffee for me.

Herb:
A nice stiff martini for me. Since it's make-believe.

Ghost Boy:
I'll take a Jack-and-Coke. Since it's, you know, make-believe. What about you, RoboGirl?

Robot Girl:
Red wine. And it's RoBOT Girl.

[Glasses clink.]

Morgan:
I heard what Burt said about me. I don't owe him no twelve dollars.

Herb:
You and he will have to work that out off the air.
Who has a request for Morgan?

Myrna:
I do! "Delilah," remember?

Morgan:
Gee, I never get requests for that one. *[He pounds out the old Tom Jones song and wails.]* "WHY, WHY, WHY, DELILAH?"

Ghost Boy:
Robot Girl, you look lovely in the candlelight.

Robot Girl:
Thank you.

Myrna:
What about me, Ghost Boy?

Ghost Boy:
All you ladies are looking fine. You too, Herb.

Herb:
Yes, aren't we lucky to be escorting three such lovely ladies? It's too bad we have to go back to town. Down the hatch, everybody, and it's back on the carpet. We'll take a quick spin over the Ferris wheel, around the inlet, and we're on our way back to the city. Across the bay . . . and we've

landed. Thank you, callers. Another wonderful ride. Time for a commercial break. Here's a message from Jeffrey R. Downes, Attorney-at-Law. Got a problem? Jeffrey R. Downes says, "Let's talk about it."

Ghost Boy:
Nighty-night, Robot Girl.

Robot Girl:
Nighty-night.

Ghost Boy is a liar, liar liar liar, I thought drowsily as I drifted off to sleep. *He does too want a friend. Even if she is a little stiff.* That night I dreamed of bridges made of diamonds.

CHAPTER 5

I took my photo portfolio to the yearbook staff meeting. Jonah sat on a desk at the front of the room, next to Nina Fogel, the editor, so I guess he really was the art director. He didn't seem very interested in the meeting, though; he spent the whole time drawing in a notepad.

"Every staff member is responsible for at least a hundred dollars' worth of ads," Nina told the prospective staffers. "Hit all the stores in the neighborhood, your parents, your grandparents. . . . The *Yodel* needs money, people!"

Maybe Jonah hoped it looked like he was taking notes, but he was obviously doodling.

"Jonah will go through pictures from our entire history at Canton, starting in pre-K," Nina said. "If you have any old pictures we can use, please submit them. To volunteer as a staff photographer, show Jonah your portfolio after the meeting. Any questions?"

A girl raised her hand. "Can we change the name? I can't ask people to buy ads in something called the *Yodel.*"

"Let's call it the *Beatbox,*" a boy said.

"How about the *Anguished Scream,*" another boy said.

"Or the *Cry for Help,*" the first girl said.

"We can't," Nina said. "I already asked Lockjaw. He said the class of 1925 named it the *Yodel* and it's a tradition, so we're stuck. Any other questions? No? Want to add anything, Jonah?"

Jonah's pen never stopped scribbling. "No."

"Come on, Jonah. You have to say something."

"Yodelay-hee-hoo."

When the meeting was over, I joined the small group clustered around Jonah. He flipped through the other students' albums. "Fine, fine, just make sure every group shot isn't a pyramid."

He turned to me. I opened my portfolio and turned the pages, wondering — nervously, to my surprise — what he would think. Most of the photos were pretend movie stills starring me and Mom. We also did fairy tales like *Sleeping Beauty* and *Rapunzel*, Bible stories, infamous murders, and ritual sacrifices. I liked to make them as bloody and violent as possible. We went through a ton of fake blood. Our fake blood purchases alone probably kept Motorbike Mike's costume shop in business.

"Who's this?" Jonah pointed to one of my favorites, Salome with the Head of St. John the Baptist. Mom wore a flowing black wig, bikini top, parachute pants, and piles of jangly gold jewelry. My body was hidden behind a table covered in an embroidered cloth so it looked like my decapitated head was sitting on the table, bearded and bloody. My tongue was hanging out and my eyes stared in glassy, frozen horror. At least, that's what I was going for.

"That's the fabulous Dori Szabo," I said. "My mother. She's Salome and I'm John the Baptist's head."

"Pretty gruesome."

"I know. Not really yearbook material, I guess."

"I like it," Jonah said. "We don't have the budget for all these costumes . . . but wouldn't it be cool to shoot the senior class photo as, like, I don't know, a pirate mutiny or something?"

Nina overheard him. "Veto. Absolutely not."

Jonah made a witchy face behind her back.

"So am I on the staff?" I asked.

Jonah shrugged. "Sure. Anybody can take pictures. Who am I to stop them?"

"I now pronounce you an official yearbook photographer," Nina said to me. "Congratulations, you're a *Yodel*er. Don't let Jonah's bad attitude keep you from celebrating."

"It's a HUGE honor," Jonah said. "We don't take just anyone. Oh, wait a minute — we do." One corner of his mouth ticked upward, in my direction. "But I'm sure you'll find a way to stand out from the crowd."

"The yearbook? Yuck," AWAE said later on Friday night. "Why would anybody want to be a *Yodel*er?"

"It would be nice if it had a less mortifying name," Anne said.

We were all at a party at Tiza's. Tiza and Anne and AWAE arranged themselves around the kitchen island, slurping cans of beer. Anne had brought me to the party, though from what I could tell, being invited to a Canton party wasn't any great sign of popularity. Most of the junior and senior classes had crammed themselves into the Rahmans' neat brick house, with a few of the cooler sophomores thrown in. Canton was such a small school that when it came to parties, the students couldn't afford to be exclusive or there wouldn't be enough people for critical party mass.

The school uniform — kilts for girls, blue pants for boys — had been replaced by a unisex weekend dress code. Boys and girls alike wore straight-leg jeans and T-shirts or oxford button-downs. I wore jeans too, but felt slightly odd in my flowered thrift-store blouse.

"Why are *you* on the yearbook, Bea?" Tiza said. "The yearbook's all about our storied past, our twelve or fifteen years growing up together, and you've been here, what, two weeks?"

"Why don't you join the Social Committee with us?" Anne asked. "We get to plan all the parties and dances."

"Not that they're ever so great," Tiza said.

"This year they will be," AWAE swore.

"I'm not the social type," I said.

"Everyone is social." Tom Garber and another boy hopped their butts up onto the kitchen counter. Tom wore his glasses propped on top of his head, so his girl-melting microwave beams could blaze all the more powerfully from his eyes. "Partying is human nature. Right, Walt?"

"Right." His friend nodded, which shook the puff of light brown curls on top of his head. I recognized him from school. He was tall and lanky and freckled, all elbows, and his hair made him look like a pencil topped with a soft brown eraser.

"This is Walt, my designated sidekick for the evening," Tom said.

"Why don't I ever get to be your designated sidekick?" AWAE asked.

Tom shrugged. "You're Anne's designated sidekick. You can only sidekick for one person at a time."

AWAE pouted. "Who made up that rule?"

"I did," Tom said.

"She's not my sidekick," Anne said. "She's my friend."

"Be real." Tom hopped off the counter. "Come on, Beatrice, I'll take you on a party tour." Walt jumped down too. "Walt's coming with us. He could use a social refresher course himself."

Walt laughed, and his puff of hair shook some more. He opened the refrigerator and grabbed three cans. "Beer for the road?"

Tom took one and gave one to me. "Good idea. Excellent work, Sidekick." He led me out of the kitchen. I glanced back at Anne.

"You'll be back in five minutes," she said. "There's nothing to see."

Tom and Walt and I trekked through a den where a few couples were making out. "This is the den, otherwise known as the Long-Term Relationship Zone," Tom said. "I never linger in this zone. Do you, Walt?"

"No, never have," Walt said.

"I barely even know these people," Tom said, studying the maker-outers as if they were animals in a zoo. "They're too busy being serious about each other. Let's move on." He crossed the room and opened a door leading downstairs. "That brings us to the Freaks. The Freaks always congregate in the basement. Shhh — we don't want to startle them."

The basement was dark and smoky and thumping with loud music. A tangle of rumpled, greasy-haired guys and girls sprawled on a plaid couch next to a lava lamp. One of the boys was smoking a joint.

"This is Justine, Harlan, Sphere, and Aislin," Walt said. "Do you guys know Beatrice?"

They lazily rolled their eyes in my direction. "No."

"Pass me that joint, Harlan," the black-haired Aislin said.

"Oh no, you don't." Tom snatched the joint out of Harlan's fingers. "Too quick for you, huh?" He took a hit, then passed it to Walt, who passed it to me without puffing.

"No, thanks," I said. "I'm paranoid enough as it is."

"Me too," Walt said. He gave the joint to Aislin and took a sip of beer. Harlan eyed the can.

"Somebody go get me a beer?" Harlan said. "I can't handle the ozone up there."

"Get me one too." Sphere looked at Justine as if he expected her to make the run.

"What?" Justine smacked him on the arm. "Do I look like your slave girl?"

"My slave girl would have one of those Cleopatra cuts and lots of black eyeliner like an Egyptian chick," Sphere said. "So no, you don't."

"You want a beer, go get it yourself," Aislin said.

"I think we've seen enough of the Freaks," Tom said. "You get the idea, Beatrice. Basically, stay out of the basement."

"Fuck off, Garber," Harlan said.

"On to the back porch, where the Cigarette Smokers lurk." Tom led our small parade back up the stairs.

"Hey, bring down some beers!" Sphere called after us.

"The Freaks are very lazy," Tom said.

"It's probably all that weed," Walt said.

"Right you are, Walt."

Walt smiled at me. "Awesome tour, right?"

"Awesome," I said.

"Where did you move here from?" Walt asked.

"Iceland," I said.

"Iceland?" Walt said. "Really?"

He looked at me funny, like he wondered if something was wrong with me. I'd seen that same look on Anne's and AWAE's faces too. I wasn't trying to be weird, but I felt like a weirdo. I didn't know why I'd said Iceland. The word just popped out of my mouth. Maybe I was feeling icy. Explaining it would only make me seem stranger.

"I mean Ithaca."

"Ithaca, New York?"

"Yeah."

"That's kind of different from Iceland."

The kitchen was packed now, but Anne and AWAE were gone. Walt and Tom traded their empty beer cans for fresh ones, and we stepped outside to the porch.

"You're back," Anne said. She and AWAE were smoking Camel Lights. "How was the fabulous tour?"

"It's not over yet," Tom said. "Beatrice, these are the Smokers."

"I'm not a smoker," Anne protested.

"Then why are you smoking?" Walt said.

"It's just this once," Anne said.

"Just this once every weekend," AWAE said.

It was a warm night, still no hint of fall. Tom plopped himself into a hammock strung between two trees in the yard. "Come on, Beatrice! This is the hammock part of the tour." He patted the tiny space beside him.

I looked at Walt. "The Hammock Tour is optional," he said.

"Good." I sat on the porch railing instead.

"Why did you say you were from Iceland?" Walt said. "That was kind of weird."

I hesitated, acutely aware of the blankness on my face, the stiff way my head moved. But Walt had asked and so I had to answer, to complete the task. That's what robots do.

"I don't know," I said. "I heard this thing on the radio once. On the BBC. They said some scientists had studied everybody in the whole world and found that the happiest people on earth are hair-dressers in Iceland. I guess that little fact got stuck in my brain somehow and decided to pop out on its own." *Searching circuits for relevant data*, I thought to myself. *Stupid robot dork.*

"Hairdressers in Iceland? Really?" Walt said.

"I swear."

"What about Swedish hairdressers?" Walt said. "Are they sec-ond happiest? How about Icelandic garage mechanics?"

"They didn't get into that. Just that Icelandic hairdressers are the happiest. No one knows why."

"Huh," Walt said. "That's a very interesting fact. Got any more interesting facts to share?"

"Fresh out," I said. My mind was blanking, as if all the facts I ever knew were slowly draining away.

I watched the smokers puff away and the drinkers sip from their sweating cans. Tom Garber rocked on the hammock and I felt uncomfortable. I wanted to like people. It worried me that I didn't.

"I can't stay too late," I said.

"I don't blame you," Walt said. "But you should stay late, any-way. If you leave, who will I talk to? What will become of me?"

"You could go back to being Tom's sidekick."

"Sidekick for Tom is a dead-end job," Walt said with a lopsided grin. "No hope of advancement."

I set my empty beer can on the porch railing. "Where's the bathroom?" I asked. The easiest way to get a boy to stop talking.

Walt pointed into the house. "Through the kitchen, under the stairs."

"Thanks." I went inside, just as three skinny girls in sundresses came out. "Uck," Anne muttered. "Radnor bitches."

The tallest skinny girl, a blonde, stepped out on the smokers' porch and waved to Anne and AWAE. "Where's Tiza?" she asked. "Oh, look who's on the hammock."

Tom sat up and scooched over. "Plenty of room, Meredith. Room for all three of you."

The blonde laughed. "Tom always has plenty of room for everybody."

I left them all outside, laughing and chattering. I tried the bathroom door but it was locked. "There's another one in the basement!" a girl shouted at me from the other side of the door.

I wasn't dying to go back down there. *Stay out of the basement* struck me as the wisest words Tom Garber had said all night.

I toyed with the idea of trying upstairs, but decided to brave the Freak Zone. I stopped at the fridge and grabbed a six-pack to placate the Freaks, as a sort of toll for crossing their territory.

Halfway down the basement stairs, I stumbled upon a white blob in the darkness. Jonah. He was sitting on the steps alone. Just sitting there. I sat next to him.

"Hey," I said. "What are you doing here?"

"Partying," Jonah said.

"Me too," I said. "Beer?"

"You're making yourself useful. I like that." He tugged a National Bohemian out of the plastic ring that bound the cans together. I took one too.

"Hey — who's up there?" one of the Freak boys shouted from the couch.

I stood up and peeked over the railing. "I was just on my way to the bathroom."

"Is someone spying on us?" Aislin yelled.

I swung the beer cans in their plastic noose and started down the stairs. Jonah followed me.

"It's the new girl!" Harlan bellowed. "What's your name again?"

"Beatrice," I said.

"Beatrice!" Sphere said. "You brought beer!"

I tossed the beer on his lap. "Here you go. Where's the bathroom?"

Justine pointed at a dark corner. "Back there."

I went into the bathroom, switched on the light, and shut the door. While I peed, I could hear Harlan say, "All hail Beatrice!"

"Beee-ya-triss!" the basement kids yelled, all together. "Bee-ya-triss!"

It wasn't easy to pee with people just outside the door calling my name, but I really had to go.

"Oh look, it's Ghost Boy," Harlan said. "Didn't see you there, buddy."

"Ghost Boy, where you been? Out haunting people?" Sphere said.

"That's right," Jonah said. "Boo."

"Do you still go to Canton?" Justine said. "I never see you anymore."

"I'm in your Calculus class," Jonah said.

"You are?"

I came out of the bathroom. "Want to get out of here?" Jonah said.

"Yes," I said. "Get me out of here. Future Beatrice thanks you in advance."

He led me upstairs. "Hey!" Harlan said. "Where are you taking our beer girl? Beer girl, bring back another six!"

"I call her Gertie," Jonah said, patting his car's vinyl dashboard. "Slow, dowdy, big-hipped, and I can't help loving her. Like a grandma."

"Is your grandmother named Gertie?" I asked.

"Mine isn't," Jonah said. "Wasn't. But somebody's is."

Gertie was a roomy, maroon, ancient Pontiac. We left the tidy houses of Rogers Forge behind and drove downtown. The houses got bigger and the yards got leafier as we turned onto Roland Avenue.

"Where are we going?" I asked.

"I don't know. You want to see a movie? *Female Trouble* is playing at the Charles tonight. Midnight show. Ever see it? I love it when Dawn Davenport kicks over the family Christmas tree because she didn't get cha-cha heels and the father says, 'Nice girls don't wear cha-cha heels!'"

"What are cha-cha heels?"

"Some kind of cool shoes, I guess."

"Then what happens?"

"The mother starts crying, 'Not on Christmas, not on Christmas. . . .' I don't want to spoil the rest for you."

"I should probably get home," I said. According to Gertie's dashboard, it was eleven o'clock. I didn't have a curfew, exactly, but even my out-of-it parents would probably notice if I didn't come home until two in the morning. "Tell me the rest of the movie," I said. "I promise to see it another time."

"Okay. After Dawn Davenport has a meltdown on Christmas, she runs away, rapes herself, and gets pregnant. She has the baby alone in the woods. She doesn't have a knife or anything so she bites off the umbilical cord herself!"

"Ew!" I said. "Wait — what do you mean, she rapes herself?"

"Oh. Well, Dawn Davenport is played by a man — a cross-dresser named Divine. So in the scene where she gets raped, Divine plays Dawn *and* the scary hick rapist. Dawn Davenport ends up becoming a serial killer."

"I've got to see this movie," I said.

"You really do," Jonah said.

We drove past the Cathedral of Mary Our Queen, a marble monolith lit up like Cinderella's castle. The more austere Canton campus nestled up to it, right next door.

"Make a left here," I said. The turn for my street, St. Dunstan's Road, was across from the Canton entrance. Jonah turned left and drove the three blocks to my house.

"This is it?" he said.

"This is it," I said. "Not much to it, is there?"

He shrugged. "It's a house. They're all just houses."

"Yeah. Well, see you at school on Monday." I got out of the car.

"See you."

The house was dark and quiet. I went upstairs, giving my parents' door a knock to let them know I was home. Then I went into my room and turned on the radio, as I had so many nights before. It felt different this time, though. This time I knew someone else who was out there listening too.

CHAPTER 6

The next night I felt restless. It had been a summery Saturday but by evening the wind shifted and a dry chill blew in from the north. There was no party to go to, not even a dull party from which my future self would need to be rescued.

Mom and Dad went out to a "Welcome New Faculty" dinner at the Hopkins Club. First they had a big fight over whether Mom should wear a blouse she'd made out of the kitchen–chicken curtain material. Dad thought it might make a bad impression on his new colleagues. Mom said she didn't care how silly it looked — she was meeting these people for the first time and needed the chickens for moral support.

"Bea, what do you think?" Dad turned to me to break the stalemate. My usual role.

"I say no chicken blouse," I said. "Sorry, Mom."

Dad smiled triumphantly while Mom did the Pinch. But she changed her blouse — thank God, because Anne Sweeney's mother would probably be at the dinner, and I didn't need Anne going all Fashion Police on my mother at Assembly on Monday morning.

"You win," Mom said to Dad. "But I'm not going to be friendly to *anyone*."

After they left, I sat on the front porch and read until it got too dark to see. Then I watched night come to the neighborhood.

Dressed-up couples drove off for Saturday-night dates. A group of kids — eighth or ninth graders — clustered in the alley across the street, then wandered off to loiter somewhere else. Three boys rolled by on skateboards, wheels clacking on the uneven sidewalk.

I was just about to go inside when a big old Pontiac chugged down the street and paused in front of my house. Jonah stuck his head out the window and squinted at the porch, as if he was trying to figure out if anyone was home.

"Hey." I waved. "What's up?" I half ran down the steps to the car and peered in.

"Get in," he said. "We're going downtown."

"What for?" I said.

"To celebrate!" he said.

"To celebrate what?"

"I'll tell you in the car."

"Is it something good?"

"Celebrations usually are," he said. "This one's kind of mixed, though."

I hesitated. Would Mom and Dad get mad if they got home and found me gone? I could call Dad on his cell and ask, but what if he said no? That would be inconvenient, since I really felt like going out. "I'll be right back," I said. I ran inside and jotted a quick note. *Went out for a little while with* — I paused — *a friend from school.* Dad would like that. *Back soon.*

I changed out of my shorts into jeans and stuffed some money and lip gloss in a small bag. My cell phone glared at me from my desk. I reached for it, then stopped. Mom and Dad could reach me on my cell if they were worried, but I hated that. Just when you were away from them and having fun, the portable babysitter rang and interrupted everything. Lately I'd been "forgetting" to take it with me, and I saw no reason to change my policy that night, so I left the phone on my desk and went back out to meet Jonah.

"Ready?" he asked, revving the engine.

"Ready."

"Let's go."

He drove downtown. "So what are we celebrating?" I asked.

"Wait till we get there," he said.

"Get where?"

"You'll see."

We turned onto St. Paul Street, rounding past Johns Hopkins. The brick rowhouses gave way to skyscrapers and the flash of downtown: the newspaper offices, the hospitals and hotels, the Washington Monument lit up on its hill. Traffic was light. Jonah turned onto Charles Street and parked on an ornate but faded block of stores and apartments. We walked up a few stairs to a store-front. Printed on the glass in chipped gold letters: CARMICHAEL'S BOOK SHOP AND BEER STUBE.

"They never card here." Jonah opened the door. "They're too busy being insane."

We walked into a used bookshop. I kicked a dust bunny across the splintered wooden floor. A potbellied, gray man — gray hair, gray skin, gray ash hanging off the end of his cigarette — sat reading behind an old cash register. He glanced up at us, nodded, and went back to his book. From below I heard voices and the rolling swell of a blues piano.

Jonah led me downstairs to a dark bar filled with rickety mismatched furniture. The walls were covered with dusty memorabilia: old photos, framed newspaper stories from the 1940s and 50s, taxidermied animal heads, hats, machine parts. A poster advertised an upcoming show:

Monday nights at Carmichael's — The Amazing Loudini. He knew Houdini! And he does card tricks.

A wizened blue-black man in a suit and fedora pounded on the piano, accompanied by a glass of whiskey and a large tip jar.

We took a table by the piano. The other tables were occupied by college students, young couples on dates, and a smartly dressed older couple on a nostalgia trip. A skinny, sweaty, bug-eyed man and woman twitched in the corner. The woman was missing one of her front teeth.

The waiter, rumpled and gray like his upstairs counterpart, took our order.

"Two bottles of Boh," Jonah ordered. The waiter wiped his nose and shuffled away.

"It's best to stick with bottles," Jonah told me. "The glasses here are filthy. I think they wash them with spit."

"Ew," I said.

"But this place is cheap," Jonah said. "Beer's only a dollar."

The customers talked right over the music, clapping when the piano player finished his song. He nodded and picked up the tip jar, teetering around the room and shaking it suggestively. Everyone tipped him except for the junkies in the corner, who pretended not to see him. Maybe they really didn't see him. They were arguing in a heated whisper.

Jonah stuffed two dollars in the tip jar. The waiter brought our beers. I wiped the mouth of my bottle with a napkin, just in case.

"Taking a break," the piano player announced. He sat at his piano bench and polished off his whiskey.

"My parents used to come here on dates," Jonah said. "When they were in college, and just after. Everybody's parents did. The place was different then. Not as scuzzy."

We sipped our beers. I waited a polite amount of time for him to tell me his news. I counted to five. He said nothing.

"So —" I said. "We're here. Now can you please tell me what we're celebrating?"

"Okay." He took a long swig of beer. "But it's kind of a long story." He swigged again. "Here goes. I just found out that someone I thought was dead is alive."

I gasped. "Your mother?"

He narrowed his eyes at me. "How do you know about my mother? Oh, right. Bigmouth Sweeney."

"Is she alive?"

"No." He scowled. "Now you're spoiling my mood."

"I'm sorry. Who's alive?"

"My twin brother, Matthew." He paused. "Do you know all about him too?"

I picked at the damp, sticky label on my bottle. "Only a little bit."

"Good," he said. "Then I'll tell you the rest."

I nodded. He continued.

"I answered the phone this afternoon and some woman said, 'Mr. Tate? This is Mrs. Trevanian. I thought I should let you know that Matthew has had a seizure.'"

"That's very weird," I said.

"At first I thought it must be a wrong number, but she called me 'Mr. Tate,' right? So even though my head was spinning and I could hardly think, I just kind of said 'Mm-hmm,' and let her keep talking. She said that Matthew was in the infirmary, and they were going to try a new medication. So I said, 'All right, fine,' trying to sound like my father, and she hung up. Then I sat down and wondered what the hell she was talking about."

"But how could it be *your* Matthew? Couldn't it be a mistake? There must be other Matthew Tates in the world." I spoke as lightly as I could, hoping not to upset him.

"I thought of that. I mean, he was *dead*." Jonah stared across the room, his eyes unfocused. "I went to the funeral. I saw the two coffins. One for my mother and one for Matthew. I visited their graves. He was dead. They both were. But now he's alive again. Like magic."

I nervously tore at my damp napkin. What if Jonah was delusional? It seemed more likely that there'd been some kind of mistake than that his twin brother had come back from the dead. But I didn't dare say what I was thinking. "Did you ask your father about it?"

"He was out at a hospital board meeting, so I had to wait hours for him to come home. I almost went crazy trying to figure out what was going on. Finally, he walked through the door and I pounced. I told him about the phone call and demanded to know what it meant."

"And — ?"

"He said, 'You caught me by surprise,' and sat down kind of hard." Jonah gave a rueful laugh. "He's not used to being greeted by me when he gets home. We try to avoid each other as much as possible. But I knew something was up because his hands were trembling. That's not like him. He's always in control. Almost always."

With every revelation I felt myself being drawn into Jonah's world. And it was scary and thrilling. The mysterious Ghost Boy was telling *me* the disturbing details of his family life. Secrets no one else knew.

"He told me everything," Jonah said. "It's true. He admitted it. Matthew is alive."

"But how can that be?"

Jonah paused to gulp his beer. "My mother was killed in a car accident, and my father told me Matthew had died in that accident too. But it turns out Matthew wasn't even badly hurt. It's just that my father didn't see how he could take care of Matthew without my mother around. And he thought Matthew and I were too close, that I was imitating Matthew and acting all brain damage-y when I'm supposed to be normal. This was the perfect chance to separate us — and I couldn't protest. So he shipped Matthew off to an institution, secretly."

I just listened, fascinated. This was like a gothic novel, like *Jane Eyre* or *Rebecca*.

"'It's a very good place,' he told me. 'The staff knows how to take care of people like Matthew, much better than I ever could.' All so I could be free — that's what he said, 'free of that burden,' as if I ever felt Matthew was a burden — and live a normal life and make friends and blah blah blah. He insists he did it for me. For my own good, and Matthew's."

Jonah still stared in that unfocused way, and the look on his face was so bitter I was afraid to say a word.

"He won't tell me where Matthew is. He thinks I'm better off not knowing. 'Just forget about this whole incident,' he said. 'Trust me.'" Jonah shook his head. "Trust him? How can I trust a man who told me such a terrible lie? He actually buried an empty coffin in a grave marked with my brother's name! My own father! And I'm supposed to *trust* him?"

Jonah picked up his beer bottle. It left a wet ring on the table. He put it down and picked it up again, leaving a circle of rings like a flower.

"All this time I've had this weird feeling, like a phantom limb," he said. "You know how, when they cut off your leg or something, they say you can still feel it even after it's gone? Your foot itches, you go to scratch it . . . but there's nothing to scratch. That's how I've felt for ten years. Like something — or someone — is connected to me by an invisible cord, and it's always tugging, tugging, tugging . . . but when I try to reel it in, there's nothing on the other end."

He looked to me for a reaction then. I sighed, unsure what to say. It was such a wild, dramatic story, full of life and death, deceit and revelation. I felt dull and ordinary next to Jonah. Unworthy.

"What are you going to do now?" I asked. "Are you going to look for Matthew?"

"I don't know where to start."

"Find that woman, Mrs. Whatever, the one who called you," I said. "Look her up on the internet."

"Even if I find her, she won't tell me anything. If my father wants something kept quiet, he knows how to do it. He's a lawyer. He majored in intimidation in law school. Look how he convinced everyone that Matthew was dead all these years."

My parents weren't always honest with me — but this was deception on a whole different level.

"So you know he's alive but you can't see him?" I said. "Or call him, or write him, or anything?"

"You're right. What am I celebrating?" He dug a fingernail into a scratch on the table. Then he smiled, just a little with his mouth but a lot around the eyes. "I do have something to celebrate. He's alive!"

He held up his bottle and I clinked it with mine. "Cheers," I said. "To Matthew."

"To Matthew."

"We'll find him," I said. "I'll help you."

Across the room the junkie woman screeched at the junkie man, "You're a fucking liar! You fucking stole it, and you're a liar!" She jumped up and knocked over the table, spilling beer and whiskey, the glasses crashing to the floor.

I flinched. The boyfriend — or whatever he was — grabbed the woman, but she yanked her arm away and ran out. He kicked the fallen table, kicked a piece of broken glass. "Bitch!" he yelled. "Stupid bitch!"

The other customers looked up at the commotion, but no one seemed too rattled.

"Sorry, folks. She's crazy." The boyfriend held out his arms in a half shrug. "Can't do nothing about it." His mustache seemed to move instead of his lips. "Stupid crazy bitch."

He stalked out. The piano player muttered, "Goddamn junkies." He played "Pennies from Heaven" while the tired gray waiter swept up the broken glass.

The cashier thumped down the stairs, stopping halfway and peering over the banister at the waiter. The wooden steps creaked under his weight. "Did they pay for their drinks?"

The waiter shook his head without looking up.

"Goddammit!" the cashier said. "They're never coming here again, you understand? You see them, you tell me, and I'll kick them out myself."

The waiter asked if we wanted another beer. "Let's get out of here," I said. It was midnight, and by now my parents were probably dialing my cell and listening to it ring in my room.

We left through the bookshop and stepped out onto the quiet street. Jonah started the car. Its engine purred beneath us as we drove up Charles Street.

"I'll be listening to the Night Lights tonight," I said. "You going to call in?"

He shrugged. "Who knows what the night will bring?"

Since it was after midnight, the show was already on the air. Luckily, my parents still weren't home.

Dottie:
Hello, Herb. This is Dottie.

Herb:
Hi, Dottie. How's life treating you?

Dottie:
Herb, you know, to be honest, I've got the blues.
I've got 'em bad.

Herb:
I'm sorry to hear that, Dottie. What's the matter?

Dottie:
Everything. . . . I'm just blue. What I want to know is, what do I do? How do I get rid of 'em?

Herb:
Everybody gets the blues, Dottie. They'll go away eventually.

Dottie:
You think so?

Herb:
Sure. You've just got to weather those hard times, and, before you know it, the sun is shining again. Maybe some of our listeners can help you out.

Dottie:
That would be nice. *[fairy music]* Guess I better go. Nighty-night, Herb.

Herb:
Nighty-night, Dottie. Cheer up! Next caller, you're on the air.

Kreplax:
Herb, Kreplax here.

Herb:
Hello, Kreplax. Been to the future lately?

Kreplax:
Funny you should ask, Herb. You know that lady, Dottie, might try a little time travel. It's like

magic — you go to another time and leave your troubles behind. Poof! Works for me.

Herb:
That would be nice, but it doesn't sound very practical.

Kreplax:
Practical, shmactical. Lighten up, Dottie! I called for another reason. I want to invite all the listeners to a party at my house in West Baltimore. Saturday, October 4. It's a Party for People from the Future.

Herb:
A what?

Kreplax:
Think about it, Herb. Let's say you're a young guy in the future, say a hundred years from now. You're hanging out next to the time-travel machine, bored, and one of your friends says, "Let's go back in time." You got nothing better to do, so you say, "What time should we go back to?" You scroll through history, looking for a fun time to check out. You see that a hundred years ago, in Baltimore, Maryland, some people had a Party for People from the Future. A party specifically for you! Wouldn't you want to go?

Herb:
I guess I would.

Kreplax:

I figure if I advertise it well enough, kids from the future will find out about this party and get in their time-travel machines and come back — just for the party. It's going to be hot, Herb. Super smokin'.

Herb:

I'll do my darnedest to get there.

Kreplax:

And listen, people, this is important. There's a big conspiracy at NASA. It's all going to come out in a few years, but the sooner you know what's going on, the better off you'll be.

Herb:

Is this the cover-up of the lost UFO files?

Kreplax:

Bigger. When our astronauts landed on the moon in 1969, they found ruins.

Herb:

Ruins?

Kreplax:

Ruins, Herb. Ruins of an ancient civilization. We colonized the moon centuries ago! And there's proof. The government forced the astronauts to keep quiet. But I've got a copy of the tape. You can hear the astronauts describing the ruins!

Herb:

Ruins on the moon? How —?

Kreplax:

It was the Egyptians, Herb! How many times do I have to say it? The Egyptians were way more sophisticated than we give them credit for. They had a lot of help from the Martians — the same Martians who built the pyramids. *[Fairy music plays.]*

Herb:

Interesting notion, Kreplax. Next caller, what do you think?

Burt:

Herb, I've been on hold for thirty-five minutes! I've been trying to get through!

Herb:

I'm sorry about that, but everybody has to wait their turn.

Burt:

You wanna know what I think about this Kreplax guy? I think it's all bull — *[bleep].*

Herb:

Burt, you've been warned about language before. You're banned from the show for the rest of the night. Next caller?

Myrna:

Myrna here. I think that Kreplax guy is on to

something. Some nights when I look up at the moon, I swear I see the shadows of abandoned malls and such. Things sure have gone downhill since I was a little girl. For all I know they've been going downhill for centuries. Maybe everything was better in the olden days, when the spacemen built them pyramids and Elvis's ancestors ruled the earth. Who knows?

Herb:
Who knows, indeed.

Myrna:
And I wanted to say something to Dottie. Dottie honey, we love you. We all get the blues sometimes, but you got to fight it. When I get the blues, I fight like crazy, and every once in a while I have a hot fudge sundae. That really does help.

Herb:
Good advice, Myrna.

Myrna:
I wrote a little poem I hope will cheer Dottie up. Can I read it, Herb?

Herb:
Be my guest.

Myrna:
Okay. Here goes:
Late one lonely night I heard
Miss Dottie has the blues.

Think how lonesome YOU would feel
If you were in her shoes.

So all the Night Lights gather round
To bring our Dottie cheer.
Think of what would perk you up,
Your grandchild, or a beer.
Just reach out through your radio,
Let Dottie know we're here.

Herb:
Very nice, Myrna. Lovely.

Myrna:
If that doesn't do it, I don't know what will. *[fairy music]* Okay then. Nighty-night! Love ya, Herb! Love ya, Dottie!

Herb:
Nighty-night.

Poor Dottie. All night long people called in to help her get rid of her blues. I wondered if it worked. Who knows, maybe the next morning she woke up feeling bright and happy as a three-year-old child.

I didn't call in. I didn't know how to help Dottie. Jonah didn't call in, either. I wondered what he was doing, what he was thinking, lying alone in his room in the dark. Maybe his father was lying in the dark too, in his room down the hall, blinking at the ceiling. Just like Jonah, and just like me.

CHAPTER 7

It was a stupid plan. I don't know why we thought it would work; we certainly didn't think it all the way through. But we had to try something.

I made an appointment with Mr. Tate. I didn't bother using a fake name; he'd never heard of me. I asked Mr. Tate's secretary for his first appointment after lunch: one-thirty.

Jonah and I cut out of school at lunchtime and drove downtown to the tall, old building where his father worked. Jonah waited in the hall while I walked into Mr. Tate's office, forty-five minutes early, when I knew Mr. Tate would be out to lunch. His secretary sat at her desk, eating a salad out of a deli container.

I was dressed for the occasion in a skirt and flats so it would look as if I really had business to discuss with a lawyer. Jonah and I had argued over which story to tell his father. Jonah preferred Option 1: I was terminally ill — or, even better, planning my own suicide — and wanted to make out my will; but I liked Option 2: I hated my parents and wanted to apply for emancipated minor status. We'd read about teen movie stars who became emancipated to keep their parents from controlling their careers and stealing their earnings. It sounded lovely and glamorous to me. If only I'd had any earnings, I would have tried the same thing.

Jonah waited just outside the office door. Mr. Tate's secretary had met him before, of course, and would recognize him. So we'd planned a signal: I'd knock twice on the outer office door to let him know when the coast was clear.

The secretary put down her plastic fork and looked up at me. "May I help you?"

"Hi, I have an appointment with Mr. Tate at one-thirty," I said. "My name is Beatrice Szabo."

"You're early," the secretary said. "He's not back from lunch yet. But you can sit over there and wait if you like."

"Thank you." I sat on a couch in the little waiting area and picked up a *Baltimore* magazine. I pretended to flip through it for a few minutes. The secretary munched on her salad. Framed certificates and photos hung behind her on the wall: *Thank You from the Boys and Girls Clubs of Baltimore, Big Brothers of America Contributor of the Year, Honorary Chairman of the Council of Independent Schools Scholarship Committee.*

I stood up and approached the secretary again. "I'm sorry to bother you, but may I use the ladies' room?" I could be very polite when I needed to be.

"Sure," she said. "It's just around the corner. Here's the key." She reached under her desk and handed me a wooden block with a *W* painted on it and a key attached.

"Thank you," I said. I took the key to the bathroom and opened the door. Inside were three stalls and three sinks. I took all the toilet paper out of each stall and dumped it in the garbage can. I covered the rolls with a few crumpled paper towels, in case anyone looked in the trash can and saw all the toilet paper and wondered what kind of lunatic had sabotaged the women's bathroom. I felt bad about wasting so much paper, but it was necessary for the plan.

I went back to the secretary's desk and said, "I'm sorry to bother you again, but there's no toilet paper in the bathroom."

"Really?" The secretary looked bewildered. "That's funny — there was plenty this morning."

I shrugged and shook my head. "I don't know, but there isn't any now."

"Huh." She stood up and started toward the bathroom. I followed, giving the outer office door a couple of quick knocks on my way.

The secretary took the key from me, and together we went into the bathroom. She checked all the stalls. "You're right. I'll get some toilet paper for you. Sorry about that."

"It's okay," I said. I stepped into the hall and watched her go to a supply closet next to the bathroom. I glanced toward the reception area, but couldn't see anything. The plan was for Jonah to sneak into his father's office while I kept the secretary busy. Once inside, he'd have half an hour or so to snoop around before his father came back from lunch. We hadn't really figured out how we'd get him out of there yet. The rest of the plan involved a lot of finger crossing.

The secretary loaded six rolls of toilet paper into her arms. I offered to help, and she handed two of them to me. We went back into the bathroom and put two rolls in each stall.

"Thanks again," I said.

"You're welcome," the secretary said. She went back to her post.

I peed and washed my hands. I felt nervous. Would I really have to face Jonah's father and pretend I wanted to hire him to make me an emancipated minor? I was beginning to wonder if I could pull it off. Maybe I should just tell the secretary that I had to leave and would reschedule my appointment for another day.

I walked back out to the reception area and smiled at the secretary. I sat down, picked up the *Baltimore* magazine, and glanced at Mr. Tate's closed office door. Had Jonah made it inside?

I checked my watch. Five to one. I really, really wanted to leave. But I couldn't abandon Jonah. He might need me to distract the secretary again, so he could get out of the office before Mr. Tate came back.

The outer office door opened and a tall, thin man walked in. His fine white hair circled a shiny bald spot. He wore a dark suit. His eyes were large and pale and looked just like Jonah's, only waterier.

My stomach knotted. This, I felt sure, was Mr. Tate, back from lunch, early.

"Hello, Melanie," he said to the secretary, who quickly stashed her salad container under her desk and wiped her mouth. Mr. Tate put a large plastic-wrapped brownie on her desk. "I thought you might like a treat."

"Thanks, Mr. Tate," Melanie said. "I'm dieting."

"Don't be silly," he said. "A brownie every now and then can't hurt."

"Yes, but you bring me one every day," Melanie said.

"Because I know you like them," Mr. Tate said. "And you won't buy one for yourself."

"That's because I'm dieting," Melanie said.

"And I told you dieting is silly." He started for his office.

I stared at the smooth wooden door. Jonah was in that office doing God knows what, probably rifling through a secret file. Mr. Tate was about to catch him in the act of snooping. I had to stop him somehow.

"Oh — Mr. Tate, your one-thirty is here," Melanie said, gesturing toward me. I stood up.

"Hello, Mr. Tate," I said. "I'm Beatrice Szabo. I'm really looking forward to talking to you, but I was wondering if we could go downstairs and get a cup of coffee or something?"

Mr. Tate eyed me suspiciously. As an estate lawyer, he probably didn't have many (or any) seventeen-year-old clients. But he was polite. "Pleasure to meet you, Beatrice," he said. "I've just had lunch, so I'd rather talk in my office if you don't mind. I'm sure Melanie would be glad to get you a cup of coffee, if that's what you want."

"Thank you."

"I'll call for you when I'm ready."

"All right," I said.

He turned and started for the door. My pulse thrummed in my forehead. I had to stop him, I had to stop him, but I couldn't stop him, I didn't know how. I had no idea what to do. My brain emptied, useless as a rusty tin box.

I watched helplessly as Mr. Tate opened the office door, stepped inside, and closed the door behind him.

I stared at the door and waited for something to happen. Nothing happened.

Melanie retrieved her salad container and stuffed a few last bites into her mouth before throwing it in the trash under her desk. She swallowed some diet soda and put that away too. "Want this brownie?" She held it out to me.

"No, thanks," I said.

She sighed and unwrapped it. She picked at it with her fingers. "He gets me one every day, and every day I eat it. What else am I supposed to do?"

I shrugged, gripping the magazine in my hands. I could not take my eyes from the door. Not a sound came from inside. I sat frozen, squeezing that magazine until it accordioned, for fifteen minutes.

Jonah must not be in there, I thought. His father would have shouted or kicked him out or something by now. But if Jonah wasn't on the other side of that door, where was he?

At last Melanie's intercom buzzed. "Please tell Miss Szabo that I can't see her today," Mr. Tate said. "Ask her to reschedule her appointment — if she sincerely wants to."

"Yes, sir." Melanie looked at me across the reception area. "Sorry," she said. "Would you like to reschedule?"

"No, that's okay." I hopped up off the couch, dropped the crumpled magazine on the coffee table, and hurried toward the outer door. "Thanks, though."

I half expected to see Jonah crouched in the hallway, but he wasn't there.

He had to be in the office. Maybe he'd told his father about our trick. I was lucky to get off so easily.

But now what? I took the elevator downstairs and stood outside the office building. I watched the business people hurry up and down the street — the khaki suits, the sensible pumps, the sweaty messengers. I waited for Jonah. I almost wished I smoked so I'd have something to do. It felt like a Barbara Stanwyck moment, a tense black-and-white scene from a film noir. She always had a cigarette ready for times like these.

After another fifteen minutes, Jonah appeared beside me, looking shaken. "What happened?" I asked.

"Nothing," he said.

"Did he catch you?"

"Yes, he caught me," Jonah said. "He found me digging through a file drawer."

"And —?"

"And nothing."

"Something must have happened."

"Come on, let's go back to school." We walked to where we'd parked Gertie. The parking meter had run out, but luckily we didn't have a ticket.

"What happened?" I said. "I can't believe you won't tell me after I sat there and waited, all ready to pretend I wanted to be an emancipated minor —"

"Get in the car." He opened the door and sat in the driver's seat. I got in and closed the door.

"Did you find out anything about Matthew?" I asked.

"No. And my father says I never will."

"He said that? What else did he say?"

He started the car, and we drove up Charles Street back toward school. Jonah said he'd refused to leave the office until Mr. Tate told him where Matthew was. Mr. Tate said Jonah was wasting his time. Mr. Tate would never tell. For Jonah's sake. He kept saying that: He was doing it for Jonah.

Then the two of them sat and stared at each other for fifteen minutes without uttering a word.

Finally, Mr. Tate stood up and opened the office door. "I have work to do," he said. "Leave, or I'll drag you out. I'll ask Melanie to help if I need to."

"He wouldn't really do that," I told Jonah.

"Of course he would," Jonah said. "Haven't you figured it out yet — he'll do anything!"

"So you left?"

"I don't want to be responsible for poor Melanie breaking a nail while dragging me out of my father's office," Jonah said. "Plus I knew you were probably wondering what the hell was going on."

"I was."

"Well, that's what was going on. Nothing."

Jonah leaned on the gas, and we zoomed through the city. I was late for English, but I didn't care. Nothing seemed less important than being on time for English.

"What are you going to do now?" I asked. "You're not giving up, are you?"

"No," Jonah said. "I don't know what to do next. But I'm not giving up."

LY AUGUST SEPTEMBER OCTOBER

CHAPTER 8

Now that Jonah and I were officially friends, Anne Sweeney gave up trying to weave me into the social fabric. When I was with Jonah, everyone else in school seemed to drift away. He wasn't very friendly to anyone but me, which didn't help. Anne and AWAE and Tiza and Carter stopped asking me to sit with them at lunch. I preferred to sit with Jonah, anyway.

I asked him for his cell phone number and email address so we could IM in the middle of the night and text during class like everybody else.

"I don't have a cell phone," he said. "In my room I have a rotary phone from the sixties. It takes forever to dial, which keeps me from making impulsive calls." We were sitting in the senior hall, leaning against our lockers with our legs sticking out. People walked by, stepping over our feet.

"Who would you make impulsive calls to?"

"The Night Lights. You. People on my Enemies List."

"Who's on your Enemies List?"

"Pretty much everyone." A boy tripped over Jonah's shoe. Jonah didn't blink. "I'd rather talk to you in person, anyway, so I can see your weird little fang."

It's true, I have a tiny, pointy canine tooth. It gives my mouth a rickety quality I'd never liked until that moment.

"If we're in class, pass me a note the old-fashioned way," Jonah said.

"Okay with me." I was leaning away from techno-communication myself. What did I need a cell for, anyway? It's not like anyone ever called me.

Jonah had a laptop, and he wasn't above using it when he needed information. He scoured the internet for institutions that might be housing Matthew, and sent emails to doctors, nurses, and administrators asking for information. The people who bothered to respond usually brought up patient confidentiality and refused to answer any questions. I did some Googling myself, to help out, but I had to be careful since my mother had no sense of boundaries when it came to privacy. Diaries, emails, search histories, phone calls — she considered nothing of mine off-limits from her prying, which was pretty hypocritical of her considering how guarded she was with her own secrets.

On Saturdays, Jonah went to the library to use their computers, since his father was often rumbling around at home, and Jonah didn't want him to stumble across his secret mission. I went with him, helping search the internet and sometimes skimming through old phone books from the year Matthew "died," hoping to find some outdated clue the internet had missed. We read medical journals and books about treating brain-damaged patients, following up every mention of a doctor or institution that worked with them, starting in Maryland and working our way outward — north, south, and west across the country — hoping it would lead us to Matthew.

Jonah took the phone numbers home and dialed them after school before his father came home from work, day after day after day, asking for Matthew Tate, hoping to find a trace of him. But so far he hadn't found anything.

I avoided going to Jonah's house because I didn't want to run into his father. I was afraid Mr. Tate would yell at me for trying to trick him.

We listened faithfully to the Night Light Show and looked forward to Kreplax's Party for People from the Future. October 4 came at last. I spent that afternoon polishing my college application essay, but I was too excited to concentrate. Maybe my college self would show up at the Party for People from the Future and tell me where I'd get in — somewhere good, I hoped. Then I'd only have to fill out one application.

Over the summer, I'd visited campuses from Maine to Philadelphia with Mom and Dad, settling on a nice array of just-below-Ivy schools to go with my solid-not-stellar SATs. The colleges shone like warm beacons along the Eastern Seaboard, each a small lighthouse: Bowdoin, Bates, Wesleyan, Vassar, Haverford. Professor Dad endorsed them all — cozy and safe, yet intellectually stimulating. I tossed NYU in there to shake things up, the one urban school on the list. Maybe, when the time came, I wouldn't want cozy and safe. Maybe I'd want glamour and danger. Why not keep my options open? By next year I could be a whole new person. Anything was possible in the Future.

Jonah came over to my house after supper to get dressed for Kreplax's party. Meeting people from the Future seemed to demand costumes.

"Do you think any of the other Night Lights will show up?" I asked. "I want to meet Myrna. And poor, sad Dottie."

"I doubt Dottie will be there. She hasn't called since that night she had the blues. I think she's still sad. Plus, she's probably scared to go to West Baltimore."

My Costume of the Future was a silver minidress with silver tights, white go-go boots, a crimson wig, and white plastic sunglasses. In my mind I guess the future of fashion happened in the 1960s.

Jonah wore a mechanic's jumpsuit sprayed with glow-in-the-dark paint, and goggles decorated with red sparkles. Kind of a Devo look. We weren't the weirdest-looking people at the party, though. Not by a long shot.

A wrinkled man in a snappy suit and panama hat guarded Kreplax's doorway. "Are you from the future?" he asked us.

"No," Jonah said. "Are you?"

"Do I look like I'm from the future?" The old man trained his bloodshot eyes on the next guests. "I want to meet somebody from the future. I want to know what's going to happen to my grandbabies."

Kreplax lived in a rowhouse not far from the Art Institute. The next block over was rubble, boarded up and abandoned. He'd hung a large banner from a second-story window that said, in spray-painted letters, WELCOME, PEOPLE FROM THE FUTURE. Guests flowed through the house, from the front stoop to the weedy backyard.

"How many of these people do you think are actually from the future?" I asked Jonah.

"You ask dumb questions sometimes," he said, taking my hand. "Come on, I want to meet Kreplax."

In the kitchen, the refrigerator door hung open, heavy with beer. Everything from the top of the stove to the jelly jar glasses was coated with a greasy film. The white ceramic of the sink had gone rusty. The cupboards were papered with cutouts from magazines, pictures of UFOs, the pyramids, the Grand Canyon, and a few naked women.

A guy in a leather vest and no shirt but lots of tats pumped beer out of a keg. "Are you Kreplax?" Jonah asked.

The guy shook his head.

"Do you know where he is?" Jonah asked.

"I don't even know who you're talking about," the guy said.

We wandered through the house, past ratty furniture, cracked linoleum, and wallpaper that looked like it had been clawed off in places.

"Are you from the future?" Jonah asked a chubby kid with a green mohawk.

"No, I'm a shape-shifter," the kid said. "But I can see how you'd make that mistake." He touched the sharp edge of his hairdo.

"What's a shape-shifter?" I asked.

"Sometimes I turn into a reptilian creature," the kid said. "I'm unconscious when it happens, but my friends have actually witnessed it. Once it happened while I was riding my bike."

"When you shape-shift, do you turn into a reptile with a green mohawk?" Jonah asked.

"No, but I get a kind of fin thing that runs down my back."

"Cool," Jonah said. "Can you do it now?"

"Do what?" the mohawk boy said.

"Shape-shift into a reptilian," Jonah said.

"I'll try." The boy squeezed his eyes shut, concentrating. Nothing happened.

"It's not working," he said. "Sorry."

"That's okay," I said. "Maybe later."

"It never works when you try to do it on purpose like that," the boy said.

We found Kreplax in the basement, showing off a half-built wooden canoe screwed onto a rack. We knew he was Kreplax because he wore a large sign around his neck that said I AM KREPLAX. He had a gray beard and wore a togalike dressing gown and a Roman centurion helmet made of tinfoil. He noticed us and said, "Welcome, time travelers. How far have you come?"

"From another world," Jonah said. "Homeland. And Roland Park."

"Homeland is the past, not the future," Kreplax said. "This is Tita and Gryphon. They're from Toronto, 2110."

"Greetings," Tita said.

Tita and Gryphon didn't look particularly futuristic. Tita had flowing gray-blond hair and wore a print housedress and a wreath of dandelions. Gryphon — tall, thin, giant Adam's apple poking from his long neck — wore a kind of brown pilgrim suit.

"Did you come just for the party, or —?" Jonah asked.

"No, we've been living in this time thread for a while," Gryphon said. "Somebody brought back some 'shrooms from an earlier time trip, and we wanted to pick up some more. Your era's drugs are much mellower than ours."

"Really?" I said.

Tita nodded. "And more organic."

"Are these the fashions of the future?" I asked.

Tita shook her head. "We bought these here in your time thread. At the Salvation Army. We couldn't get away with 2110 fashions here."

"We'd be arrested!" Gryphon said.

"Why? What do they look like?" I asked.

"Very revealing," Tita said.

"We have holes cut out where our sex organs are," Gryphon said. "To let them breathe."

"Your scientists haven't discovered this yet, but the sex organs need plenty of air," Tita said.

"You should have worn your real clothes to the party," Kreplax said. "You're among friends here. We would have understood. We would have reveled in it!"

"Yeah, I'm dying to see everybody's organs," I said.

"Instead, you'll have to make do with my Powwow canoe." Kreplax waved his arm over the half-built boat. "Are you entering a craft?"

"Powwow?" I asked.

"It's a big canoe race," Kreplax said. "We hold it every June. Anyone can enter a canoe, but it must be homemade. We launch them off the industrial beach past Pigtown. The winner gets an Indian headdress."

"Huh."

"There are bands, food, and balloons filled with nitrous oxide," Jonah said. "Five dollars for a big one."

"So it's a party," I said.

"A wingding," Kreplax said. "The police never come to that part of town. There's nothing there but abandoned factories and toxic waste."

"Sounds great."

"Some people see Powwow as just an excuse to huff nitrous," Kreplax said. "But to me, it's a Clash of the Titans."

Jonah and I admired the canoe. Then we went back upstairs and settled on a lumpy couch in a second-floor den filled with charts, maps, and books.

Two guys sat on another couch across the room, drinking cans of Fresca. Their eyes flicked over us, barely taking us in. "This Kreplax guy's out of his mind," one said.

"Seriously."

"At least we landed in the right thread this time." He glanced at his BlackBerry — at least, that's what I thought it was. "Dude, it's almost my birthday! We've got to get back. I don't want to spend my birthday with a bunch of twenty-first century Neanderthals."

"Let's bounce."

They disappeared into the bathroom.

"What would you say if I told you *I* was from the future?" Jonah asked.

"From when in the future?" I said.

"Say, fifty years from now. I'm my own grandson."

"I'd say bullshit."

"But how would you know for sure? You wouldn't even wonder for a minute?"

I looked at his pale Casper face, with its snowy eyebrows and lashes. He did kind of look like a mutant strain of human developed in the genetic labs of the future.

"Maybe I'm the one from the future," I said.

"Sorry," Jonah said. "That's just not believable."

We eyed the bathroom door. The two guys hadn't come out yet.

"Do you ever wish you could go back in the past and change something?" Jonah said.

"What, like assassinate Hitler?"

"I mean in your own past."

"Sometimes I'd like to stop my parents from marrying each other," I said. "But then I wouldn't exist, so it doesn't seem like a very good idea."

Jonah was quiet.

"There are a few embarrassing incidents I wouldn't mind averting," I said. "And no, I won't tell you what they are. Except to say that one of them involves peeing in my seat in first grade."

He smiled but seemed far away.

"I puked all over the lunchroom table in second grade," I said. "But that's all you get."

Still quiet.

I watched the bathroom door. The future boys didn't come out.

"What are they doing in there?" I said. "Do you think they climbed down the fire escape?"

"Maybe bathrooms are portals to the future," Jonah said. "And they've left us."

"Down the drain."

Jonah picked up a beer bottle full of cigarette stubs and shook it.

"Is there something you'd like to change?" I asked him. "About your past?"

"Yeah," he said. "I'd like to go back about nine years and cut the ignition wire to my mother's car. Or fake a fever and stay home from school so she couldn't leave the house without taking me with her."

"Maybe we could get one of these time travelers to go back for us and fix everything," I said. "But that might start a different chain reaction. . . . Some other horrible thing could happen instead. Maybe *you'd* be killed —"

"I wouldn't care," Jonah said. "That would be better than this . . . this —" He touched his chest, groping for the word he couldn't find.

"Stop." I couldn't stand it. "We'll find him."

I had to do something. In a romantic comedy, I would have been able to wipe all his troubles away with a single kiss. But that wasn't going to happen — not the kiss, not the troubles vanishing with it. I felt so close to him, but I didn't want to kiss him. And I didn't get the sense that he wanted to kiss me. So when it came to helping, all I could think of was those two Fresca-drinking time-traveler boys in the bathroom-slash-portal-to-the-future. Maybe they could show us how to zip back into the past and make everything turn out right. I'd make it happen. I'd find a way.

I got up and knocked on the bathroom door. "Hello? Fresca drinkers? Are you in there?"

No one answered. I opened the door.

The bathroom was empty.

TEMBER OCTOBER NOVEMBER

CHAPTER 9

"See that guy?" Anne pointed out a schlub sporting a cardigan and shaggy sideburns. At his side stood a surprisingly perky brunette. "That's Clayton. He's the head of the Neurobiology Department. His wife is a bed stylist."

I had to clamp my jaw shut to keep from yawning. Caroline Sweeney's annual pre–Thanksgiving faculty dinner was so boring it made my teeth ache.

"What's a bed stylist?" I asked.

"She works for Homewares, when they shoot their catalogs," Anne said. "Her whole, entire career consists of arranging the beds so they're artfully rumpled in the pictures. Like someone just had great sex in them."

"That's her job?"

"Yeah."

"For real."

"Yeah."

We snickered. I ate another gingersnap.

Anne's mother, Caroline, crossed the room, sweeping us up in her wake. She was trim and attractive, a classic brunette in pearl studs and red cashmere. "Anne, stop making fun of Clayton's wife. Why don't you and Beatrice take that tray of crab balls out to the sunporch and pass them around?"

"Okay," Anne said, her voice thick with reluctance. "Come on, Bea."

Caroline disappeared through the swinging kitchen door. My parents mingled on the sunporch — Dad telling a joke to a circle of laughing admirers, Mom hovering on the edge of the circle, staring out the window. The main attraction of the Sweeneys' backyard was a stone birdbath, iced over.

"Crab ball, Mom?" I offered her the tray.

"No, thanks, honey."

Anne offered crab balls to Dad and the others, who gobbled them up with cocktail sauce. Dad glanced back at the kitchen door, still swinging, and rattled the ice in his glass.

"Time for another scotch." He headed for the bar. The circle broke up.

"The students adore your father," a perfumed woman said to me. "Aren't you lucky to live with such a charming man!"

"He's even more charming at home," Mom said. "Isn't he, Bea? He rides a unicycle through the house —"

"— even up and down the stairs," I added.

"He juggles eggs as he makes breakfast every morning —"

"— which he serves to us in bed, of course," I said.

"— and pulls fragrant bouquets out of his ass," Mom finished. "He's just a joy."

The perfumed woman's chin jiggled. She couldn't tell if we were joking or not, but decided to play it safe and assume we were. She coughed up a brittle laugh and excused herself.

"We shouldn't do that," I said. "People will think we're weird." Actually, I didn't mind if people thought *I* was weird. But for some reason, I didn't want them to see that side of Mom — if it was just a side, and not her whole personality.

"Faculty spouses have to work hard to be liked," Mom said. "Look at that poor bed stylist person with her tight smile. I don't have it in me."

Dad didn't come back from the bar. The kitchen door was swinging again.

"Do you want to go home?" Mom asked.

"Now?" I knew the rules of faculty parties, and that would be breaking them. "We haven't had dinner yet."

"I'm not hungry. Anyway, we've got French Bread Pizzas in the freezer."

"Won't Dad be mad?" I asked.

"I'm not sure," Mom said. "I imagine he'll have mixed feelings."

The party was dull, but I didn't feel right leaving so early. It seemed rude. And I didn't want a French Bread Pizza.

"I think we should stay through dinner," I said. "This party is a big deal to Dad."

Anne tugged on my sleeve. "Let's get out of here before my mother makes us freshen people's drinks. My room."

I checked with Mom. "Go ahead," she said, and headed for the bathroom.

I followed Anne upstairs. Riding trophies and plastic horse figurines crowded her shelves. She had a vanity in the corner draped with jewelry, makeup, and nail polish bottles. On her desk was a pile of college catalogs, with Vanderbilt on top.

"We have to stick together," Anne said. "There are more faculty parties to come. A *lot* more."

"I hate them," I said. "I always feel so stiff around adults when they're trying to have fun. I get embarrassed for them, like they're trying too hard and they don't know everyone can see it."

Anne shot me a curious look, like she was thinking, *Look who's talking, party-bot.* "There is no way out," she said. "I've tried them all. Short of being hospitalized for meningitis, you've got to show your face at the faculty parties."

"I don't see why. It's not like anyone really wants to talk to us."

"We're proof they can reproduce." Anne kicked a white sneaker aside and sat on her bed. I sat beside her. She lay back and stared at her ceiling. I did the same. The ceiling was white and smooth except for a grapey lump where an old lighting fixture used to be.

"So, you've been hanging with Jonah a lot," Anne said. "Speaking of stiff."

"Uh-huh," I said.

"It's not . . . you know . . . a *thing*, is it?"

I pretended not to know what she was talking about, just to annoy her. "What do you mean?"

"You know. Carter says she saw the two of you kissing in front of the Morgue, but I told her no way, you had to be sharing a ciggie or something. Right?"

Jonah and I had never kissed, and neither of us smoked. I didn't know what Carter saw, but it wasn't a kiss. All I said was, "I don't smoke."

Anne sat up and faced me, propped on her elbow. "So it *is* a thing? I've been telling everybody that you're one hundred percent just friends."

"Why does everybody care?" I asked.

"They don't, really, except we're all so bored we've got to talk about something," Anne said. "And since Jonah hasn't had a friend in like ten years, it makes people wonder, that's all."

"Why hasn't he had a friend in ten years?" I thought I half knew the answer — something about his family tragedy, and Jonah's withdrawal — but that couldn't be the whole explanation.

"You know," Anne said. "The ghost thing. The way he's kind of not really *there*. It's not all our fault. He's never been the chummiest guy in the world. Or much of a friend."

"What do you mean?"

"He makes stuff up. You can't trust him. He lies, or at least exaggerates. When we were really little, he used to talk about these cats he had. He would try to get me to come over and play by telling me he had these two amazing cats who did all sorts of incredible tricks, and it was a total lie. He didn't have any cats. I went over to his house lots of times, and I never once saw a cat."

"He was just a kid," I said. "Maybe he was lonely."

"Don't you get it? It's manipulative. It's one thing to be lonely, but don't try to trick people into playing with you, that's all."

"Maybe he grew out of it."

"Maybe. But some people don't grow out of it. They just get better at manipulating you."

I thought she was overreacting to the whole cat thing, but I didn't say so. I didn't want to hear any more about it. She was implying that I couldn't trust Jonah, but could I trust Anne? I didn't know her well enough to say. I wanted to believe in Jonah.

"You're cleverly evading my question," Anne said. "You and Jonah. If you don't smoke and you don't kiss, and you never go to parties anymore . . . what do you guys do — read comic books?"

What could I tell her? *We listen to the radio, we think about heartbreak, we look out for time travelers, we cut yearbook meetings, we go to the library, we call institutions looking for Jonah's lost secret twin. . . .* All of that was part of a different world, a foreign country to Anne and everyone else at school. She wouldn't understand — except maybe the part about cutting yearbook meetings.

And besides, I couldn't explain it. Some of it, I didn't understand myself. We were best friends. Were we in love? Were we headed that way? I didn't know, and I didn't want to bring it up with him. It was like the one thing we couldn't talk about. Our friendship was delicate, like a bubble, and I was afraid it would pop if I asked the wrong question. *Where is this going?* definitely felt like the wrong question.

"We just hang out," I said. "It's no big mystery."

"You know what Garber told me?" Anne said.

"What?" Since I'd become friends with Jonah, Tom Garber had stopped trying to microwave me. I didn't know if he'd given up or thought Jonah's proximity tainted me in some way.

"He's lonely," Anne said. "He hasn't had a girlfriend since the summer."

"Three whole months. Poor guy."

"No, really," Anne said. "He's in a tight spot, kind of like a prince or a movie star. He's already been out with most of the cute girls at Canton at least once or twice over the years, if you start counting at around sixth grade, and he's hit all the hottest Radnor and St. Mary's girls too. He's running out of options."

"How does that make him like a prince or a movie star?" I said.

"Our social world is small and exclusive," Anne said. "Like, you know how a prince can only marry other royalty, pretty much, and there are only so many princesses to go around? And movie stars have to marry each other because their lives are so weird no non-celebrity can understand them."

"Tom's cute but he's no movie star or prince. Maybe he should relax his standards. There, problem solved."

"Relax them to what?" Anne said. "Who's he going to go out with, some grit from Glen Burnout with feathered hair and a Bawlimer accent?"

"I have no idea what you're talking about," I said, though actually I did understand a little bit from things I'd picked up on the Night Light Show. The callers' accents varied by neighborhood — the bluer the collar, the heavier the accent. The Canton kids — who mostly lived in North Baltimore and the suburbs — had slight drawls, barely noticeable. "What about you?" I asked. "When's the last time you had a boyfriend?"

"I went out with a lifeguard from the pool last summer," she said. "I'm not interested in Canton boys anymore. I'm holding out for college. I can wait."

"So Tom can wait too. Sorry, but I just don't feel bad for him."

"You don't understand," Anne said. "He's smart and he's good at sports, but girls are part of his identity too. It's sad to see him without a girl; it's like something's missing. He's got no one left to chase — except for you."

"Boo hoo hoo." This idea that I must succumb to Tom for some vague greater good, like a virgin sacrificed to pacify a dragon, disgusted me, but it also thrilled me, and that was a secret I would reveal to no one, definitely not Anne, not even Jonah.

"He hasn't paid much attention to me lately," I said. "I think he's lost interest."

"He thinks there's something between you and Jonah," Anne said. "Once I reassure him that there isn't, I bet he'll ask you out. So what should I tell him? Is there, or isn't there?"

Is there or isn't there *what*? How do you define a boyfriend? If a boyfriend is the first person you think about when you wake up in the morning and the last face you see before you fall asleep, then I was in love with Jonah. But if a boyfriend had to involve physical chemistry and kissing and sex and stuff, then, no, he wasn't that.

"It's too complicated for yes or no," I said.

"Bullshit," Anne said.

Someone knocked on the door. "Anne? Is Beatrice in there with you?"

"Yes," Anne called. Her mother opened the door. Dad hovered behind her in the hall.

"Bea, have you seen your mother?" he asked.

"She was downstairs a minute ago," I said. "She went to the bathroom."

"We can't find her anywhere," Caroline said. "Could she have gone home?"

"She wasn't feeling well," I said, covering for her.

"Her coat's still here," Caroline said.

I knew Mom had left. I could see her now, picking her way down Charles Street in her high heels and party dress, shivering in the November dusk.

Dad cursed under his breath. "She might have said something if she wanted to leave. I'd better go find her."

"I'll go," I said.

Dad hesitated.

"It's okay." I got up off Anne's bed. "You stay here, in case she comes back."

"Take the car," Dad said. "I'll walk home."

"I'll drive you home later," Anne's mother said.

"Will you call as soon as you find her?" Dad said.

"I will."

Anne followed me to her parents' room, where the bed was piled with coats. I picked out my peacoat and Mom's black velvet with the fur collar.

"What's the deal with your mom?" Anne said.

I shrugged into my coat. "I guess she hates these parties even more than we do."

We lived about a mile from the Sweeneys. I slowly cruised the streets, keeping an eye out for an underdressed, wobbly woman. She was halfway up the front steps when I reached our house.

I parked in the alley and went in through the back door. By then she was already upstairs. "Mom?" I called. The only answer was her shoes thunking to the floor as she kicked them off. I went upstairs. She was lying on the bed, still dressed in her wool shift and stockings.

"Why did you leave like that?" I said.

"The food in that house didn't smell right," she said. "Did you smell that stench from the kitchen? It was making me sick."

She closed her eyes and breathed deeply. End of discussion. I should have known better than to bother asking.

Caroline Sweeney dropped Dad off around eleven. He found me in the kitchen making a peanut butter sandwich. I'd forgotten to eat dinner.

"Where's your mom?" he asked.

"Asleep. She's been asleep since we got home."

"Great," Dad said. "That means she'll be up half the night trying eye shadow combinations in the bathroom mirror."

"Is that what she does all night?"

"Usually. Sometimes she dials the time and just lies next to me, listening to that automated voice count off the seconds. *At the tone the time will be* . . ." He shuddered.

"The party went late," I said.

"You should have come back for dinner — Caroline roasted a goose. Have you ever eaten roast goose before?"

"I don't think so."

"It's delicious. Well, good night, honey. Maybe I can snatch a few hours of sleep before the makeup seminar begins."

"Good night, Dad."

He went upstairs. I sat in the kitchen eating my peanut butter sandwich and drinking a glass of milk, one eye on the clock, waiting for the magic hour of midnight to strike. I imagined Mom lying awake with the phone next to her ear blaring, *At the tone the time will be . . . twelve . . . midnight . . . and no seconds. Beep.*

I went back to my room and turned on the radio.

Don Berman:
DonBermanDonBermanDonBermanDonBerman!
[Click.]

Herb:

Nighty-night there, Don. Next caller, you're on the air.

[The scratch of a needle on a vinyl record, the pop of a record player, and a cheesy old song plays. Lots of strings and horns, very Vegas 1976.]

Herb:

Is that you, Larry? Sounds like Larry from Catonsville. He never says much, just treats us to an old song every once in a while.

[The song plays, then fades out.]

Larry:

Hi, Herb. That was an oldie but goodie, "After the Lovin'" by Engelbert Humperdinck.

Herb:

Thanks for that walk down memory lane, Larry. I want to take a moment to remind everybody about the annual Night Light Christmas Luncheon. This year's event will be held as usual at Mario's Italian Palace on Route 40, in the heart of beautiful downtown Catonsville, on Saturday, December nineteenth at eleven A.M. I hope to see you all there. This is the perfect chance to see old friends and meet some of the voices you hear on your radio night after night. I'll be there — I'm hosting the luncheon personally. Reservations are required — call the station. What do you say, Larry? Will you make it this year?

Larry:

I'll be there, Herb. Wouldn't miss it.

Herb:

Glad to hear it. And now a message from our sponsor, Mr. Ray's Hair Weave. Gentlemen, is your hair thinning? Do people think you're older than you really are? Patch up that thatch at Mr. Ray's! Our professionals sew genuine human hair right to your skull. . . .

I dialed Jonah. It was late, but I didn't care. He had to be listening.

"We're going to the luncheon," I said.

"Your wish is my command," he said.

"Have you ever been before?"

"I wanted to go last year, but I felt weird going by myself. And I didn't have anyone to take with me. Until you came into my life, darling. You know, even after the lovin', I'm still in love with you. Funny how that works. How was La Sweeney's party?"

"Yawn. How do you think? What did you do tonight?"

"I sat in my room and drew a portrait of my closet door. Wait till you see it. It looks so true-to-life."

"I've seen closet doors before."

"Not like mine. It takes blankness to a new level." He paused. "So did she say anything to you? Did she tell you any big secrets from Our Collective Past?"

"Who?"

"You know who."

What kind of secret was he afraid Anne would leak to me? That silly thing about the cats? "No," I lied. "We talked about faculty parties and what a drag they are. Not much else. I had to leave early because of Mom."

"What did she do this time?"

"Nothing, she just left early."

"But she did it in some bonky way, right?"

How did he know? "Not that bonky. She just didn't say goodbye to anyone. And she forgot her coat."

"I knew it. I love that woman."

He did seem to like my Mom stories. That would have annoyed me except that I understood why: They made us more alike, more equal on the family weirdness scale. In the dysfunction sweepstakes Jonah would always win, but at least Mom brought me into his league.

"The show's back on," I said. "It's Kreplax. Talk to you later."

I clicked off and turned up my radio.

Kreplax:
Salutations from the World of Tomorrow, Herb.

Herb:
How was the party for the People from the Future, Kreplax? Sorry I couldn't make it.

Kreplax:
The party was fabulous. Several Futurians showed up and dropped hints about what lies ahead for our troubled human race. One major prediction was making the rounds. It's a shocker, and I thought your listeners should know.

Herb:
What's that?

Kreplax:
A comet, Herb. A deadly comet is coming this way.

Herb:
When, exactly?

Kreplax:
I'm still working out the details. Basically, it's
huge, it falls into the ocean — some disagreement
as to which ocean, which is of course crucial —
and floods the coasts, big time. Not only that,
it carries horrible viruses we have no cure for,
as well as a few tiny aliens with a fascist takeover
in mind.

Herb:
Sounds pretty bad. Are you sure about this?

Kreplax:
Oh, I'm sure.

Herb:
Well, I don't know what we can do to prepare,
except say our prayers.

Kreplax:
[snorts] Good luck with that, Herb. God died in 1945.

Herb:
Thanks for the update, Kreplax. Not a very cheer-
ful outlook for the holidays, is it? Next caller, welcome to the Night Light Show . . .

After a few hours, I drifted to sleep with visions of aliens in my
head — aliens dropping tinsel bombs all over town.

CTOBER NOVEMBER DECEMBER

CHAPTER 10

Every year before Christmas, the Canton fourth-year language classes performed holiday skits for the rest of the school. It was a special Holidays Around the World Assembly Week, and our French teacher, Mr. Meath, announced that our class's theme would be "Christmas at the Movies," or *"Cinémathèque Noël."* We would split into teams and write our own skits in French. Tom Garber volunteered me to be on his team, which also included Anne and Walt Carrey.

"Instead of doing live skits," Walt said in class, "why don't we film our skits and show them to the school like a movie?"

"Bonne idée, Jean-Pierre," Mr. Meath said. Jean-Pierre was Walt's French name.

The next question was: What movie should we spoof in our skit? Our team met after school at Anne's house to figure it out. We each nominated a film. I rented *Female Trouble*, the John Waters movie Jonah had told me about, and showed my skitmates the scene where Dawn Davenport expects cha-cha heels for Christmas.

"It's not really in the Christmas spirit," Anne said. "It's just kind of icky."

"I think it's funny," Walt said. "Everybody else will be ripping off *Elf* or *Miracle on 34th Street*. Nobody will think of this."

"That's for sure," Garber said. "What the fuck, let's do it."

That's how I ended up spending a week's worth of free periods with Garber, Anne, and Walt, translating, rehearsing, and filming our French Christmas skit on Anne's video camera, much to Jonah's annoyance.

"You don't understand," I told him. "I have to do it. It's for French."

Jonah took Latin, the one language class exempt from performing holiday skits. Instead they did a parade of Caesars on the Ides of March, or something.

"You don't have to do it with *them*," Jonah said. "Why can't you be in Harlan and Sphere's skit? Or some other geek's?" Harlan and Sphere were doing *Harold et Kumar Vont à White Castle à la Veille de Noël*, or "Harold and Kumar Go to White Castle on Christmas Eve" — two stoners get the munchies for candy canes, and White Castle is all out.

"I was assigned to Garber's group," I said. The disgusted look on his face told me that he sensed this was not the complete truth.

Garber looked surprisingly cute as Dawn Davenport, in his pencil skirt and bouffant wig, kicking down the Christmas tree and attacking his horrified parents, played by me and Walt. *"Mais qu'est-ce que c'est? Je veux cha-cha heels! Où sont mes cha-cha heels? Je vous déteste!"*

"Cut," Anne said. She owned the video camera, so that made her the director. "Beatrice, you're too stiff. You look like a mannequin. Loosen up!"

I wasn't trying to be stiff; I guess I just came off that way on camera. Garber defended me. "She's playing the mother. The mother is a stiff. Leave her alone."

Anne sighed. "Whatever. Let's go again."

The real problem — besides my innate physical stiffness — was the contrast between the way Garber and I played the scene. I was playing it straight, to honor the spirit of the original. Garber hammed it up as Dawn, telegraphing *this is a joke* with every girlish sashay. That was the wrong approach, I thought, but I knew he wouldn't change it for me. The skit was supposed to be a joke; it was just a stupid school project, anyway. It wasn't worth arguing about.

"You're doing *Female Trouble*?" Jonah said after catching a glimpse of my script. "I can't believe you. I told you about that movie, and now they're desecrating it."

"We translated all the dialogue into French," I said. "That gives the scene a totally different feel."

"They're *desecrating it*," he repeated. "*You're* desecrating it."

I felt like a traitor. But why should I? What did Jonah want from me? Was I supposed to flunk French on principle, just to avoid people Jonah didn't like?

"Why are you so jealous?" I said. "It's not like you're my boyfriend or anything. Are you?"

A shocked glare from Jonah. Then he looked away. I couldn't believe I'd let those words out of my mouth. They rang in my ears, pushy and demanding, the questions of a conventional girl, something Anne or AWAE would say, not me.

"*Boyfriend* is such a stupid word," Jonah said. "No, I'm not your boyfriend. I thought we were way beyond that. What we are cannot be described with trivial words like *boyfriend* and *girlfriend*. Even *friend* doesn't come close to describing it."

"I know," I said. "I'm sorry. I didn't mean that."

"Look, do what you have to do," Jonah said. "I'm sorry I'm being a prick about it. I really don't care."

Maybe that was the problem — I wanted him to care. But he didn't utter another word of protest about *Trouble Feminin*, even after we screened it at Assembly to laughs and cheers. Jonah and I kept up with our nightly radio rituals and our search for Matthew as if nothing had changed. But something had. I could feel it in my

clanky metal joints. Somehow I had let Jonah down. He was starting to treat me like I was just another person.

I was one of *them* now.

We still hung out. I still tried to help.

"This is it." Jonah slammed the Walla Walla, Washington, phone
book shut. The muffled thud echoed through the monumental hall
of the Enoch Pratt Library. "If Matthew is not being held captive at
the Walla Walla Home for Invalid Boys, he is not in the continental
U.S. And why my father would bother sending him to Europe or
Hawaii or somewhere just to strap him to a bed and feed him mush
three times a day, I don't know. Though maybe the institutions in
Mexico are cheaper."

"I'm sure they're taking good care of him, wherever he is," I said.

"I'm sure they're not," Jonah countered. "No one would take
care of him like I would." He thumbed the flimsy white pages. "I
could swear she had a Baltimore accent, just a touch of one —"
I knew he meant Mrs. Trevanian, the woman from the home who'd
called his father about Matthew back in September. "He's probably
somewhere nearby, maybe Virginia or Pennsylvania —"

"But we've called every institution in the area five times," I said.
"They won't tell us anything. It makes sense, Jonah. You wouldn't
want just any random caller to know your business —"

"I'm not a random caller," Jonah said. "I told them I was family,
but it didn't matter."

"Maybe you should ask your father one more time," I said.
"Maybe he's changed his mind. Maybe he'll tell you this time —"

The lids dropped over his eyes, like steel doors slamming shut.

"He won't. I've begged him. I've knelt on the kitchen floor in
front of him and pleaded for him to tell me where Matthew is. I
grabbed his ankles, trying to stop him from going to work, swore
I wouldn't let him leave until he told me, but he jerked his legs

away. Now he won't even admit that Matthew is alive. He tells me I must have dreamed that phone call."

"He's gaslighting you," I said. Mom and I had watched *Gaslight* many times back in the pre-crazy days. It was an old Ingrid Bergman movie about a husband who tried to convince his wife she was losing her mind.

"I don't know what to do," Jonah said. "I don't want to give up. But I can't find him. I can't find him. I can't find him."

"We'll find him," I promised. "There must be someplace we haven't looked. Some secret place in your house, maybe —"

"Stop it," he snapped. I was afraid if I touched Jonah's hand at that moment, my skin would stick to it and tear off, like a tongue on a frozen rail. "You're making me crazy. Why do you even care about Matthew? He's *my* brother. But you keep saying, *We can do it, if we just stick together and wish on a star.* . . ."

My breath caught, trapped in my lungs. "I'm not like that at all," I said. "Anyone who knows me even a little bit knows —"

"I don't care," Jonah said. "I can't think with you around. Leave me alone."

"What? Jonah —"

"I said leave me alone!"

"Shhh!" The librarian, a chubby bald man, glared at us from behind the checkout counter.

"Jonah," I whispered, desperate to make him hear me.

"Give it up," he said loudly. "You can't help me. Why don't you go to your real friends, Anne Sweeney and those people. That's who you belong with."

"Why are you saying this to me?" Now my breath was heaving and damp, the tears fighting their way to the surface. "I don't deserve this."

"Go away."

"It was a school project. I couldn't get out of it. But it's over now —"

"Go away."

He dropped his head on top of the phone book. The marble floor screeched under my chair as I slowly stood up, my eyes on Jonah. I picked up my coat, my book bag. But I didn't walk away yet. I waited.

He didn't move for ten long seconds. At last he looked up. "What are you waiting for?"

I glanced at the librarian, whose eyes were shooting death rays at us. Why didn't he pick on the bums sleeping in the periodical stacks? I had more to say to Jonah, but I wanted to say it without making noise. So I stiffened my torso and bowed from the waist, jerking my arms the way I had over Goebbels's dead gerbil body.

Jonah scowled. "What the hell is that?"

"I'm yelling at you," I said. "In Robot."

He pushed to his feet so fast his chair fell backward, clattering on the floor. "You want to learn a new language? Here's how you say *Go to Hell* in Ghost."

He walked away. His shoes squeaked on the floor. The door moaned as he opened it, then slammed shut, the crash echoing through the hall.

The mid-December days dragged without Jonah. Every night I listened faithfully to the Night Lights, hoping Ghost Boy would call, but he didn't. Myrna read a poem about how excited she was about the upcoming Christmas luncheon, Larry from Catonsville played old Frank Sinatra carols on his record player, and Dottie reported that she got the blues worse than ever this time of year. I worried about the luncheon, if Jonah would still go with me, or if I had the courage to go by myself. I didn't think I did.

"How come I never see you with Jonah anymore?" AWAE asked the week before Christmas break. We were in gym, camped on the sidelines during a basketball scrimmage. Our gym uniforms consisted of boxy blue mini-dresses that snapped down the front, with poofy matching bloomers underneath. We looked like dowdy flight attendants on the Starship *Enterprise*.

"Did you finally realize he's not worth it?" Tiza said.

"No," I said. "I don't want to talk about it."

"I told you, you can't depend on him," Anne said.

This was beginning to look kind of true, but I still didn't want to admit it.

"You don't have to tell us what happened," AWAE said, and I swear I saw specks of foam in the corners of her mouth, so eager was she to hear the dirt. "Just know that we're here for you now."

"Thanks." I'd never admit it, but I did feel a little lonely. I'd gotten used to having someone to talk to, someone to go out with, a reason to leave my disheveled tomb of a house. The Christmas video was finished, so I'd drifted away from Anne and Walt and Tom Garber, hoping to appease Jonah. I called him instead, but he never answered. I pictured him glaring at the old black dial phone in his room as it rang. I approached him at school, but he ghostwalked away. I even showed up for a yearbook meeting, but he didn't. Nina told me to tell him that the job of Art Director could not be done from home, and, if he didn't show up next time, she'd try to get him fired. I wasn't too worried about that happening, since I doubted Nina could find anyone else who'd want the job.

If he didn't want me, he didn't want me. I had to find other ways to fill my time.

When gym mercifully ended, I followed the rest of the blue-bloomered herd downstairs to the locker room. My face was sweaty, my hair flopping out of its ponytail holder, and I had pit stains under my arms. Loitering outside the girls' locker room was a freshly showered Tom Garber.

"Stop, in the name of the law." He blocked my way with a *halt* gesture. I stopped.

"What law?" I said.

"The Law of Nature," he said. "The Law of Thermodynamics. The Law of the Divine. Pick a law, any law."

"I wouldn't dare break the law," I said. "What do you want?"

"I would like to invite you out for pizza," Tom said. "Have you been to Alonso's yet?"

"No."

"Then you're obligated by law to accompany me there this Friday night."

"What law is that again?" I asked.

"A local statute of the City of Baltimore. Alonso's is a neighborhood institution and every Canton student must eat there at least once before graduation. You can go downtown to City Hall and check the books."

"I believe you," I said. He smelled like tea-tree-oil shampoo.

"Good," he said. "I'll pick you up at seven."

"Okay."

He breezed away, and I pushed through the locker room door, dazed, as if I'd had the wind knocked out of me. I checked my pits for BO. Yecchh. I hoped he hadn't gotten a whiff of that.

Anne, half dressed already in her kilt and small white bra, smiled knowingly. "So, what was all that about?"

"Did he ask you out?" AWAE asked.

"Just for pizza," I said. "No big deal."

"I told you he likes you." Anne tugged on the hem of my gym uniform. "Any guy who finds you attractive in this outfit deserves a chance."

"I guess." I stumbled, still dazed, to the bathroom for a quick shower, and wondered what Jonah would think if he found out I was going out for pizza with Garber. It would probably only make him hate me more, I decided.

But what could I do?

It was the law.

CHAPTER 11

"Sit on my side," Tom said. "Next to me."

I moved over to his side of the booth, and the Prince of Roland Park rested his arm on my shoulders. It was just another Friday night at Alonso's, a cozy old tavern near Hopkins, where high school and college students ate pizza and downed beer by the pitcher. The waitress, a ponytailed blonde, said, "Something to drink?"

"Ginger ale, please," I replied.

"Make it two," Tom said.

"Why aren't you having a beer?" I expected lacrosse players to drink beer at every opportunity.

"Why aren't *you* having a beer?" he asked back.

"I'm trying to keep my wits about me."

"Well, *I'm* trying to keep *my* wits together too." Tom smiled. "So you can't take advantage of me."

The waitress sighed. "Nobody's having anything if you keep this up."

"Ginger ale," Tom said, smooth as vanilla pudding.

"Back in a minute," the waitress said.

Tom glanced at the menu. "Pepperoni okay?"

I nodded. "Or mushroom."

When the waitress brought our sodas, Tom ordered a large pepperoni and mushroom pizza. He removed his arm from my shoulders and played with the pepper shaker. "Are you going away for Christmas?"

"No," I said. "Are you?"

"Vail," Tom said. "Do you ski?"

I shook my head. "Not really."

"Do you play any sports?"

"I like to swim when it's hot out," I said.

"Hey, so do I!" He held out his hand. I slapped it five. "What else do you like?"

"Um . . . I like to watch *Columbo* reruns."

He nodded soberly. "I'm heavily, heavily into *Columbo*. I was named to the first All-City Team in *Columbo*-watching last year. What else?"

"Driving around aimlessly with the radio on is good," I said.

"Way good. Hit me again. I'm loving these juicy Beatrice factoids."

I strained to come up with something cute. "I enjoy being a girl."

"That's my hobby too! I've got the video to prove it. We've got so much in common. Give me five."

I slapped his hand, but he caught it and curled his fingers around it. Maybe Anne was right; maybe Tom deserved a chance. Just because Jonah thought he was shallow didn't mean it was true. And what was so bad about shallowness, anyway? Sometimes it was kind of a relief. I thought about Dad and how he didn't get bogged down by misery the way Mom and I did. Maybe that was how people were supposed to be. Shallowness might be something to strive for.

The waitress returned. "Excuse me, is your name Beatrice?" she asked. I nodded. "You have a phone call at the bar."

"A phone call? At the bar?" This had Jonah's prints all over it. But how did he know where I was? "It must be my mother."

Tom was looking at me funny. "Don't you have a cell phone?"

"Guess I forgot it." I got up from the table. "Sorry. I'll be right back."

The bartender passed me the phone with a wet hand. "Hello?" I said.

"Bea, I've got to see you."

"Jonah? How did you find me?"

"Your mom blabbed," Jonah said. "I can't believe you. Alonso's with Garber? How trite can you get? I'll rant about that later."

"What do you want? I thought we weren't speaking." Was he just trying to ruin my evening? Could he be that petty?

"I need to see you right away."

"Why?"

"Please, just come see me."

"Jonah, I'm busy now. Can't it wait a few hours?"

"No. Bea, I'm sorry, it's an emergency. It's big. Remember that first night we went to Carmichael's? When I had something important to tell you?"

"Yes, of course I do."

"This news is that big. Bigger."

"What is it? Something about Matthew?"

"Yes," Jonah said. "I found him."

"Oh my God!"

"Please, Bea, I'm bursting. I have to show it to you."

"Show what to me?"

"Just come! Meet me at Fanny's in ten minutes."

He hung up. I stared at the phone for a second, buzzing with a mixture of annoyance, excitement, and curiosity.

He'd found Matthew. But how?

I looked at Tom in our booth, patiently waiting for me and the pizza to arrive. I desperately wanted to see Jonah. Jonah needed me. Tom didn't deserve to be abandoned on our first date, but I couldn't imagine staying, wondering the whole time how Jonah had found Matthew, knowing the only other person on earth who cared was me. Tom was okay, but we were just pretending to like each other, hoping that eventually, if we pretended hard enough, it would turn real. Maybe it would and maybe it wouldn't. But Jonah was already real. Even Matthew was real, though I'd never seen him. And they made me real.

I went back to the booth.

"Everything cool?" Tom asked.

"There's kind of an emergency. I need to get to Fanny's somehow."

"Fanny's Bar? In Hampden?" Tom said. "That's where the emergency is?"

I nodded, and he didn't press me, even though it sounded ridiculous. "I'll take you," he said. "Let me get the check."

He paid the check and told the waitress he'd stop back in a few minutes and take the pizza to go. I tapped my toes on the floor, trying to shake out the energy suddenly flowing through me. Jonah was back.

Tom and I hurried to his Saab. He opened the passenger door for me, very gallant. I felt like a wife in a TV movie, going into labor while her husband rushes her to the hospital. "To Fanny's!" Tom cried. "I'll get you there in no time."

We zipped down Cold Spring Lane and across Roland Avenue into Hampden. The houses and yards and trees suddenly shrank, and Christmas decorations seemed to have snowed down from the sky. Tom pulled up in front of a grimy storefront with a pink neon sign that said FANNY'S, the Y shaped like a martini glass.

"Want me to come in with you?" Tom asked.

"No. I'll be fine. Thanks for everything," I said. "I'm sorry I had to cut this short."

"Make it up to me," Tom said. "Go to Carter's party with me."

"New Year's Eve?" I'd heard rumblings about a party at Carter Blessing's house, but I'd planned to skip it.

"You have other plans?"

"No."

"Then go with me. You owe me."

He'd been a good sport about our interrupted date; I did owe him another one. And I'd never had a date on New Year's Eve before. "Okay. I'll go."

"Call me if you need a ride home or whatever. Okay?"

"Okay. Thanks, Tom."

I hurried inside. The bar was heavily Christmased out, hardly an inch of wall or ceiling left undecorated. A TV high up in a corner played *It's a Wonderful Life*, the volume low.

Two drunks sat at the bar. The bartender, a haggard fortyish woman, clenched a cigarette between her teeth. Jonah sat waiting at a rickety table, rubbing his hands over and over.

"Bea," he said.

"What is it? What happened?"

"Did I get you at a bad time?" He didn't even smile when he said it.

"You're kidding, right? Is there a bomb you want me to defuse? Is civilization as we know it at stake? This better be a real emergency, or I'm walking out of here —" I tried to think of something threatening, but the best I could come up with was the superlame "— in a huff."

"Wait till you see this. It will make up for everything." Jonah reached into his black backpack and pulled out a Christmas card: Jesus in the manger, surrounded by Mary, Joseph, the usual farm animals, and a haze of golden sparkles.

I opened the card. *O COME LET US ADORE HIM*, it said. *SEASON'S GREETINGS. THE STAFF OF THE ST. FRANCIS HOME AND HOSPICE.* No signature, but a bit of yellow and black fuzz was stuck to the card with a smudge of red clay.

"St. Francis," I said. "In Lutherville. That's one of the places we called."

"They refused to tell us anything," Jonah said. "They were one of the cagier institutions."

I looked at the card again. "I don't get it," I said.

"It's from him," Jonah said. "From Matthew. He sent me a card!"

"How do you know it's from him?" I said. "It doesn't mention him."

Jonah pointed to the yellow and black fuzz. "It's Catso. Matthew's favorite toy. That's a bit of Catso's fur. Look, I've got his twin." He pulled a small stuffed cat out of his backpack. The cat was old and worn, black with yellow stripes and golden button eyes.

"When we were little, my mother gave me and Matthew matching cats," Jonah said. "This one was mine. I named her the Evil Miss Frankenheimer. Matthew's was the opposite, yellow with black stripes. He couldn't talk, so I named his cat Catso. They were our favorite toys. We took them everywhere with us."

I patted the Evil Miss Frankenheimer, then touched the fuzz on the card. The fur had the same texture.

"I assumed Catso had been buried with Matthew. After my mother died, I put Miss Frankenheimer away in a box in my closet and left her there."

The Christmas lights blinked across Jonah's face. Red. Shadow. Red. Shadow.

"It's — you really think this is —"

"I don't know how he did it," Jonah said. "But somehow Matthew sent me this card. He's calling out to me. And now I know where he is."

"You two going to order a drink?" the bartender snapped from behind the counter. "This ain't a bus stop, you know."

I stood up. "I'll get it. What do you want?"

"Ginger ale," Jonah said.

"Two ginger ales," I ordered. "One plain and one with whiskey."

"Whoop-de-doo," the bartender said. She gave me some flat yellow liquid in two fingerprint-coated glasses. I left her a three-dollar tip. Spirit of Christmas.

"Great. Now I can buy myself that fur coat," she said.

"Which one has whiskey in it?" Jonah said.

I took a sip and gave him the whiskey glass.

"What are you going to do now?" I asked.

On the TV, George Bailey stood on a bridge in the snow, crying, "I want to live again. Let me live again."

"I want to see Matthew," Jonah said.

"Maybe for Christmas," I said.

"Yeah." Jonah straightened up. "For Christmas. That's perfect." He slid the glass of ginger and whiskey over to me. "Tomorrow's the Night Light luncheon. We're still going to that, aren't we?"

"I'll go if you go." I tried not to show how happy I was.

"Good. So I'll go to St. Francis on Sunday. Will you come with me?"

I sipped the drink. "Yes. I'll come."

Jonah stared at the TV while Jimmy Stewart ran joyfully through the slushy streets of Bedford Falls.

"I can't believe you were out with Garber," Jonah said. "Has your brain dissolved? How could you consciously agree to spend time with him?"

"He's nice," I said. "And you weren't speaking to me. It has nothing to do with you, anyway. You have no say in this."

"He's sludge," Jonah said. "You'll see."

"What did he ever do to you?"

"I've got a grudge against him."

"I know what it is."

"No, you don't."

"Does it have to do with me?"

"It happened before I knew you existed."

"So what is it, then?"

Jonah shook his head. "Forget it. Just stay away from him."

"Too late," I said. "I promised to spend New Year's Eve with him. To make up for tonight."

"What? Are you trying to make me vomit?"

"It's your fault! If you hadn't interrupted us, he wouldn't have asked me, and I wouldn't have felt like I owed him."

"The interruption was worth it," he said. "Wasn't it?"

I touched the rough sparkles on the Christmas card. "Yes," I said. "It was worth it."

On TV, the movie ended in a jangle of bells. Then it started up again from the beginning.

I was back in Jonah's world, and everything was all right.

Somehow, I knew Jonah was listening when I turned the Night Lights on at midnight.

Herb:
We've been discussing a lot of different
things, but the topic that won't die, so
to speak, heh-heh, is this: Do you believe in
ghosts?

Kreplax:
We're all going to be ghosts once the comet
lands. It's going to crash into the earth on
January twenty-third. This January! Why won't you
people listen to me?

Herb:
We're listening, Kreplax —

Kreplax:

The whole east coast of North America —
flooded! The whole west coast of Europe — wiped
out! Happy New Year, everybody! Get your jollies
now because next month you'll all be dead.

Herb:

Where will you be on January twenty-third, Kreplax?

Kreplax:

I'm getting out. I'm going back to 2110, if I can
get there. If my stupid friend Tita would just hurry
up and fix the time machine —

Herb:

[music playing] Try a monkey wrench, Kreplax.
Next caller, you're on the air.

Dougal:

Hi, Herb. This is Dougal from Hampden. First-time
caller.

Herb:

Welcome, Dougal.

Dougal:

Um, I have a question for all the ghost experts
out there. I'm a mortician. I live above a funeral
home, and I spend all my time with dead
people. I've dragged bodies out of car wrecks,
I've picked them up from the hospital. They lie
in their coffins one floor below me, night after
night while I'm sleeping —

Herb:

How long have you been a mortician, Dougal?

Dougal:

About thirty years. Here's my question. I've always wanted to see a ghost. I really WANT to believe in them. I want to believe in something! But I've never seen one, ever. Never heard a creak in the night, a boo, or anything.

Herb:

That's strange.

Dougal:

I hear your callers telling ghost stories all the time, about people they've seen come back from the dead. . . . I really, really want to see a ghost. Why won't they show themselves to me? I'm right here!

Herb:

I don't know, Dougal. We'll toss that one out to the listeners. Next Night Light, hello.

Myrna:

It's Myrna. I believe in ghosts, Herb. I swear to God, one night when my late husband was in the hospital, not recuperating from his third and fatal heart attack, I was lying alone in my bed, and the ghost of Elvis came to comfort me. I use the word comfort as a euphemism, Herb. I'm sure all the ladies out there know what I'm talking about.

Herb:

Seems like most of our listeners do believe in ghosts, or some kind of life after death. It's hard not to.

Myrna:

It sure is. How can I just disappear when I die, in a POOF!, like that? I can't! I can't imagine it. I'm here, I'm real, my thoughts, my spirit, where would they go? *[Music starts.]* One last thing, Herb. I want everyone listening tonight to know that when I die, I'm not going anywhere. I'll still be here, driving down the streets of Baltimore, and all you better watch out. If you cross me, I'll haunt you up so bad your hair'll fall out and won't never grow back. And all of us people, men and women, bald or beehived, we all love our hair. We sure do.

Herb:

Amen. Nighty-night. Next caller, you're on the air.

Larry from Catonsville:

Everybody needs to calm down, Herb. There are no ghosts or evil spirits. There's only love and heartache. This song is called "Don't Let the Sun Catch You Crying." I think that's good advice. *[A needle drops on a record. The song plays.]*

For some reason, listening to that song, I started crying. I thought about Jonah, how he'd missed Matthew all these years, lived without him like living without a leg or a lung, and now they were about to be reunited. It had nothing to do with me, really, but every time I thought of that Christmas card with its little patch of yellow fur, a current of feeling flowed through me. I wasn't used to that. It hurt.

I wondered if Mom was awake too, sitting in the bathroom putting eye shadow on or whatever she was into these nights. She acted as if she was missing something too, but I had no idea what it could be. What had she suddenly lost that had marooned her so far from me and everyone else? Why couldn't she tell me what it was?

I took Larry's advice. It was two-thirty in the morning and the sun was nowhere to be seen. By dawn I'd be dry-eyed and the sun would never know what I'd been up to all night.

CHAPTER 12

A certain kind of Baltimore bride — the kind who goes through a can of hairspray a day — had her dream wedding at Mario's Italian Palace. "Their motto should be, 'If it's not made of crystal, gold, or marble, we spit on it!'" Jonah said as we walked through the splashy Hall of Fountains. Mario's real motto (as advertised on the Night Light Show) was "You *can* buy class."

Eighteen Night Lights showed up for Herb Horvath's Christmas luncheon. Herb sat at the head of the long table, greeting everyone and passing out name tags. He was slicker-looking than I expected, sixtyish, with thick white hair and a square jaw.

"Nice to see you, uh, Robot Girl," he said, reading the name tag on my scarlet sweater. Then he laughed. "Oh, *you're* Robot Girl. You haven't called in much, but who could forget the name?" It was strange to hear that mellifluous voice come out of a person instead of the radio.

"Thank you," I said. "I'm really excited to meet everybody."

He turned to Jonah. "And Ghost Boy, what an honor. It's wonderful to see young people at our luncheon. We don't get too many young callers on the show, as you probably know."

"We love the show," Jonah said. "We listen every night."

To my right sat a small woman with silver cat's-eye glasses and blue-black hair teased into the tallest beehive I've ever seen. Her pink face was heavily powdered, eyes lined like Cleopatra's, inky eyebrows drawn on. Her name tag said *Myrna*.

"Myrna from Highlandtown?" I said.

"That's me, sweetheart." She read my tag. "Robot Girl! I don't believe I've heard you call since we took the carpet to Ocean City."

"Oh, I'm way too shy to call," I said.

Jonah was talking with a chubby middle-aged man with stringy hair, a goatee, and a smug look on his face. His hands and jowls trembled. Don Berman.

"Don, we're huge fans," I said.

"*Don, we're huge fans*," he shot back in a high-pitched voice meant to mock me.

What a jerk, I thought, but I didn't care, because he was Don Berman, and that's what Don Berman did.

The waitresses brought out iceberg salads with Italian dressing. Across from me sat a large black man wearing dark glasses. I saw the white cane next to his chair and realized he was blind.

"Here you go, Larry," Herb said. He reached over and slapped a name tag on the blind man's jacket. Larry from Catonsville, who liked to play old records, especially Engelbert Humperdinck.

I took his hand, shaking it. "Hi, Larry. I'm Robot Girl. I love that song you played the other night, 'Don't Let the Sun Catch You Crying'? And you're turning me into an Engelbert fan."

"Blech, not me," Myrna said. "Engelbert's too mushy. Elvis has guts."

"Elvis had guts all right," Larry said, patting his belly. "But Engelbert's got that mellow sound. If I had a wife, I'd sing 'After the Lovin' to her every night."

"Elvis can do mellow," Myrna said. "What about 'In the Ghetto'?"

"That song's sad, not mellow," Larry said. "Besides, he over-orchestrates it. And what does Elvis Presley know about the ghetto?"

"Plenty," Myrna said. "Elvis knows pain."

She showed me her Elvis charm bracelet, with a little head of Elvis — "Young, pudgy, mutton-chop, I like them all, every incarnation" — a guitar, a tiny Graceland, a Priscilla in a bridal veil, a little Lisa Marie, a hound dog, and a pair of men's shoes.

"They're supposed to be blue suede shoes," Myrna said. "You can't tell from looking at them, but it's obvious."

"Hey, Herb." Burt from Glen Burnie reigned at the far end of the table. "Where's Peggy? Couldn't make it?"

"That Burt's so mean," Myrna said. "He knows darn well Herb's sensitive about Peggy. Herb's a widower. Why shouldn't he have a girlfriend? I don't know how Burt even found out there was a Peggy."

After the salad we had veal parmesan with a side of spaghetti. "Wait till you taste Mario's famous spaghetti sauce," Burt growled. "It's like watery ketchup."

Herb tapped his glass and stood up. "I'd like to make a toast. Thank you all for coming. I hope that you, my most dedicated listeners, realize how much you mean to me, and I'm pleased to give you this chance to meet one another. To the new listeners, welcome." He raised his iced tea. "Here's to the power of radio to reach out and make a community out of those who prowl sleeplessly through the night."

"Hear, hear." Jonah and I clinked glasses. Burt muttered, "I gotta work at night. I'm no insomniac loser like the rest of you all."

Myrna shook her head and clucked. "Why do they let Burt come to these luncheons? They should ban him."

"You're right, Myrna," Larry said.

"No, they shouldn't," Jonah said. "Burt's the greatest. I love it when he calls in from the Amoco station and you hear some kid in the background ask for a pack of Kools and Burt tells him to go to hell."

"He upsets Herb," Larry said. "That's no good."

Myrna elbowed me and gestured toward Jonah. "Is that fella your boyfriend?"

"No," I said. "We're just friends."

"Really?" She peeked at him. "He's nice-looking, in a bleached-out sort of way. I can see why he calls himself Ghost Boy." She leaned close and whispered, "What's your real name, honey? I won't tell anyone."

I looked through Myrna's cat's-eye glasses into her warm hazel eyes. Something about her made me want to tell her things. And my real name wasn't a secret. I just enjoyed having an alias.

"Beatrice," I whispered.

"And your boy's?"

"Jonah."

"Thanks for telling me," Myrna said. "I don't mind that you use fake names on the radio, but I can't be friends with a person who won't tell me her real name."

"I understand," I said.

"So why don't you go out with him?" she asked.

"Jonah? I do like him," I said. "I like him a lot. He's my favorite person in the whole city of Baltimore. Maybe the world."

"So what's the problem?" Myrna said. "Sounds like love to me." She lowered her voice. "Is he — you know — funny?"

"He's very funny." Then I realized my mistake. "Oh, you mean gay. Um, I don't think so." I'd never really thought about it. Was Jonah gay? Did he like girls? I had no idea. He never talked about boys *or* girls, except to say how much he didn't like them. He was an equal opportunity disliker.

"You'd make a real cute couple," Myrna said. "What are you waiting for?"

"Myrna, I've got bionic hearing like the Six Million Dollar Man, and I can hear every word you say," Larry interrupted. "What are you bothering that girl for? She don't want a boyfriend, she don't need to be pushed. She and Ghost Boy will fall in love when they're ready."

"But they're meant for each other," Myrna said.

"Sure, like crabcakes and crackers," Larry said. "I didn't say they wouldn't get it on *sometime*."

"Isn't it the Bionic Woman who has super hearing?" I said.

"I wouldn't know," Myrna said.

I glanced at Jonah. He was deep in a baseball argument with Don Berman.

"The O's are the Devil's team, that's why they don't win," Don said. "They're on the side of Darkness. And Darkness never wins in baseball."

"You're crazy," Jonah said. "What about Steinbrenner and the Yankees? You ask me, Steinbrenner *is* the Devil."

"Steinbrenner is just a good businessman," Don said. "And don't call me crazy again. I'm touchy about it."

"Sorry, Don."

"Don *Berman*."

"Sorry."

"'Sorry, *Don Berman*.' Say it, kid, before I punch you in the face."

"Sorry, *Don Berman*," Jonah said. "Jeez."

"Are you taking Our Lord's name in vain?" Don Berman said. "No wonder the O's stink. It's the people of this city. Your souls are lacking! Lacking, I tell you!"

"Keep it down, Don Berman," Larry said. A strand of spaghetti stuck to his chin.

"Tell your boyfriend to stay away from Don Berman," Myrna said. "He starts fights with everyone."

"He's not my — oh, never mind."

When the plates were cleared, Myrna said, "I need to tinkle. Come with me to the little girls' room?"

I didn't have to tinkle, so I said no, thanks. Myrna got up and flounced away on her high heels, jangling with every step.

"She wears a lot of jewelry, doesn't she?" Larry asked me.

"Yes," I said.

"I like that. What about a wedding ring? You notice one?"

"No, just a really big blue cocktail ring," I said.

"She's one fine woman," Larry said. "I wonder if she likes blind guys. We're the best lovers, you know."

"Makes sense, I guess."

When Myrna came back, I whispered to her, "I think Larry from Catonsville likes you."

Larry tapped his right ear. "Bionic."

"Next time you have to tinkle, we'll talk in the ladies'," Myrna said to me. "You can't hear through walls, can you?" she asked Larry.

"Maybe I can and maybe I can't," Larry said. "Wouldn't you like to know?"

"I've got nothing to hide," Myrna said.

"I don't believe that for a second," Larry said. "Any woman worth the time's got plenty to hide. That's what I like about women."

"You don't want to know *my* secrets," Myrna said.

"Yes, I do, and I've got ways of finding out," Larry said. "Let's show these kids how it's done, Myrna. Go out with me."

Myrna didn't say anything.

"I should warn you, I don't drive," Larry added.

"I don't date people I only know from the radio," Myrna said.

"What better way to know someone?" Larry said. "I listen to your voice every night and think, *That's a good woman, cheering people up with poems and funny little ideas. And with a voice like that she must be fine-looking too. Is she, Robot Girl?*"

"Very," I said.

"I knew it," Larry said.

"Well, *you're* not so good-looking," Myrna said. "You're no Elvis, I tell you that. You're not even Tom Jones."

"Elvis is a pretty high standard to hold a man to," Larry said.

"Too bad," Myrna said. "That's my standard. Elvis is my ideal and I'm sticking to it." She set her mouth in a firm ruby-red line.

Larry was quiet for the rest of the lunch. During dessert I heard him humming "After the Lovin'" under his breath. Myrna heard it too.

"Don't count your chickens, Larry," she warned.

After lunch, riding home through the city in Gertie, Jonah said, "Are you disappointed?"

"Disappointed?" I tugged at a nylon thread poking out of the vinyl upholstery. "No. Why?"

"To meet those radio people in person," he said. "To see what they look like. To watch them interact in real time, with food between their teeth and moles on their chins and white canes to help them walk and cheap brown shoes."

"Well, I —" Some of the Night Lights did look different from the way I'd imagined. But once I saw them, my imaginary pictures popped like cartoon bubbles and their real selves solidified in my mind. "I could tell by his voice that Don Berman wore cheap brown shoes."

"But you never actually thought about it, right?" Jonah said. "You never thought, *I bet his shoes are ugly.* If I asked you, *Do you think Don Berman wears cheap brown shoes?* you'd probably say yes. But unless someone mentioned shoes, all you thought about was what he was saying. What the world inside his head must look like. That's what I did."

"Not me," I said. "I pictured apartments and houses and clothes and hairstyles for all of them. I imagined Burt's Amoco station and his oil-stained gray workshirt. . . . Of course, I was wrong about a lot of it. I thought Myrna would be a redhead, for some reason. I thought Herb would be handsomer. And I didn't guess that Larry was blind. . . . Are you disappointed?"

"I don't know," Jonah said. "I like them all — it's not that. But I've been listening to the show for four years. This is the first time I've seen any of those characters. In my mind, they were almost mythological, like pirates or fairies or witches." He shook his head, as if to shake the visions away. "It's my own stupid fault. My brain's all messed up."

"The show will be just as good now, you'll see," I said. "Maybe even better. Before, the other callers were like characters in a play. Now they'll be like family."

"Maybe that's what I'm afraid of," Jonah said.

"Oh." I slumped in my seat, realizing what I'd just said. "You're right. Well, we won't let them be family the way *we* know family. They'll be characters . . . in a movie we live in."

"That's better," Jonah said.

We were quiet the rest of the way home, lost in our own thoughts. I was thinking about Myrna, wondering what she'd say if she ever met Mom. I didn't know what Jonah was thinking, but he was probably thinking about Matthew and our visit the next day. When he pulled up in front of my house, he said, "I'll pick you up at noon tomorrow."

"I'll be ready," I said.

Matthew was less than a day away.

CHAPTER 13

The St. Francis Home occupied the grounds of an old estate in Baltimore County. The main building was a rambling stone mansion, ivy-covered, manicured, and elegant except for the iron gates on the windows.

On Sunday afternoon, Jonah and I approached a nurse sitting behind glass in the reception area. "My name is Jonah Tate, and I'm here to see my brother. Matthew Tate."

The nurse looked up, surprised. She riffled through an appointment book. "I don't see your name here —"

"I didn't call," Jonah said. "It's kind of a spur of the moment thing." Jonah was afraid that if he made an appointment to see Matthew, his father would find out and try to stop us.

"You should have made an appointment," the nurse said.

"I know, but I'm an impulsive guy," Jonah said. "Come on, it's Christmastime. See that wreath? Hear those carols? My poor brother is lonely."

"Just a second." The nurse disappeared into a back office. A few minutes later she reappeared and said, "Dr. Kramer will be with you shortly."

We sat on a bench under a giant wreath and waited.

"Will he look like you?" I whispered. "Are you identical?"

"We are," Jonah said. "We'll find out what I'd look like without motor control."

Dr. Kramer walked toward us down the long hall, her heels clicking on the waxed floor. She was a thin, neat woman with stiffly coifed hair and a tidy brown tweed suit. She carried a file under one arm.

"Jonah?" We stood up. She offered him her hand to shake. "This is a surprise. I'm Dr. Kramer. I'm the supervising administrator of St. Francis."

"This is my friend Beatrice Szabo," Jonah said.

"Where's your father?" Dr. Kramer asked.

"He didn't come."

"I see. Do you have his permission to be here?"

"Do I need it?" Jonah asked back.

"You're a minor, aren't you?" Dr. Kramer opened the file and ran a finger along a page. "Sibling: Jonah Martin Tate. You're Matthew's twin brother, correct? So you're only seventeen."

"I'll be eighteen in the spring," Jonah said, and a note of plaintiveness crept into his voice that I'd never heard before.

"Perhaps I should call your father and ask his permission," she said.

"He'll say no," Jonah said.

"Well, he's in charge of Matthew's care," Dr. Kramer said. "We have to respect his wishes."

"What about Matthew's wishes?" Jonah said. He brought out the Christmas card. "He sent this to me. I know he wants to see me."

Dr. Kramer took the card and looked at it. "This isn't from Matthew. I don't know how you got this, but Matthew has no way of sending mail."

Jonah pointed out the bit of Catso's fuzz. "It *is* from him. This fuzz comes from his favorite toy. I can prove it."

"That's not necessary." Dr. Kramer returned the card.

"Has my father come to visit Matthew?"

"Not for a while," Dr. Kramer admitted.

"Please let me see him," Jonah said. "Just for a short time. What harm could it do? Dad never has to know. Who's going to tell him?"

"You could," Dr. Kramer said. "Or your friend."

"Trust me, we won't," Jonah said. "Have you ever met my father?"

"No, I've only spoken to him on the telephone."

"If you had, you'd know that behind his back is the best way to deal with him," Jonah said.

"Dr. Kramer," I said. "He reached out to Jonah. Matthew reached out."

"He can't reach out. It's some kind of mistake." She frowned at the card. She looked at me and Jonah, sizing us up. Jonah straightened his posture.

"He's in the dayroom," she said. "But prepare yourself, Jonah. It looks calm and pretty in the main building but the patients . . . most of them are neither calm nor pretty. You might get upset."

She called a nurse. "Will you please take Mr. Tate and his friend to see Matthew Tate in the dayroom?"

The nurse nodded. Dr. Kramer said to Jonah, "If you would like to speak to me afterward, the nurse can bring you upstairs to my office. Good luck. And don't stay long."

"Thank you," Jonah said.

We followed the nurse through an enclosed walkway to another building. This one was no mansion, more like an elementary school.

A buzz grew louder as we walked down the hall. The nurse opened the door to a large, gym-like dayroom, and the buzz became a roar. Sunlight filtered through high, gated windows that ran along the ceiling. The dayroom reminded me of a cafeteria, full of squirming, shaking, shouting, muttering people, many in wheelchairs with helmets on their heads to protect them from falls. Most of them were adults, but there were a few children and teens clustered together at a table around a hunk of yellow clay. An aide stood nearby, keeping a girl from stuffing the clay into her mouth. No matter how many times the aide told her no, the girl wouldn't stop trying to eat it.

A boy sat at the table in a wheelchair, helmeted and propped up with straps. He pounded a lump of clay with one hand. Before the nurse said a word, I knew it was Matthew.

Scraps of blond hair peeked out from under the helmet. His bleary, unfocused eyes were a familiar white-gray color, but they lacked the sharpness, the bite of Jonah's. If Jonah's eyes were pond ice, Matthew's, in his slack face, were skim milk. You could tell they were twins, yet Matthew didn't really look like Jonah at all.

"Here he is," the nurse said, leaning toward Matthew. "Matthew, this is your brother, Jonah. He's come to visit you." She straightened up and said to Jonah, "I don't know if he understands or not. He can't talk or communicate in any way, so it's hard to tell."

But Matthew's eyes sharpened slightly. He recognized Jonah.

"Hi, Matthew. Merry Christmas," Jonah said. "I should have brought you a present, but I didn't know what you'd need."

"I'm sure your visit is a present enough," the nurse said.

"But he might like something, as a treat," Jonah said. "Something special. A book, maybe? A book with pictures?"

"I don't know how much it would mean to him. He loves pounding clay. And he loves that stuffed cat. He brought it with him when he arrived. It's practically falling apart."

The stuffed cat — small, dirty, yellow, with black tiger stripes and worn fur — sat in Matthew's lap, leashed to the arm of his wheelchair. It was the negative image of the Evil Miss Frankenheimer, only much more worn. Jonah reached for it slowly.

"Catso," Jonah said.

Matthew jerked. "Uh! Uh!"

"I think he understood you," I said.

"I don't know," the nurse said. "Sometimes it seems like they understand you, but they don't. It's just a coincidence. Or they're reacting to something else."

"That's crazy," Jonah said. "Of course he knows Catso. Matthew's had him since he was a baby."

He picked up Catso and danced him around in front of Matthew as if he were fencing an invisible opponent. Matthew watched carefully, then jerked again and shouted, "Uh!" He hit the yellow clay.

"Catso and the Evil Miss Frankenheimer used to sword fight all the time," Jonah said. "Matt loved it."

The other patients watched Jonah play with Matthew, their faces slack, their eyes following Catso's every move. Jonah looked different in the fluorescent glare of the dayroom: more solid, somehow.

An aide appeared beside the nurse and said, "I'm taking Matthew. It's time for his medication." The aide stood behind Matthew's wheelchair, ready to roll him away. Jonah jolted.

"We just got here. Give us a few more minutes. Please."

"We're on a strict schedule," the aide said. "You can visit him another time."

"That's the problem," Jonah said. "I don't know if I can. I haven't seen him in ten years."

"Really? Huh," the aide said. "Then you can wait a week or two before you see him again. Come on, Matthew." He wheeled Matthew away. Catso's leash pulled taut and Jonah tossed him onto Matthew's lap. Matthew didn't turn around to look at us. Maybe he couldn't. He just kicked his legs a little.

"Is he coming back soon?" Jonah asked. "From medication time?"

"No. Visitor's hours are over," the nurse said. "Would you like to see Dr. Kramer?"

"Not now," Jonah said. "I'll be back soon. What are the visitor's hours on Saturday?"

*   *   *

"I think he remembered me," Jonah said in the car on the way home. "Do you think he remembered me?"

"I know he did," I said.

"Everything is going to be different now," Jonah said.

CHAPTER 14

On Christmas morning, Mom fell down the steps, ripping the garland of holly off the banister. Then she threw up.

She seemed okay after that. "Just let me rest here a minute," she said from the hall carpet. "Then we can open our presents."

Dad and I drove her to the emergency room, anyway, to make sure she didn't have a concussion.

"Your mother's a wreck," Dad said. We sat in the hospital waiting room on yellow vinyl chairs. Mine was torn. I picked at the tear, making it grow.

"What tipped you off?" I said.

Mom didn't have a concussion. Her ankle hurt a little. The doctor figured the vomiting was a coincidence. She'd been throwing up a lot lately, and she just happened to do it again after she fell down the steps.

We drove home and continued our Christmas customs (after I cleaned the puke off the rug) as if everything was normal. We sat by the fire and opened our presents one at a time, taking turns, while Bing Crosby played on the stereo. Then we had breakfast, even though it was two-thirty already. Our Christmas was running late because we'd spent so much time waiting at the hospital.

We called my aunt and uncle and cousins in Denver to wish

them a Merry Christmas. We called Gran in Florida. At six o'clock it was time to eat. We always ate Christmas dinner at six.

But we weren't that hungry, because we'd just had breakfast. And the turkey wasn't ready. It was pink inside. Dad said we couldn't eat it yet or we might get violently ill. "I think we've had enough illness for one day," he said, and put the turkey back in the oven.

"We should have made chicken instead," Mom said with teary eyes.

I banged my head on the table. Dad patted my hair. "I sympathize," he said. "But don't hurt yourself."

At eight, I fixed myself a plate of stuffing, mashed potatoes, and creamed spinach and went into the living room to watch *It's a Wonderful Life*. I could watch that movie a million times. I could watch it every day for the rest of my life and never get sick of it.

People think *It's a Wonderful Life* is a sappy movie, but they're wrong. It's sad. George Bailey is no saint. He's angry. He hates his family. He wants to travel the world and have adventures, but his family keeps stopping him. He even says to his wife, "Why do we have to have all these kids?" People tell themselves George doesn't mean that, he's just upset at that moment. But he *does* mean it. Sure, he loves his wife and kids, in that helpless way people love their families. He's stuck with them, so he makes the best of a bad situation. He's a hero because he makes something good out of a life he doesn't want. I'd like to be able to do that. I hope it's something you can learn.

By ten or so the turkey was ready. Dad and I sat in the kitchen and ate it with cranberry sauce. Mom had already taken a hot water bottle to bed in the guest room.

"Good turkey," I said, mostly to be polite.

"A little dry," Dad said.

And that was Christmas.

* * *

"Why do you want to spend New Year's with those horrible people?" Jonah said to me the next day. "The way you start the year is the way you'll spend it."

"That's a superstition, and you don't even believe it yourself," I said.

"I do so," Jonah said. "I completely and utterly believe it."

I lounged in the window seat in my bedroom, wrapped in a blanket. Jonah was sketching me in pen and ink. He had to draw a self-portrait for his art-school portfolio. For some reason he was drawing me instead.

"I thought we'd spend New Year's Eve together," he said. "Maybe take the Flying Carpet out to Ocean City or something."

"You mean spend New Year's Eve listening to the Night Lights?" I said. "The show will be on all night. We can listen after the party."

"We could go down to the station and say hello to Herb. Wish him a Happy New Year."

"I'm sure he'd love that."

"We could go downtown. They always do something crazy at Carmichael's. Or maybe Kreplax is having a party."

Jonah wasn't saying what he really wanted to do. He wanted to go to St. Francis and ring in the New Year with Matthew. But the home was closed to visitors that night.

"Come to Carter's party," I said. "That way we'll be together."

"But you'll be with that creep."

"He's not all that creepy when you see him up close."

"Yes, he is. He's wrong for you. And he's not nice. Everyone thinks he is but he's not. You know why he wears those glasses? So you can't see the evil gleam in his eye."

"Just because he's cute doesn't mean he's evil." I got up to see how the portrait was progressing.

"What are you doing?" he said. "Sit back down there."

"I want to see." I looked over his shoulder. The portrait was very good. The funny thing was, even though the drawing clearly showed me, the physical me — my lank brown hair, my round face, my skinny neck — something about it did remind me of Jonah. It was as if he were trapped inside me, staring out through my eyes.

"Go back to your pose, art slave," Jonah said. I returned to my window seat, flared my nostrils, and smushed my cheeks together with my hands to make an ugly face.

"Stop that."

"Not until you promise to go to Carter's party."

"Okay, I promise."

"Really?"

"Really."

"Swear?"

"Would you please stop making that face? It's hideous."

"Swear?"

"Swear."

I released my cheeks and let my face return to normal.

"Oh, thank God." He resumed drawing. "You're not going on the ski trip next week, are you?"

"No, of course not." The Outing Club had organized a one-day ski excursion to the Poconos. "I hate being cold."

"Damn. Nina's on my ass to get some pictures of it. For the *Yodelay-hee-hoo*. You know, jerks hotdogging on their skis, posing with their butts out, Meath falling into a snowbank with lots of girls toppled on top of him. . . ."

"Guess you'll have to get somebody else to do it," I said. "Or go on the trip yourself."

"I'm not riding a bus for six hours just to stand in the cold and take pictures of people in goggles."

"Why did you become the photo editor, anyway?" I asked. "It seems so unlike you."

"For control," he said.

"What are you talking about?"

"As photo editor, I get to shape our class's history. I choose which pictures go and which will stay."

"But you also have to organize a lot of corny group shots and cover field trips," I said.

"It's the price I pay."

"But why? Why do you care about our class's history?"

"I just do. Besides, I need something to put on my art-school applications besides 'Locks self in room and draws all day.' Even art schools won't take a psychopath."

"I guess."

Carter Blessing lived out near horse country, in a glassy modern house in Owings Mills. Tom Garber parked at the end of a long line of cars and we walked down the dark wooded road. A crust of snow crunched under my boots. Inside the house, the music was loud, the lights were dim, and everybody was dressed up, trying to pretend that this was a glamorous event, not just another house party.

"Happy New Year, you guys!" Carter squealed. Her sequined dress flashed. "Perfect timing — my parents just left. Here — take a hat, and a noisemaker, and some confetti or whatever else you want." She strapped a cardboard cone on Tom's head.

"Is Jonah here yet?" I asked.

"Who?" Carter made a face. "I don't know."

"He'll get here." Tom took my arm. "You're my date, not Jonah's."

Earlier that evening, before Tom picked me up, Mom and I did our hair together in her bathroom. She seemed better since Christmas. She and Dad were going to a New Year's Eve party at the Hopkins Faculty Club that night.

"Be careful when Tom kisses you tonight," she said. "If you see silver sparkles, you're in trouble."

"Silver sparkles?" I said.

"You'll want to see those sparkles again," she said. "They're like a drug. They're like, I don't know . . . cocaine or something."

I stared at her. "Are you on coke?"

"That's not the point," she said.

"So you *are* on coke?" Maybe drug addiction would explain her odd behavior.

"No, Bea." She pinned up her dark hair with a Chinese rooster clip. "Don't be ridiculous."

"Have you *ever* done coke?"

"Stop it, honey. I'm talking about love, not drugs."

"Well, if you're talking about love, why did you bring up cocaine?"

"I was making an analogy. Forget it. . . ."

"What are you trying to tell me?" I said. "That I shouldn't kiss Tom tonight?"

"No," she said. "I don't mean that you shouldn't kiss him. . . . It's just, if you see sparkles when you kiss him, then you'll know . . ."

"Know what?"

"He'll haunt you," she said. "That's all. The silver sparkles are addictive. Oh, right — *that's* why I brought up drugs."

"And that's how you know you're in love?" I said. "Silver sparkles?"

"Not in love. Hooked. Two different things."

She wouldn't meet my eye. She was trying to give me advice, but as usual her advice was crazy.

"What if he melts you into a greasy puddle of processed cheese?" I said, thinking of Tom's microwave stare. "Is that the same thing as seeing sparkles?"

"Processed cheese? I never should have said anything." She turned on the blow dryer. End of conversation.

I expected to kiss Tom at midnight. To me, he was more of a melter than a sparkler, but then, I'd never kissed him, so what did I know?

"Let's get a drink," Tom said. "Beer or champagne?"

"Champagne, please," I said.

We went to the kitchen and Tom got us drinks. Through the sliding glass doors I saw people smoking on a back patio, staring at a waterless fountain.

"Is that Meredith?" Tom took off his party hat and peered at the smokers. "No, she never wears her hair up like that." He smiled at me, then looked outside again. "Is it? No. Couldn't be."

It *was* Meredith, one of the skinny Radnor girls who'd shown up at Tiza's party in September. I could have told him that, but chose not to. I was pretty sure he knew.

Anne Sweeney came into the kitchen with AWAE and Tiza. "You've got to dance. Nobody's dancing."

"All right," Tom said. "Want to dance?"

"Okay."

We danced in a group — Tom, Anne, AWAE, Tiza, and me. A couple of boys joined in. People wandered through the house. Walt Carrey sat on a couch by himself. He waved to me.

"Hey, dork." Tom playfully kicked Walt's feet. "You gonna come dance with us, or are you going to sit there by yourself all night?"

Walt got to his feet. "If you insist."

"I insist you stop being such a dork," Tom said.

Walt danced, shaking his fluff of hair.

"Spaz Mo-Dee, we call him," Tom said. "For such a good lacrosse player, you sure are a spaz."

Walt shook his hair harder. Tom laughed. I assumed he was teasing Walt in a friendly, jocky, designated-sidekick way.

"I'm going to get another beer," Tom said. He disappeared. I finished my champagne and danced some more with Walt and the girls. An old Gnarls Barkley song came on, "Crazy." The girls shrieked with delight and started waving their arms in the air.

"Ever do the Batusi?" Walt shouted over the music.

"The what?" I said.

"The Batusi. You know, Batman." He demonstrated, making a peace-sign V with each hand, then placing the Vs over his eyes to suggest a Batman mask. He dragged his fingers across his eyes while wiggling his hips, his face completely deadpan. "Uma Thurman and John Travolta did it in *Pulp Fiction*."

"Oh, the Batusi!" I remembered now. I was a Batman fanatic when I was four — the campy 1960s *Batman* show, not the dark, scary movies. Mom had the complete series on DVD.

"You be Catwoman, and I'll be the Caped Crusader," Walt said. "Holy Hipwiggles, Catwoman! No man can live on crime fighting alone."

Among the sea of swaying girls, Walt and I Batusi'd. Tom didn't come back. When "Crazy" segued into "Rehab," I thanked Walt and asked Anne if she knew where Tom had gone. She shrugged and shook her head in time to the music: *no, no, no*.

I checked the kitchen and the patio, but Tom wasn't there. I left the group of dancers and wandered down the hall, following the laughter to a noisy game room. Tom sat on a couch in front of a large screen playing *Grand Theft Auto*. Long-legged Meredith sat beside him, cheering him on.

"Get him! Get that one! Kill him!" she said.

"*K-prrrh!*" Tom made an explosion noise. "The cops got me." He sensed the weight of my shadow on his back and turned around. "There you are. Sorry, Bea, I can't resist *Grand Theft Auto*. My mom won't let it into the house."

"My turn," Meredith said.

"Oh — Meredith, this is Beatrice."

"Hi, Beatrice." Her straight white teeth clacked out my name.

"Hi."

"Turns out it *was* Meredith smoking out on the patio," Tom said. "I've just never seen her with her hair up before."

"And you never will again." Meredith took the controls from him. "It makes my face look horsy."

"You're crazy," Tom said. "It makes you look — I don't know — good."

"Good like a horse," Meredith said.

"Quit fishing for compliments," Tom said. "You want to play next, Bea?"

"No, thanks. I'll watch." I hate video games.

While Tom and Meredith took turns killing off thugs, I thought about Kreplax. And the comet. The end of the world was only three weeks away. At that moment wiping out humanity didn't seem like such a terrible idea.

Tom's watch flashed. Eleven-thirty and still no Jonah.

I left the game room to wander the house, peering into dark bedrooms, asking people in the bathroom line if they'd seen Jonah. No one had.

One of the beds had a pile of coats on it, still cold and fresh-smelling from the night air. Another had bodies tangled up in the dark, giggling. Out on the patio, the smokers filled the empty fountain with cigarette butts. Justine, Aislin, Harlan, and Sphere passed a joint around.

"Have you seen Jonah?" I asked them.

"Nah. Do you think he'd really come to a party like this?" Aislin said. "It's not his scene."

"What else would he do for New Year's?" I asked.

"I don't know," Harlan said. "Sit home in the dark and watch the *Star Trek* marathon? That's what I'd be doing if Sphere hadn't scored this hash."

But Jonah had promised me. He told me he'd come. He swore.

Maybe something had happened to him. A car accident.

I imagined Gertie skidding off a dark, icy road and crashing into a tree. Jonah slumped in the front seat, a bloody gash across his forehead.

What else could have happened? Car wouldn't start? House caught on fire? Escaped convict climbed through his bedroom window and tied him with duct tape? Poison eggnog?

Or maybe I just didn't matter enough to him.

Anne pulled me back inside the house. "Come on, it's almost midnight!" she said. "Where's Tom?"

"I don't know. The game room, I think."

"Well, get him! The countdown's about to start!"

Someone had turned on a TV and we saw the crystal ball sparkle in Times Square, ready to drop. I hurried into the game room.

"Ten! Nine! Eight!"

I pushed past couples guzzling champagne, past revelers shooting curly paper horns in my face.

"Seven! Six! Five! Four!"

The whole way I searched for Jonah. I didn't want him to be alone at the stroke of midnight. I was supposed to be with Tom, but I wanted to be with Jonah.

"Three! Two!"

I couldn't help opening the front door, just to see if he was out front, crunching over the gravel driveway. But no one was there.

"One! Happy New Year!"

Everyone shouted and kissed. I worked my way through the crowd and into the game room to find Tom. I was a second too late.

Meredith was in his lap, and he was giving her a New Year's kiss. They kissed like two starving people who'd just discovered ice cream.

So much for silver sparkles.

I gave him the finger. He didn't see it.

I went back to the main room. Everyone but me had someone to kiss, even if it was just a friend. I bit my lip. *It's better this way*, I thought. *Feelings make you crazy.* I had to keep reminding myself of that. *You're Robot Girl. Made of metal.* I thunked my stomach for old times' sake, *thunk thunk.*

"Hey." Walt tapped me on the shoulder. "Happy New Year."

"Happy New Year," I said.

He put a paper crown on my head. "Show me your best Queen Elizabeth face."

I scowled.

"Are you okay?" he said.

"Yeah."

He looked at me expectantly, but I wasn't sure exactly what he expected. "Want to dance or something?" he asked.

He was sweet, but I couldn't help it — I was bitter.

"Not right now," I said.

"How about a drink?"

"Okay."

Walt loped off to the kitchen.

"Happy New Year!" Anne threw her arms around me and kissed me on the cheek. "Where's Tom?"

"In the game room."

She frowned. "With Meredith?"

I nodded.

"That jerk. They went out in ninth grade. Guess he likes her again."

"I thought you said he didn't repeat," I said. I felt ridiculous for even caring at this point.

Anne shrugged. "I was wrong."

"Listen — now that it's midnight, do you think you'll go home soon?" I said. "I need a ride."

"Now? The party's just getting started!"

"What about an hour from now?"

"We'll see. I'll give you a ride if you need it, but not yet."

"Okay. Thanks."

Walt reappeared with two plastic cups. "Club soda?"

"Thanks." I took the cup. We clicked them together and I drank, suddenly very thirsty.

I had to drag Anne Sweeney out of the party at two A.M. We dropped off AWAE and Tiza on the way home. It was almost three by the time Anne left me in front of my house.

I paused on the front porch, fumbling with my key. A voice said, "Hey."

I jumped. Jonah stepped out of the shadows.

"How was the party?" he said.

"Sucked," I said. "Why didn't you come?"

"I just couldn't," he said. "But I'm here now. I didn't want to start the New Year without you." He kissed me on the cheek. "I wish you a happy year."

"Thanks," I said. "Happy New Year to you too." I hugged him. It was cold. Our breath mingled in the frozen air. "Want to come in for a New Year's hot chocolate?"

"What about your parents?"

"If they're asleep, we'll try not to wake them. If they're awake, we'll suffer their presence."

"Okay."

I unlocked the door. "Is that you, Bea?" Dad called from upstairs.

"Yes."

"How was the party?" Mom peered down at us from the top of the stairs. "Oh," she said when she noticed Jonah. "I guess you didn't see sparkles."

"No, no sparkles," I said. "I'll tell you about it in the morning."

"Okay. Good night."

Jonah and I settled in the kitchen. I put some water on the stove to boil.

"So where's your hot date?" Jonah said.

"He reunited with an ex at the party."

"That's evil. I'm sorry." He clamped his lips together. It must have been the struggle of his life to keep from saying "I told you so."

"Go ahead. You're dying to say it."

"No. No, I won't." He jiggled his lips with his fingers to loosen them up, making a *b-b-b-b-b-b* sound. "So what did you do?"

"I gave him the finger," I said, demonstrating. "That's *fuck you* in Robot."

"That's *fuck you* in any language," Jonah said. "Not really, but it should be."

The water boiled. I ripped open two packs of hot chocolate mix, poured them into mugs, and added water.

"I have a confession to make," Jonah said. "I purposely busted up your Alonso's date with Garber."

"I thought so," I said.

"It wasn't a total fake-out. I really did find Matthew's card when I got home that day. And I really was excited. I needed to see you. But pulling you away from Garber didn't bother me much."

"You did me a favor."

"You want to know the real reason I don't like him?"

"Yeah," I said. I gave him his mug and a spoon and sat down at the kitchen table with him.

"Garber is the one who started that whole g-g-g-ghost thing," Jonah said. "In seventh grade he started a rumor that I was dead. I don't know why. Then, when I showed up, he screamed like he was seeing a ghost."

"Anne told me about that," I said. "On the first day of school. But she didn't tell me that Garber started it."

"He held a mock funeral for me. He gave this ridiculous joke eulogy about how no one would miss me because I'd never really existed in the first place."

"That's awful," I said. "Why was he so mean to you?"

Jonah stirred his hot chocolate. "I don't know. People did a lot of mean things in seventh grade. Not just Tom, and not just to me. And in a way, secretly, I kind of liked it. That funeral brought me more attention from the other kids than I'd gotten in years. Then they forgot about me and moved on to other targets."

"You liked it? I don't believe you."

"No, really. Part of me felt like, Matthew died, and now I'm dying. It's the way things are supposed to be. I forgot that after you die, people forget about you."

"Not everyone forgets. You didn't forget."

"That's why it surprised me," Jonah said. "When they forgot."

"Well, I'm glad you told me, even though it's too late," I said. "Tom already burned me."

"You wouldn't have listened to me before."

"Maybe I would have. But thanks for trying to protect me, anyway."

"I wasn't just trying to protect you," Jonah said. "I was jealous too."

I focused on my mug, trying to keep my face from showing my surprise. "Jealous?"

"Not like that," Jonah said. So he wasn't going to confess his love for me. I felt relief and disappointment, mixed. I wasn't sure I wanted to hear a confession of love, but it would have given the night a dramatic kick.

"I was jealous as a friend," Jonah said. "An all-consuming friend. I don't want to share you with anyone, not even your parents. I know it's weird and not fair, but that's how I feel."

"I want you all to myself too," I said. The two of us in that kitchen felt more like a family than I'd ever been with my parents.

He laughed. "Don't worry. You have zero competition."

"Except Matthew," I said.

Jonah laughed again and nodded, as if the idea of competing with Matthew were ridiculous. But it wasn't.

"These curtains are hideous, by the way," he said, tugging on the chickens.

We stayed up the rest of the night listening to psychics on the radio make predictions for the coming year. An earthquake. A celebrity wedding. The comet. Then we fell asleep on the living room couch, curled up together, half covered by an afghan, as the first day dawned gray, pink, and frozen.

NOVEMBER DECEMBER JANUARY

CHAPTER 15

The day of the big comet disaster, January 23, came and went without fanfare. No comet crashed to earth. The coasts of the great continents were not deluged, no plagues sickened the world's people, no alien fascists invaded the planet. Not on that day.

Herb:
How do you explain that, Kreplax?

Kreplax:
I must have miscalculated the astronomical date.
I've never been good at math —

Herb:
You might have told us that before you scared us
all with your predictions of doom.

Kreplax:
Yeah, I might have. But then you wouldn't have
listened to me.

Herb:
I believe that's my point. . . .

Jonah picked that day to visit Matthew again. He had tiptoed around the idea with his father, who firmly repeated that there would be no visits to St. Francis. So Jonah had to be careful not to alarm Dr. Kramer or anyone else at the institution. He wanted them to think it was okay for us to visit, that we had Mr. Tate's permission. If Dr. Kramer called to check and Mr. Tate forbade our visits, they would end.

I knew that would crush Jonah. After so many years without his brother, one half-hour visit had reawakened some lost part of him. Jonah showed an easy, unqualified affection for Matthew that I'd never seen him show for anyone else. Including me.

This time Jonah brought the Evil Miss Frankenheimer with him. She was much less worn than Catso. While the Evil Miss Frankenheimer had sat in Jonah's closet all these years, Matthew had carried Catso everywhere with him. The nurses at St. Francis patched him up to keep him together. It seemed that if Catso fell apart, Matthew would too.

We were led to the dayroom. This time, the patients listened to music while nurses and aides moved their arms and legs around for them. A workout of sorts. When exercise period was over, we approached Matthew. He seemed less lively without a pile of clay in front of him. He slumped in his chair, a thread of drool trickling down his chin.

"Hi, Matthew," Jonah said. "Look who I brought."

Matthew lifted his head. I don't know if it was the sight of Jonah or the Evil Miss Frankenheimer, but he brightened. Jonah walked Miss Frankenheimer up Matthew's leg and made her kiss Catso. "Oh, Catso, I missed you so much," Jonah said in a girl voice. Matthew gripped Catso as if he were trying to move her, but couldn't. Or maybe he was clinging to her, trying to protect her.

"You know what I missed the most?" Jonah said in his Frankenheimer voice. "The sword fights!"

He bounced Miss Frankenheimer around, attacking Catso and making funny fighting noises. Matthew's mouth fell open and his head dropped back.

"I've never seen him do that before," the nurse said.

"He's laughing," Jonah said.

It was hard to tell *what* Matthew was doing. He wasn't shaking, the way most people do when they laugh. But he kept dropping his jaw open in an expression of glee. And every time the nurse picked up his head, he tossed it back. On purpose.

"Stop picking up his head," Jonah said to the nurse. "Let him do it."

"I don't think it's good for his neck," the nurse said.

"You don't think laughing is good for him?" Jonah said.

"I'm not sure that's laughing," the nurse said gently.

"You don't know him at all, do you?" Jonah said. "He's lived here ten years and nobody really knows him."

"Jonah —" I touched his shoulder. His voice was rising.

"You heard what she said," Jonah said. "She's never seen him do this before. And I'm telling you, this is how he laughs. That means in ten years, Matthew has never laughed. Not once."

"I've only worked here for two years —" the nurse said.

"Even so," Jonah said. "Two years. Can you imagine not laughing for two years straight? What kind of hellhole is this?"

"I think you'd better calm down," the nurse said.

"Is there a problem here?" A large man, an orderly, came over and set his hands on his hips in an intimidating way.

"This visitor is causing problems," the nurse said.

"I'm causing problems? *I'm* causing problems? Did I put my brother in a wheelchair? Did I lock him away in this place? Did I neglect him so much he looks dead in his eyes, until he sees me? Those are real problems. Not a little noise!"

The orderly took him by the shoulders. "Come on, kid. Time to go."

Jonah struggled, but the orderly was strong and used to manhandling difficult people. "No! I've got fifteen minutes left in my visiting session!"

"You just forfeited them. Next visit, don't give the nurse a hard time, or you'll be banned forever. Hear me?"

"We hear you," I said, taking Jonah by the hand and leading him away. "Come on, Jonah, we'll be back soon."

He looked back at Matthew, whose head had dropped forward again, eyes shut. His body went slack, except for his left arm, which pounded Catso against his cheek.

Someone from St. Francis made a call to Jonah's father. They told him that Jonah had visited and upset the nurse, the orderly, and Matthew.

"What bullshit," I said.

"He was so pissed," Jonah said. "*So* pissed. I haven't seen him that pissed in a long time. Usually he's just calm and cold, like a big scary iceberg."

"What did he say?"

"He said I'm not allowed to go to St. Francis ever again. He told Dr. Kramer to make sure I was kept away, even if they have to post a mug shot in the front office. He said I have no business butting into Matthew's care. I should do as I'm told, stop worrying about Matthew, and worry more about myself, because I'm in danger of turning out to be a huge loser if I don't buckle down and concentrate, make some friends, go to college, et cetera, et cetera. All in a voice of doom at ear-splitting decibels."

I couldn't imagine Mr. Tate yelling like that. He'd seemed so controlled when I met him.

We sat in the courtyard outside the Upper School building, shivering in the weak winter sun. The bell rang. It was time for Assembly.

"What are you going to do?" I asked.

"What do you mean?" Jonah said.

"About Matthew."

"Oh. I don't know."

But I knew him, and I knew that now that he'd found Matthew, he wouldn't give him up. Somehow, Jonah was going back to St. Francis.

"What are you doing after school?" I asked Jonah at the Morgue one Friday. "Want to go junk shopping?"

"I can't," Jonah said. He didn't say more.

I finished my grilled cheese.

"Why not?" I finally asked.

"Homework," Jonah said.

"Homework?" I said. "You never do your homework."

"And *Yodel* stuff," he said.

"Bullshit," I said.

"Think whatever you want. It's true," he said.

No way was it true. Something was up.

"You're going to St. Francis, aren't you?" I said.

"No."

"Yes, you are. What are you going to do, sneak in there?"

"I don't know yet," he said.

"Can I come?"

"Not this time. Why should we both get arrested?"

"Do you think they'll arrest you?"

"Who knows?" He raised his pale eyebrows, two streaks of vanilla on his snowy face, and his eyes glittered.

"Have you been back since the last time?" I asked.

He nodded. I felt a stab of disappointment. He'd gone without me, without even telling me. "They wouldn't let me in," he said. "Dad must have threatened them. He controls the money. They'll do what he wants."

"So what are you going to do?" I asked.

"Promise you won't tell anyone?"

"Who would I tell?"

"I'm going to disguise myself. Wig, glasses, dress —"

"Dress?"

"I'll say I'm a social worker or something. We'll see what happens. As long as they don't suspect it's me, they won't call the police."

"They'll know it's you. You're going to get into huge trouble."

"I don't care. I've got to see Matthew. I want to make sure he's okay."

"Do you need to borrow any clothes?"

"Maybe. I was going to hit the Salvation Army but if you've got something that will fit me —"

"I'll help you," I said. Mom and I hadn't taken any fake-movie photos in months. I missed dressing her in drag and pointing a gun at her head. But she wasn't into it anymore. "I've got tons of stuff — props, costumes, makeup. . . ."

"As long as I look real," Jonah said. "Remember, I have to look real."

I studied his haunted face — the pale skin, the spooky eyes — and thought, *That might not be so easy.*

"Come over after school," I said. "We'll do what we can."

At seven o'clock that night, the doorbell rang. Dad was eating at the Faculty Club, so Mom and I were having chicken pot pie in front of the TV. *Jeopardy!* was on. I was picking out carrots and avoiding peas.

I'd spent the afternoon helping Jonah disguise himself in a wig and a dress and glasses. I did the best I could to make him look like a real female, then watched him drive off to St. Francis.

Ding-dong.

"Maybe that's Jonah." Visiting hours would be over by now. I got up to answer the door. It was him.

"Here." Jonah stuffed the curly blond wig into my arms. His face, still rouged, looked sunken. I could tell immediately that his plan hadn't worked.

I pulled him inside. "Mom, we're going up to my room."

"Wait. Stop. You didn't finish your dinner," Mom said without taking her eyes off Alex Trebek.

"Ignore her," I said to Jonah. We went upstairs and sat on my bed. "What happened?"

"I managed to confuse the receptionist long enough for her to let me in," he said. "But I guess I don't walk like a girl or something. She followed me down the corridor. I started to run, like an idiot."

"Oh, Jonah."

"So she yelled 'Stop!' and chased me. I didn't stop, so she screamed her head off for security. They tackled me and tore off my wig and said 'Ah-ha!' They actually said 'Ah-ha.' Then they threw me out. They said next time they'll call the police."

I went to my dresser and dunked a Kleenex in cold cream. "You're lucky they didn't arrest you this time."

"Yeah," he said. "Lucky." His head bobbled on his neck, unconsciously dodging me as I tried to rub the rouge off his face.

"Hold still," I said. "Did they call your father?"

He shrugged. "I don't know. Probably. I haven't been home yet." He kicked off my moccasins, the only girl shoes we'd managed to stuff his feet into. "We've got to get Matthew out of there."

"But he needs special care," I said. The Kleenex turned red. I threw it away.

"I can take care of him," Jonah said. "Once school's finished, I can stay with him all the time. I used to help my mother take care of him. It's hard, but I can do it."

He was serious, and I knew it, but I didn't think about what he was really saying.

"What will you do until school's out?" I said. Graduation was six months away.

"I don't know," he said. "Think. Plot. Plan."

"I'll help you think and plot and plan," I said.

"Okay," he said. But his rueful half-smile really said, *You can't.*

DECEMBER JANUARY FEBRUARY MARCH

CHAPTER 16

I hate February. It's the bleakest month of the year, and that February was even bleaker than usual. It snowed half a foot, then freezing-rained for a week until the whole world seemed carved out of metal-gray slush.

In March, it snowed again and then just plain old rained. The few sunny days were cold and windy and fluorescent in a glaring, turn-that-light-down way, exposing the bare trees and brown grass and other ugly wounds of winter no one was ready to see. They blended together, February and March, into one long, lonely winter's end.

Dad had a heavy course load and spent long days on campus. Mom hunted for a job, some kind of arts work, but nobody was hiring. I often found her on the phone, speaking quietly, as if she didn't want me to hear. *An odd way to talk to prospective employers*, I thought, but I didn't ask. I just wished she'd get a job so she wouldn't be ghouling around the house so much when I got home from school.

The winter left her thinner than ever, dark hollows shadowing her eyes. She started seeing a therapist — Dad made her go — and she said that was helping. If it was, I couldn't tell. Maybe she didn't nap so much, but she still did spacy stuff like parking on a hill without the emergency brake. She came out of Louie's Bookstore to find the Volvo had rolled backward down Charles Street and crashed into another parked car. After the car was fixed, she left it running in the driveway all night without realizing it. She hung a plastic chicken *and* a St. Christopher medal from the rearview mirror, but they didn't bring the poor Volvo much good luck.

As for me, I stayed up all night listening to the radio, and, in the mornings, I tunneled to school through the World of Gray Slush. I avoided Anne and the other girls when I could; ever since New Year's Eve, I felt embarrassed around them. Tom and Meredith were together now, and everybody knew how it had happened. The whole Tom thing was kind of humiliating. I was over him, but, despite my denials, AWAE and Tiza and Carter seemed to think I was crushed by his rejection. *Just like Lucy Moran*, they said. Sure, I had circles under my eyes and dirty hair and a wrinkled uniform, and I slouched around school staring at the floor as if my dog had just died, but that had nothing to do with Tom.

Jonah skipped school at least once a week, claiming to be sick. But he was there one morning in Assembly when Lockjaw announced that the art teachers were accepting entries for the Spring Art Show in April.

"Let's do a project together," I whispered to him while Nina Fogel took over the podium to hector the seniors about looming *Yodel* deadlines and how missing them would ruin their lives.

"I can't," he said. "I've already started my project."

"You have?" I stiffened. "What are you doing?"

"It's a secret," he said.

"Tell me," I said.

"I can't."

"Yes, you can."

"No, I can't."

I fumed in my seat for a few seconds while Nina ranted, "I'll print blank pages if I have to, I really will. . . ."

"Tell me," I said again.

He shook his head.

"Quiet, you guys," Anne said. "You're missing Nina's Mussolini act. You can see the spit-spray from here. The first two rows should be wearing raincoats."

Right after Assembly, Nina collared me and demanded I start taking yearbook photos immediately, since I had, in fact, volunteered for the job. So that afternoon I found myself in the gym, begging the Varsity boys' lacrosse team to please be quiet and stand on the bleachers for their team picture.

Their coach finally settled them in order, sticks in their left hands, helmets under right arms, Tom Garber front and center. As I aimed the camera at him, he flashed his brightest grin, and I wondered if future generations of girls, looking at this team picture, would be microwaved by it, through the filter of film and paper and years. Maybe Tom would microwave girls from beyond the grave, his laser-beam eyes the lasting legacy of Canton Lacrosse.

Walt sprouted up behind Tom. He smiled at me too, and looking at the two grins, one above the other, I marveled at the difference between them. Tom's was brighter, but Walt's was warmer, if you could make it out through the glare gleaming off Tom's teeth. Walt patted the fluffy top of his hair, trying in vain to flatten it.

"On three," I told them. "One, two —"

On three, Walt flashed two fingers over Tom's head, the devil's horns, warmly grinning all the while. Perhaps another photographer would have asked for a second shot, but I decided the first one was a keeper.

"That's perfect," I said. Thanks to Walt, the record had been corrected for posterity.

Girls of future generations had been warned.

The next day, I brought a shopping bag full of glasses and masks and hats to school for the Yearbook Committee photo. Jonah had asked for them, saying he had a concept for our group portrait.

Ten *Yodeler*s gathered in the yearbook office after school for their picture. I gave Jonah the bag of props and asked, "So what's the concept?"

"The concept is: Everybody wears a hat or something."

"That's it?" I said. "That's your brilliant idea?"

"Why do we have to wear anything?" Nina said.

Jonah handed her a cowboy hat and bandanna. "It's fun."

"Fun?" Nina said.

"Don't you like your cowboy hat?" He pointed her to the window so she could see her reflection. The hat gave her a saucy look completely at odds with her personality.

Nina grinned at her reflection. "Sure, I like it."

"Okay then." Jonah waved a rubber Richard Nixon mask. "Who wants to be a disgraced ex-president?"

"I do." Aislin took the Nixon mask. I wore a pirate's hat and a robber mask. Jonah chose a ski cap and plastic Halloween cat mask. The others wore wigs and hockey masks and false noses and goofy glasses.

"Is this so people won't know who to blame if the yearbook sucks?" Aislin asked.

"No," Nina said. "We'll print a caption under the picture with all our names, just like we always do. Right, Jonah?"

"Right," Jonah said. He pulled down his mask. "Everybody ready?"

I set the camera's timer and took my place in the cluster of masked *Yodeler*s. Nina insisted we take five shots to make sure at least one turned out okay. Then we were done.

"Why did you really want these costumes?" I asked Jonah as I packed them up.

"What do you mean?" Jonah said. "I'm the photo editor. I wanted an interesting shot."

"No, really," I said.

"Really," he swore.

One night in March I started sketching plans for my art project. I'd hoped Jonah would take Mom's role — the Anthony Perkins role — in a photo-reconstruction of the shower scene from *Psycho*, but he refused. Without a partner, the shower scene wouldn't work — it required a Janet Leigh victim (me), mouth gaping in midscream, and, at the very least, a knife-wielding arm. I could ask Mom if she'd help, but I really wasn't anxious to put a knife — even a rubber one — within her reach.

I needed a new idea, something I could pull off by myself. I sat at my desk late into the night, sketching and thinking while the radio kept me company.

Soon — in two or three weeks — we'd find out where we were going to college. Jonah had applied mostly to art schools, including the School of Visual Arts in New York. I imagined us leaving Baltimore together, driving off in Gertie to our exciting new life. New York would be perfect for us. People reinvented themselves there. You could be anybody you wanted to be in New York.

Then I remembered Matthew. I tried to imagine him in our tatty-but-cozy New York apartment, but I couldn't see him there. I couldn't make him fit into the picture. How would two college students take full-time care of a severely handicapped boy? Did Jonah really expect to take care of Matthew by himself?

He didn't, I decided. He didn't mean it. Jonah would get into art school and we'd move to New York together and we'd visit Matthew when we came home for holidays. That had to be what Jonah was thinking. I couldn't see any other way to make it work.

The Night Light Show came on. I turned up my radio.

Herb:
I'm your host, Herb Horvath, on this icy night in early

spring. Doesn't feel like spring, does it? But
warm weather is just around the corner, don't you
worry. Okay, let's get started. First caller, you're on
the air.

Myrna:
Hi, Herb. Guess who.

Herb:
Myrna! What's going on in Highlandtown tonight?

Myrna:
Not a whole lot, Herb. March is such a dreary
time of year. I hope Dottie has shuffled off
those blues, finally. I read something in the
paper about that . . . what was it? You know,
my neighbor's an old man who never throws
out his newspapers, and the other day I was
helping him clear a path from his kitchen to
his bathroom, and I happened to see an old
newspaper article that said something about this
place. . . . It's supposed to be the happiest place
on Earth.

Herb:
Disneyland?

Myrna:
No, not Disneyland. Heavens no. This was an
unexpected place, some strange place where they
have lots of hairdressers. . . .

"Iceland," I whispered to the radio. "It's Iceland."

Herb:

Gosh, I can't help you there, Myrna.

Myrna:

Oh, I know. It was Iceland! Isn't that funny? But this article said that people who get their hair done in Iceland are very happy. The happiest people in the world. Or something like that.

Herb:

That's very interesting. I wonder how they found that out?

Myrna:

I have no idea. But I love to go to the beauty parlor, so Iceland sounds like the place for me. What do you say, Dottie? Maybe you and me should take a little trip up there and see if it cheers you up any.

"I'll go," I volunteered.

Herb:

[fairy music plays] Sounds like a good plan, Myrna. We've got to take another call. Nighty-night.

Myrna:

Nighty-night, Herb.

Herb:

Hello, you're on the air.

Ghost Boy:

Hi, Herb. Ghost Boy here.

Herb:

It's nice to hear from you. How's your little friend?

Ghost Boy:

Robot Girl? She's fine. I'm sure she's listening tonight.

Herb:

And what are you up to, Ghost Boy?

Ghost Boy:

Not much, Herb. Just thinking. Plotting, planning, thinking.

Herb:

Thinking about what?

Ghost Boy:

Oh, you know. Ghost Boy things.

Herb:

I'm afraid to ask what that means.

Ghost Boy:

Probably best you don't ask, Herb.

Herb:

And what about this plotting and planning?

Ghost Boy:

A secret, Herb. Can't say much about it now. But everyone will find out about it sooner or later.

Herb:

Some great project, I suppose?

Ghost Boy:

An art project. You could call it that. Of course, you can call just about anything an art project these days, right, Herb?

Herb:

[laughing] Right you are, Ghost Boy. Some of the stuff they show in those art galleries downtown. . . . I mean, one place had a log on the floor, and that was it! A plain old ordinary log, and nothing else. I'd like someone to explain to me how that's art.

Ghost Boy:

Me too, Herb, me too. *[fairy music]* Well, guess I'd better make way for another caller. I hope you all have a wonderful night.

Herb:

Same to you, Ghost Boy. Nighty-night.

Jonah's call annoyed me. Plotting and planning? What was he talking about — his art project? I could keep it a secret, he knew I could. Instead he taunted me over the radio, sending me a cryptic message everyone could hear.

I listened late into the night, still sketching. I thought about what Myrna had said. She'd gotten the details a little skewed, but she'd obviously read the same story I'd heard on the radio, about the happy Icelandic hairdressers, and it gave me an idea.

Winter is a dead time. I sketched and sketched, searching for a way to turn the cold into a good thing. In the meantime, all I could do was wait for spring to come, for things to start happening again.

EMBER JANUARY FEBRUARY MARCH APRIL

CHAPTER 17

In the second week of April, the halls of Canton buzzed as news from colleges trickled in. My college notices were waiting in the mailbox when I got home from school on April 12. Four rejections, but I got into Vassar and NYU, so I was very happy.

I called Jonah right away. "Did you hear?"

"MICA and the School of Visual Arts."

"SVA! New York City, baby! I'll take photography classes with you."

"Yay. Whoopee."

"What's wrong? Aren't you excited?"

"Excited about what? More school?"

"It's art school, not school school. SVA won't be anything like Canton."

"God, let's hope not."

"And we'll be in New York! Together! On our own!"

"We'll see."

I didn't understand his attitude. "Jonah, it's exciting!"

"I know."

My enthusiasm seemed to annoy him, so I tamped it down. Maybe he was right. Maybe we were all excited over nothing. Just more school. What was there to celebrate?

* * *

The next weekend, Mom and I went to New York to visit schools. The idea was for me to get a feel for college life and decide where I wanted to go. Did I want to be on a bucolic campus in Poughkeepsie? (Mom and Dad: *Yes, you do.* Me: *No, I don't.*) Or did I want to dive headfirst into New York City? (Mom and Dad: *No, you definitely don't.* Me: *Yes, I really, really do.*)

"I won't be alone if I go to NYU," I told them. "Jonah will be with me." He hadn't said that he'd decided to go to SVA, but I knew he would. What choice did he have? What else could he possibly do?

"Why don't I find that reassuring?" Dad said.

"I don't know," I said. "Why don't you?"

He opened the refrigerator and rummaged through the bottles and jars. "Do we have any strawberry jelly?"

"We'll go to New York together this weekend, Bea," Mom said. "We'll visit both schools, talk to people, and go out on the town. Just us girls. It will be fun."

"The point is to stay with the students in the dorms," I said. "Not to go out on the town with your mom."

"I think it's a great idea," Dad said. He found the strawberry jelly and shut the refrigerator door. "You and your mother could use some time together. I'd like to come too, but I don't want to get in the way of your girl time."

"Girl time?" The idea repelled me. "I want to stay in the dorms. Couldn't we go to New York together another weekend?"

"No, this is perfect," Mom said. "It's all settled. We're going to New York."

This wasn't perfect. It was all wrong. I wanted to go alone. But they were both set on this plan, and I couldn't change their minds.

There was a time when I would have wanted Mom to visit colleges with me. When I would have enjoyed her company. When

I wouldn't have been able to imagine making the decision with-out her.

She'd never been the most maternal person on Earth, but, before Ithaca, she was like a big sister or a favorite babysitter. When I was little, we used to make a tent out of blankets in the living room and have slumber parties there — just me, Mom, and my stuffed ani-mals. In fourth grade, there was a boy at school who picked on me, so Mom made paper dolls of me and the bully and we acted out elaborate revenge fantasies. I never had the nerve to take vengeance on that boy in real life, but humiliating the paper version of him made me feel better.

Then, after we moved to Ithaca, she started acting weird — distant, like she had secrets from me. Maybe she'd been weird all along and I'd only started noticing. Whatever. Now she just felt like an obstacle I had to maneuver around, someone in my way.

We left early on Friday morning and drove to Poughkeepsie. Mom and I spent the day on the Vassar campus, visiting classes, looking at the art studios, eating in the dining hall. I liked Vassar, but that didn't matter — I was determined to move to New York with Jonah.

We drove into Manhattan and checked into the Washington Square Hotel. Instead of taking a campus tour, we walked around Greenwich Village and stopped at an Italian restaurant for dinner. Mom had been edgy all afternoon, and by dinnertime her face was pale green. I thought maybe she was upset about me going away to college, her only child leaving home, and the trip was making my departure seem real for the first time. *She's got a little motherliness in her after all*, I thought. *She's going to miss me.*

"What's wrong?" I asked Mom. "Don't you like your linguini?"

"It's fine." She nibbled a piece of bread. "My stomach's a little upset, that's all."

"Are you sick?"

"No. It's from spending all that time in the car today."

"What, you get carsick now?"

"Sometimes."

"You keep finding new ways to get sick," I said.

She turned greener. "I need to lie down."

We went back to our hotel room. I had to get up early for breakfast with a dean, so I went to bed. Mom stayed up watching TV.

A few hours later, I woke up to a gagging sound. Mom's bed was empty. The light was on in the bathroom. The bedside clock said 3:03.

More gagging. Vomiting.

I got up. Mom huddled over the toilet.

"What's wrong? Are you sick?" I asked.

She nodded.

"What should I do?"

"I'll be okay," she said.

"I'll call Dad," I said.

I dialed home. The phone rang four times; then our machine picked up.

"Dad, it's me. Pick up, Dad."

I waited. Dad didn't answer.

"Sorry if I'm waking you, but it's an emergency. Mom's sick."

"Is he there?" Mom asked.

I shook my head.

"Where is he?"

"Want some ginger ale or something?"

"No. I'll be okay in a minute."

"I'll try his cell." I dialed the number, but it went straight to voicemail.

"He's probably just sleeping," Mom said. "Dead to the world."

Mom's cell rang. It wasn't in her purse, but on the nightstand next to the bed. I answered it.

"Hello?"

"Dori?"

"Dad?"

Silence.

"Dad?" I said again.

The man said. "Is your mother there?"

Who could this be? I looked at the phone, but it only showed a number.

"Mom, it's for you," I said. "Some man."

"I'll be right there." She rinsed out her mouth and took the phone. "Hello?" Pause. "Where are you?"

Pause. Then, trying to whisper.

"What about tomorrow?"

Pause.

"Are you sure?"

Pause.

"But —"

Pause.

"I came all this way —"

She shut herself in the bathroom, muffling her words: She sounded upset. She came out a few minutes later, her face red and wet, and dropped the phone on her bed.

"Who was that?" I said.

"Oh. My therapist," Mom said.

"I thought your therapist was a woman," I said.

"This is a new therapist," she said.

"You're lying," I said. "Who was that?"

She collapsed onto the bed. "Bea, I told you. I don't want to answer any more questions tonight. I'm sick."

Enough, I thought.

"That's your excuse for everything," I said. "I think you make yourself sick on purpose."

"Bea, that's ridiculous. Why would I make myself sick? I'm miserable!"

"*I'm* miserable!" I said. "It's the middle of the night! I have to get up early tomorrow. We're supposed to be here for me! For my decision. An important decision about my future. Tell me — *Who was on the phone?*"

The line about "my future" was pouring it on a little thick, but I couldn't resist. Those words gave me the moral high ground and I knew it.

Mom curled up on the bed. "Bea, please. I'm sorry about this. About everything. We can talk about it tomorrow, but right now my stomach hurts and I can't think. I'll make it up to you, I promise."

"You can't make it up to me," I said. "Just leave me alone. That's all I want. If you'd only let me come by myself, none of this would have happened. Having you around makes everything worse."

She buried her head under a pillow. "Stop it! You're so cold! You're heartless, you little robot!" The pillow muffled her words, but they stung.

"I feel things," I said. "I'm not a robot!" I stamped my foot and screamed. Then I burst into tears. I touched the little wet drops and held them toward her. "See, I'm *not* a robot. This is proof."

She refused to take the pillow off her head. I wiped the tears on her pillowcase. I might have been made of metal once, but not anymore. Like Pinocchio, I'd turned into a real girl. So far it sucked. But there was nothing I could do about it.

I got into bed, leaving the bathroom light on. Mom might need it.

I woke up at eight feeling drained. Mom was asleep, tangled in her sheets, pillow on the floor. The bathroom light was still on.

I got dressed and found my way to the dean's office. I met with some students, toured the campus, ate lunch in the student center. I tried to concentrate on the school and the city, but I couldn't stop thinking about Mom. And Dad. Why didn't he answer the phone last night? Where was he? And who had called Mom?

I went back to the hotel after lunch. Mom's bed was made. Her things were packed. She lay on the bed on her back, dressed in jeans, with her shoes on.

"How are you feeling?" I asked.

"Dizzy," she said. "I'm sorry, Bea. I can't stay here. I have to go home."

We'd planned to go to the Met that afternoon. That night I was supposed to go to a party for prospective students. Was she saying I should stay by myself and do these things without her? Was she leaving me there? Or did she expect me to go home with her?

"I don't understand," I said. "Did Dad call?"

"Finally. This morning."

"Where was he last night?"

"He said he'd turned the phone off."

That didn't sound like something Dad would do while Mom and I were away and possibly needing him. Or maybe it did. I didn't know anymore.

"So . . . do you want me to go home with you?"

"I'm not leaving you alone in New York City," Mom said.

"Oh. Okay." I packed my few things and we were ready to leave. It took five minutes.

"Will you drive?" Mom said. "I'm too dizzy."

That was the end of my college weekend. We were quiet on the drive home. There was no point asking any questions. Because there was no way she was going to give me any answers.

Dad met us at the front door.

"Make any decisions?" he said. "Vassar, right?"

I walked past him without answering. Dad helped Mom upstairs. He tried to lead her into their room, but she went into the guest room and shut the door. He forced his way in. They stayed in there for hours, hissing at each other.

CHAPTER 18

For the art show, I entered a photo called "A Hairdresser in Iceland." I posed in a snowy Santaland with a candy-striped barber pole. A large Barbie makeup head played the role of beauty shop customer, propped on a box with a smock around her neck. Wearing a platinum wig, a short blue tunic, and a wide smile, I teased the Barbie's hair into a tall, yellow beehive. A sign over the mirror spelled out ICELAND in rainbow letters. Fake snow sparkled all around me. I tried to look as happy as I possibly could.

"Iceland," Walt said as he studied my entry. "You told me about that a long time ago, at Tiza's party. All about the happy Icelandic hairdressers."

"You remembered," I said.

"You should have won first place," Walt said.

"The judges thought my picture was a joke," I said.

"Want to walk around and look at the other stuff?" Walt said.

"Okay." I was dying to see Jonah's painting. Every time I stopped by his wall, he covered the painting with a sheet and told me to go away. He didn't want me to see his masterpiece without its rightful blue ribbon.

Now Jonah sat on the floor in front of his work, a blue ribbon finally stuck to the pasteboard. The large painting, "Family Portrait," took up the entire wall. It showed Matthew, crowned with his padded helmet, ruling from a golden wheelchair before a Tate family crest. Or was it Jonah in the throne, playing Matthew? The eyes were sly, more icy than milky. Catso and the Evil Miss Frankenheimer perched on either side of him like hounds flanking an English lord.

The colors and composition and technique were impressive. But the most striking thing about the painting was the look on Matthew's face. What was he thinking? Was he smiling or smirking or just making some kind of brain-damage face?

It was like the Mona Lisa. Inscrutable.

"Congratulations." I slid to the floor to sit with Jonah. "I almost can't believe you won first place, because this painting deserves it so much, and people who deserve to win hardly ever do."

"It's awesome," Walt said. "But why did you paint yourself in a wheelchair?"

"It isn't him —" I began, but Jonah interrupted me.

"Because that's how I feel," he said.

"And what are those little cats supposed to represent?" Walt asked.

"They don't represent anything," Jonah said, a note of disgust creeping into his voice.

Walt backed off. "I'm glad you won," he said. "Hey, Beatrice, can I talk to you a minute?"

"Sure," I said.

"Over here, I mean?" Walt pointed to a quiet pasteboard nook nearby — the freshman watercolor section.

I got to my feet — with difficulty, since Jonah clamped his hand down on mine. I wrested it out from under him.

"Don't go," Jonah murmured.

"I'll be right back," I promised.

I walked away with Walt. "What's up?" I asked.

"I know it's a little early," Walt began, "but I was afraid if I waited, it would be too late —"

"Too late for what?"

"Um, would you like to go to the prom with me?"

"The what?" I said.

"The prom?"

"Oh, the prom." I guess I'd known there was a prom coming up, somewhere in the back of my mind.

"Do you have a date already?" Walt said. He twisted his fingers together nervously. His eyes gleamed with goodwill and hope and anxiety.

"No," I said. "No date."

"You're not going . . . with Jonah, or somebody like that?"

"I don't think so." Jonah and I hadn't discussed it. I doubted he was very interested in a night at the prom.

"So, what do you say?"

He meant: Why wasn't I saying yes? Good question. Why wasn't I?

I could still feel the pressure of Jonah's hand on mine.

I remembered a time in Austin, a few years earlier, when a girl from school asked me if I wanted to go skiing for a weekend with her family. I wanted to, but Dad was going to a conference that weekend, and Mom and I had planned a three-day Alfred Hitchcock marathon. We could have watched those old movies any weekend, but somehow I couldn't tell Mom the marathon was off. So I didn't go. And Mom and I had fun. I'll never know for sure if I made the right decision, but it felt right. That girl was my friend, but Mom came first.

Now, Jonah came first. I liked Walt, but that was the way things were.

"I'm sorry, Walt," I said. "It's not you personally. I just don't think I'll be going to the prom."

The hope in his eyes dried to panic. "Not with anyone?" I shook my head. "Why not?"

I made up a plausible-sounding reason on the spot. "I feel weird about it. Everyone else has been at Canton for so long, and I just got here, and the prom's not my thing."

"It doesn't matter how long you've been here," Walt said. "I'll make sure you have a good time."

I shook my head.

"Will you think about it? Maybe you'll change your mind."

I started to say no, but he said, "Just think about it."

"Okay," I said.

"Okay." His body relaxed slightly, the ordeal over. "See you later."

"See you."

He walked away. I went back to Jonah.

"What did Ichabod want?" Jonah said.

"Don't be mean to him. He's nice."

"I wasn't being mean. That was affectionate. An affection-ate nickname for a tall, awkward, geeky guy who's easily spooked. It fits."

"You weren't being affectionate."

People walked by and congratulated Jonah. They looked at his painting thoughtfully, as if considering its deepest implications. But they didn't linger or talk to Jonah for long. He sent out a people-repellent vibe, a kind of *Off!* for humans.

"Did you go to the prom last year?" I asked him. The Canton prom was for juniors and seniors. He might have gone.

"What? Fuck, no," he said. "Are you thinking of going?"

"No."

"Did Walt ask you? Is that what he wanted?"

I even felt guilty telling him. "Kind of."

"Did you say yes?"

"I said no, but he told me to think about it."

"Don't go," Jonah said. "You won't like it. They rent out a ballroom downtown at the Belvedere, and everybody puts on fancy clothes and tries to pretend they don't know every pimple on each other's butts. Limos, the whole bit. Afterward, somebody has a big debauched party where they all get drunk and puke in the yard. Everybody stays out all night. Big fucking deal."

He was right. What would I do at a prom without Jonah? If you analyzed the concept, took it apart, and looked at its pieces, the prom was nothing more than a dress, a limo, and a perfunctory date.

"I'll tell you what," Jonah said. "We'll do something big on prom night. Just the two of us. After all, we're graduating too. We deserve a celebration. Our kind of celebration."

This was exactly what I wanted.

"Like what?" I asked.

"Let's run away, just for the night. Or maybe the weekend. To Ocean City."

"Yeah," I said, warming up to the idea. "Prom night in Ocean City. I'll even buy a gown to wear."

"I'll promenade you down the boardwalk," Jonah said. "We'll be king and queen of the freaks. Be sure to wear your tiara."

"I don't have a tiara," I said. "All I have is a Happy New Year crown with painful memories attached to it."

"We'll get you one, then," Jonah said. "You can't go to Ocean City without a tiara. It's a new rule I just made up."

"What about all your plotting and planning and thinking?" I asked.

"I've done a lot of it," he said. "We'll finish our plotting together, at the beach. Deal?"

How could I resist?

Of course it was a deal.

IBER JANUARY FEBRUARY MARCH APRIL MAY

CHAPTER 19

Herb:

Hello, you're on the air.

Robot Girl:

Herb, I'm just calling to wish Ghost Boy and his twin brother, Matthew, a very happy birthday. They'll be eighteen years old tomorrow. And I'd like to invite all loyal Night Light listeners — and you too, Herb, if you can make it — to a birthday party for Ghost Boy tomorrow night at Carmichael's Book Shop on Charles Street, off Mount Vernon Place. Around eight.

Herb:

Thank you, Robot Girl. I'm sure many listeners will join you for the celebration. Happy Birthday, Ghost Boy! Next caller, you're on the air.

Judy from Pikesville:

This is Judy from Pikesville? I heard that young lady, and I just want to remind her that the drinking age in this state is twenty-one, not eighteen as she seems to think. I have a good mind to go to that birthday party just to make sure she and her little friends drink nothing stronger than RC Cola. I would, too, if it weren't for my phlebitis . . .

Jonah's birthday was May 5, and by eight-fifteen, he and I were lingering in the dusty upstairs bookstore, browsing before going down to the beer stube for the party.

"I want to make an entrance," Jonah said.

"I think you're nervous," I said. I was enjoying this, teasing him and bantering with him again.

I didn't know why, but since the art show Jonah had warmed up again. He seemed excited about something. I assumed it was graduation, the end of school. No more Canton, after fifteen years. I was glad to have him back.

I pulled a heavy coffee-table book off the shelf called *Dreaming of Iceland* — full-color photos of steaming springs, Reykjavik pubs, and stark volcanic landscapes. I showed Jonah one of the pub pictures. An elfin-eyed girl fed beer to a stuffed reindeer.

"Look," I said. "Drunk people."

Jonah paged through the book. "It's missing something, don't you think?"

"Yeah," I said. "No pictures of hairdressers. No salons or barber shops. How could they leave out Iceland's greatest natural resource?"

"Mysterious," Jonah said. "Maybe they don't know the value of what they've got."

"Maybe."

Jonah reached through the gap in the shelf left by the fat picture book. There was a six-inch space between the back of the wall and the books. "This would be a good place to leave a secret package, if we were spies," he said. "Or drug dealers. The book titles would be our code. I'd send you the title of a book, and you'd know exactly where to look for the treasure."

"If only we had a secret mission to fulfill." I put the book back on the shelf. "Or treasure to hide."

"Or a big stash of drugs," Jonah said.

"Have you had a nice birthday so far?"

"No," Jonah said. "My father made a special dinner tonight to celebrate. Or, you know, had one delivered from Petit Louis."

"That doesn't sound so bad."

"It's weird. I can't remember the last time my father made a fuss about my birthday. He always gives me a present, but that's all. Last year he didn't even eat dinner with me."

"Eighteen is a big birthday," I said.

"That's not it. He was in a bad mood — a worse mood than usual. But he tried to pretend he was happy, which isn't like him at all. To make an effort, I mean. He kept looking at me in this meaningful way, but what was the meaning? As if he had something he wanted to tell me. As if the dinner had been called so he could make an announcement. But there was no announcement. When dinner was over, he excused himself, stood up, kissed me on the top of my head, took his coffee into his study, and shut the door."

"He kissed you on the top of your head?"

"Yeah. That's what freaked me out the most. He never does stuff like that. Even when we were little, he never kissed me or Matthew. Especially not Matthew."

"Never?"

"You know in *The Godfather* when a Mafia boss gives someone the kiss of death, and that means they're doomed? That's what Dad's kiss felt like. The kiss of death."

"Come on. What's he going to do — gun you down? Cut off Miss Frankenheimer's head and leave it in your bed?"

"I'm just saying the whole birthday charade was creepy."

"*Happy birthday to you —*" I sang.

"Shut up."

"Come on, birthday boy. It's time for your real party."

We went downstairs. Four other Night Lights sat at a table near the piano: Myrna from Highlandtown, Larry from Catonsville, Burt from Glen Burnout, and Kreplax from the Future. An older couple huddled in the corner, watching us. I suspected they might be Night Light listeners, only too shy to join in.

"Here he is!"

"Ghost Boy!"

"Happy birthday, hon."

Jonah let Myrna buss him on the cheek. He lit up. Unlike his father's kiss, hers was simple auntish affection, not a harbinger of doom.

A few more people arrived, including some listeners we didn't know. We pushed tables together and squeezed in. Some people brought presents. Larry gave Jonah a couple of old records, the Partridge Family and the Monkees. Myrna gave him an Elvis notebook, and Kreplax gave him a calendar for the year 2110. "It's from my home time thread," Kreplax said. "I hope you'll be able to visit me someday."

"Thanks, I hope so too," Jonah said. Then he turned to me and asked, "Where's *your* present?"

"I was going to give it to you later —"

"No," Myrna said. "Now!"

"Now! Now!" Our crowd of radio friends banged their fists on the table.

"All right." I pulled the present — a flat rectangle wrapped in pale green tissue paper — from my bag. Jonah eyed it warily.

"Is it embarrassing?"

I shrugged. "Depends on how easily embarrassed you are."

"This I gotta see," Myrna said.

Jonah ripped off the paper. Underneath was a framed print of a photo I'd made just for him.

"What the hell is that supposed to be?" Burt said.

"It's a picture," Myrna said. "It's us."

"It's the Night Lights, riding the Flying Carpet," I said.

I had set up some dolls on a small Persian carpet in front of the most elaborate starry backdrop I could paint. I did my best to make the dolls look like the real Night Lights. One of my Madame Alexanders sported a black beehive, red nail polish, and lots of jewelry. A small Buddha statue stood in for Larry, and a G.I. Joe — dressed in a natty suit — for Herb. I'd found a Casper puppet to play Jonah, and I'd put a doll's dress on a red Rock 'Em Sock 'Em Robot to make a Robot Girl.

Larry banged his white cane on the floor. "Tell me what the picture looks like, Myrna."

"Some dolls are riding to Ocean City on the Flying Carpet," Myrna said. "And the dolls look just like us! There's even a doll version of you." She patted Larry's big belly. "The sky is just beautiful. And the stars spell out something . . . 'Happiness Must Be Earned.'"

I'd copied that motto from an old Douglas Fairbanks movie, *The Thief of Baghdad*, silent version. The thief and the genie are riding on a magic carpet and the stars spell those words while the soundtrack plays Rimsky-Korsakov's *Scheherazade*. It's a lovely scene. I just wanted to go live in that night sky whenever I saw it.

"That sounds like a fine present," Larry said.

"How come I'm not in the picture?" Burt grumped.

"You are," I said. "See?" I pointed to a rubber duckie I'd stuck on the carpet, just because I liked it.

"That's not me," Burt said. "You think of me as a duck?"

"Why not?" I scrambled for something nice to say. "Everybody loves ducks."

That seemed to satisfy him. He ordered another beer.

"Do you like your present, Ghost Boy?" I asked.

"You should go to art school in my place," Jonah said. "You know how to make beautiful things."

He pressed his hand on mine, the same way he did at the art show.

"A toast to the birthday boy!" Myrna shouted. "Welcome to the adult world, hon. It's lonely, it's miserable, and God help you. But there are bright spots, and nights like tonight are one of them."

We clinked our bottles of beer in honor of Jonah the Ghost Boy. Myrna nudged the piano player, and he played "Happy Birthday." The whole room sang along. By the end of the evening, Myrna and Larry were holding hands, Burt and Kreplax were trying to bribe the pianist to play "Stairway to Heaven," and Jonah's face . . . I'll never forget Jonah's face. A light poured out of him and became the spirit of the room, like a genie released from a bottle after centuries of darkness.

CHAPTER 20

The day of the prom, a package arrived for me. Inside was an aluminum tiara decorated with rhinestones and glass rubies. The note said, *For the Benevolent Queen of the Freaks, from their Stern and Silent King. Long May We Reign.* — J

I held the tiara up to the light. It didn't sparkle, exactly, or gleam, but I thought it was beautiful. It was my first gift from Jonah, unless you counted the paper airplane addressed to Beatrice from Future Beatrice, which I kept by the radio on my night table.

After dinner, I dressed in a midnight blue gown and put on Miss-America-Gone-Psycho makeup. Mom sat on my bed and watched me glob on the mascara.

"So, Jonah's your date," she said, deadpan.

"Yep," I said.

"Funny," she said.

"Why?"

"I don't know. You never struck me as the prom type."

I concentrated on not poking my eye out with the mascara wand. "Wonders never cease."

"They never do," Mom said. "Jonah doesn't seem like a prom type either."

"It's just a dance," I said.

"Do you see silver sparkles?" she asked.

I put away the mascara and set the tiara on my head, artfully askew. "That again?"

"Silver sparkles," Mom said. "When you kiss him."

"When I kiss who?"

"Jonah."

I'd never actually kissed Jonah. Not in any way other than friendly, sisterly, fondly. Certainly not in a way that would produce silver sparkles, or visions of any kind. But he was my "prom date." Kissing was expected. So I played along.

"Not silver," I said. "Gold."

"Ah," Mom said. "That's nice." She hugged me, her back muscles tense.

Dad waited for me downstairs. "Maybe we'll stop by the Owl Bar later on and check up on you," he said when I appeared in my prom-queen-from-hell glory.

"We will not," Mom said. "We're not that screwy."

"I was just kidding," Dad said. He kissed me and straightened the tiara. "Needs to sit just right. A tiara's not an easy thing to pull off."

I heard the chug and rumble of Gertie's engine pull up outside.

"Prince Charming's here," Mom said.

The doorbell rang. Dad answered the door. I grabbed my spangled evening bag, readjusted my tiara, smudged my eyeliner, and went to meet my escort.

Jonah's powder blue polyester tux and white dress shoes emphasized his pallor. "This is for you." He handed me a clear plastic box with an orchid in it.

"A corsage! Thank you." I kissed him on the cheek and slid the corsage onto my wrist. The orchid was hideously beautiful, which suited my getup perfectly.

"I'll be back before supper tomorrow," I said.

I grabbed the small suitcase I'd packed, and we ran down the front steps like bank-robbing newlyweds dashing for their getaway car. Gertie rumbled to life. Mom and Dad stood on the porch and watched us drive away. I saw that look in Mom's eyes again, the look I'd noticed on the first day of school: *Please hurry up and leave leave leave LEAVE NOW.*

Don't worry, Mom, I'm leaving as fast as I can.

"We're off!" I leaned across the seat and rested my head on Jonah's shoulder, just for a second. Like I was his real girlfriend, and he was my real boyfriend, however inadequate those words might be. I switched on the radio. It was a beautiful evening, warm even for mid-May.

"We're off!" I cried.

We drove through the city, right past the Belvedere Hotel. Limos stacked up outside, and there were all our classmates in tasteful dresses and tasteful black tuxedos, ready to go inside and dance the night away with the same eighty or so people they'd attended every dance of their lives with. Anne Sweeney clutched Tom Garber's arm, claiming him. He'd broken up with Meredith, I'd heard, and was cycling back through his old girlfriends again. I wondered if, at the beginning of the year, Anne knew he'd do this and was in a hurry for Tom to get me out of his system, so he'd get to her faster.

"Open the glove compartment," Jonah said. "I've got another surprise for you."

I opened the glove compartment. Tucked inside were two plastic water pistols, loaded.

"One for you and one for me," Jonah said.

He slowed down in front of the hotel. We squirted our pistols out the car window. I got Tom Garber on the back of the head. Anne waved to us, so I spared her and hit Carter instead. She gave a satisfying shriek.

"Got 'em!" Jonah laughed. "Let's book."

He hit the gas and we squealed off.

"I'm so glad I'm not there," Jonah said.

"Me too," I said.

We hit the highway and drove east to Ocean City. It was dark by the time we rolled over the Bay Bridge. Crossing the Chesapeake was just like a Flying Carpet ride. The boats twinkled on the water below, and when we reached the Eastern Shore, I caught a whiff of salt on the air.

"I can't believe you've never been to Ocean City before," Jonah said.

"Is it like Atlantic City?" I'd never been there either, but I'd seen it on TV.

"Please," Jonah said. "The Jersey Shore is a pale imitation. They *wish* they had a cool place like Ocean City. By which I mean Ocean City, Maryland, not Ocean City, New Jersey."

"There's an Ocean City in New Jersey?"

"It's hardly worth mentioning."

We drove past dark, greening cornfields and grubby antique towns. Once we reached Assawoman Bay, the salt air smell grew strong, laced with French fries and cotton candy.

We crossed the 62nd Street Bridge and headed south toward the Ocean City Inlet. Fancy high-rise condos gave way to older Jetsons-style motels, then the oldest hotels and rooming houses, squat clapboard buildings below Twelfth Street. Neon lights flashed everywhere: ICE CREAM, MINI-GOLF, STEAMED CRABS, STEAKS, SEAFOOD, AMUSEMENTS. Cars cruised Ocean Highway, the boys calling to girls who darted through the traffic in tank tops and flip-flops.

"Where are we staying?" I asked.

"The Majestic," Jonah said. "Queen of the Boardwalk since 1925."

We parked behind the pool and checked in. The Majestic had a big front porch overlooking the boardwalk. Old people rocked in their chairs and watched the vacationers troop past — gangs of kids looking for trouble, tired parents with sugared-up toddlers, preening teenagers baring their navels.

Our room was small, clean, plain, and white, with twin beds and a window overlooking the parking lot. I opened it, and the roar of the ocean rumbled like a bassline under the traffic noise.

"Ready, Queen Beatrice?" Jonah said. "It's time to meet your subjects."

I grabbed a sweater and we headed out into the night, strolling arm in arm down the crowded Saturday-night boardwalk.

The moon rose full over the ocean. We passed a monstrous sand carving of Jesus's head, lit with rainbow-colored lights. A handwritten cardboard sign said, CARVED BY DAVID SMITHSON! NEVER FORGET! JESUS DIED FOR YOUR SINS!

"That Jesus guy's here every year," Jonah said. "There's usually a bunch of summer Bible school kids singing Christian folk songs in front of it."

We trolled through a trinket shop, examining bongs, T-shirts, puka shell necklaces, and gun-shaped lighters. I found a dusty Halloween mask in a forgotten corner of the store.

"Jonah, look. Casper."

Jonah put the mask over his face. The elastic string made his hair stick up in the back. I laughed.

"Looks just like you. I can't tell you're wearing a mask at all."

"You're hilarious," Jonah said, his voice muffled. He paid the cashier a dollar for the mask. "You have your tiara. I need something to wear too."

We made an odd pair, a rag queen and a ghost, but the boardwalk carnival world welcomed us. Jonah wore the mask all evening, resting it on top of his head when he ate. Children pointed at him, some laughing, some frightened. Otherwise, we blended well with the Confederate hats, the scraggly beards, the missing teeth, the cleavage.

We ate French fries for supper, then rode the bumper cars and the roller coaster. The Ferris wheel whisked us away from the noise and smells of the boardwalk for a few seconds, high over the sand

and water. The moon bleached a strip of the sea. We dipped down, down through the squeals and shouts and bangs and pops and up, up again into the fresh air, the lights of the toy city below. I wished I could live at the top of the Ferris wheel, just high enough to walk on the clouds if it's cloudy, but close enough to the ground to keep an eye on everybody.

We stopped at a photo booth and took a strip of pictures of ourselves to commemorate our prom night. Jonah pumped quarters into the machine and sat down on the stool behind the curtain. I perched on his lap.

"Take your mask off," I said.

"No," Jonah said.

A light flashed, the first picture taken.

"Come on, Jonah, take it off," I said again. "Just for the pictures."

Jonah poked his tongue through the mask's mouth hole. The light flashed again. Jonah snatched the tiara off my head and propped it over the mask. *Flash*. The third photo gone.

"Give me that." I lifted the mask. The tiara clattered to the floor. *Flash*. The glare blinded me.

"Gotcha," I said.

"You shouldn't have done that."

He pulled the mask back over his face. I picked up my tiara. We bought ice-cream cones and waited for the photos to develop. They slipped out of the machine, wet as a newborn baby. Three pictures of prom-tux Casper and me. One picture of Jonah, his bare face stricken in the light, my profile in shadow.

"They're funny," I said.

"Let me see." He stared at the strip of pictures, then folded it in half and slipped it into the pocket of his jacket.

The rides closed up around eleven. As we were leaving Trimper's Amusements, we passed a Haunted House.

"One last ride," I pleaded.

"It's a rip-off."

"That's why I like them. Please, Jonah. It's my prom night. You're supposed to spoil me. In ten years, I'll write a scathing memoir about all the innocent childhood pleasures I missed because of *you*."

"Ugh, okay."

"Last ride of the night," the ticket taker said. We settled into a cart and rested our hands on the greasy metal bar that locked us in. "Don't stick your arms out or you'll get electrocuted."

The cart jerked to a start. We glided into the spook house through double doors painted like the entrance to a coal mine. Down a long, dark tunnel. The spooky noises began. Jonah pressed a smooth bottle into my hand. "Here."

"What is it?"

"Wild Turkey."

I felt for the top, unscrewed it, and took a sip. "You've been carrying this all night?"

"For emergencies." He took the bottle back, pulled his mask up just high enough, and drank.

The first few displays were under repair. Then we rode through the torture chamber. A man was being sliced in half by a buzz saw. A speaker shot his piercing screams right into our ears.

"I hate spook houses," Jonah said. "Why did I let you talk me into this?"

"It's fun." I took his hand.

"Fun that can get you electrocuted," Jonah said.

The cart forced its way through another pair of double doors. A skeleton in a wig and a dress sprang out at us, cackling. We jumped in our seats. Jonah yanked his hand away.

We rolled outside, along the balcony, a brief respite of reality, the boardwalk below us emptying quickly. Then back inside for more scenes of horror: a man in a guillotine overseen by a black-masked executioner, a pile of bloody heads in a basket at his feet; a golden-haired maiden who lowered her hand mirror to reveal a ravaged face; a rocky ride through a world of fake flames, lorded over by a red devil.

In the final chamber, a careworn judge banged his gavel in a courtroom, pointing his long bony finger at us. "Guilty!" he screeched. "Guilty!"

"We're guilty all right," Jonah said. "Guilty of paying way too much for ten minutes' ride through a dump. And a firetrap." He took another sip from the bottle and stashed it in his jacket.

The cart emerged into the yellow haze and jerked to a stop. We stumbled out, bleary, and strolled up the boardwalk to our hotel. Kids clustered in pools of lamplight, up to no good. The beach seemed vast and dark, an ocean of sand. Distant squeals drifted on the breeze.

Back in our room, Jonah switched on the clock radio and turned the dial to the Night Lights. I went into the bathroom and changed out of my prom dress into a T-shirt and sweatpants. I hung my tiara on the mirror. Jonah put on pajamas. Cool night air poured in through the window, riding the roar of the waves. We sat on our beds, separated by a night table, and listened to the show.

"I wonder how the prom went," I said.

He shook the pint of Wild Turkey at me. "Still got a little left."

I took a sip and passed it back. My whole head felt warm. The voices murmured on the radio, the sea crashed faintly outside, the bathroom light fixture buzzed.

"I wish we could live here for the summer," I said. "Or longer. Forever."

"Yeah." Jonah drained the bottle. "I wish Matthew could live with us too. He'd like it here. He'd see the ocean and breathe the salt air —"

"— watch the sun and moon rise over the water —" I said.

"— and listen to the waves for hours and hours," Jonah said. "He can do all those things. That's a life."

"A good life."

Jonah sank down against his headboard.

"If we were characters in a movie, we'd rescue him," he said. "We'd break into St. Francis and kidnap Matthew."

"Yeah," I said. "We'd bust him out."

"We'd take him someplace no one would find him," Jonah said. "Like . . . here. Ocean City. Lose ourselves in the crowd." He rolled onto his stomach and looked at me. "We could rent a cheap room. I'd run rides at Trimper's, and you'd waitress at Phillips."

I laughed. "You'd work at night and I'd work during the day," I said. "We'd take turns watching Matthew. We'd be a family on the run, wary of snoops, always looking over our shoulders for the cops. . . ."

"Maybe Matthew would get better," Jonah said. "He'd have fresh air and real stimulation. He wouldn't be stuck in a home. St. Francis is so depressing. He's going downhill and they won't let me see him. . . ."

Jonah rolled off the bed and took a sketchbook and pen from his bag. "We should do it. We should bust him out."

"For real?"

"Why not?" Jonah said. "We'll save my brother's life."

"But how?" I said. "How are we going to break into St. Francis and sneak out a boy in a wheelchair?"

"Simple," Jonah said. He drew a map of the hospital, all the windows, entrances, and exits he could remember. "We'll do what they do in the movies. We'll make a plan."

I woke up the next morning draped across the still-made bed, Jonah sleeping next to me. The radio chattered. I switched it off.

My head ached. The sun hurt my eyes. The empty bottle of Wild Turkey lay on the carpet. I kicked it away.

The floor was littered with paper, drafts of our big plan to kidnap Matthew. The details were a little fuzzy, but we'd come up with something that had seemed amazingly brilliant at the time.

Jonah and I checked out of the hotel, loaded our stuff into Gertie's trunk, and walked a few blocks to a diner for breakfast. My mouth was cotton-dry but I felt good, anyway. Maybe it was the ocean air, and having a plan of action, however drunkenly conceived.

Jonah's mind was still buzzing. "We should do it during the day, when there's traffic, people coming and going. . . . We're less likely to look suspicious. At night there are alarms to deal with, security guards, and, who knows, maybe dogs."

"And we're settled on the date?" I said. "This Saturday?"

"Right. In one week."

"We're really going to do this?"

"Yes. We're really going to do it." He poked a quivering blob of egg with his fork. "Bea, I'm serious about this. You are too, right? Because if you're not, I'll find a way to get Matthew by myself."

I felt dizzy. Scheming at night had been delirious and fun, but the plan looked a little crazy in the light of day. Were we really going to bust Matthew out of an institution?

On the other hand, this was a chance to do something real, something that mattered. After all the years of reading and writing and adding and subtracting, schoolwork and swimming lessons and learning how to behave, I was ready to make a big, dramatic gesture. Wasn't this what it meant to be adult — taking action?

"I'm serious," I said.

"Good. We'll keep it simple. We'll just walk in, wait until they leave Matthew unattended, and walk out with him. Drive that wheelchair right out of there."

The plan wasn't quite that simple.

On one of his visits, Jonah had met a large family, the Keanes, whose disabled aunt lived at St. Francis. The Keanes visited often. They had a daughter our age named Georgia. Georgia looked a little like me, Jonah said — stick body, lollipop face — only blond.

I planned to disguise myself as Georgia Keane and say that I'd come to visit my Aunt Candy. Jonah would rig up a fake photo ID in case the receptionist questioned me. I'd only been to the hospital twice, and Jonah didn't think the staff would remember me, especially if I wore a blond wig.

Jonah, also disguised, would pretend to be a friend of mine. We'd get him past the receptionist somehow.

We'd leave the car at a side door, an emergency exit near the dayroom, where Matthew was sure to be waiting out visiting hours. We'd grab him, race the chair down the hall, out the emergency exit (which would probably blare an alarm, but that didn't matter), into our waiting car, and speed off. We'd drive straight to Ocean City, find a cheap room in one of the old boarding houses off the main drag, and start our new life.

That was our plan.

We had a few weeks of school left, but we didn't care. We were just killing time in our classes. We could show up for graduation if we really felt like it, then zip back to Ocean City and our real lives. Swimming in the ocean, running the rides, pushing Matthew down the boardwalk in his wheelchair, watching him get stronger every day. . . .

The whole summer stretched out before us, long, hot, endless. September flashed like a tiny red warning light in the distance, but if I squinted, I could ignore it. I decided to squint for a while.

"It's going to be wonderful," I said.

I broke my promise to my parents and got home after dinner .on Sunday night. I found Mom sitting on the front steps, smoking a cigarette. Which I had never seen her do before.

"Where's Dad?" I said.

Mom said, "He left."

CHAPTER 21

"God, I am so punished," Anne Sweeney said at Assembly on Monday. "AWAE and I were up for thirty hours straight."

"That's rough," I said. I was pretty punished myself, but in no mood to explain, not to Anne of all people. "What happened to Tom?"

"He passed out by four A.M. and one of his friends dragged him home."

"Lightweight."

"And then I come home for dinner last night and find your dad sitting at the kitchen table. Like, shocker."

"My dad had dinner at your house?" I said.

"My mom felt sorry for him."

I'd seen Dad later that Sunday night, in the dorm room where he was staying.

"Dad," I said when I found him. "What the fuck?"

He flinched. "You never used to speak to me that way."

"You never used to live in a dorm," I said.

"I'm not living here," Dad said. "It's only temporary."

"Only temporary? Where are you going to move to from here? The Sweeneys' house?"

"That's not fair," Dad said. "Caroline Sweeney is a good friend, that's all."

"Then why is Mom so crazy?" I said.

"I don't know why she's so crazy," Dad said. "I love your mother. I tried to understand what she's going through. But after a while I got tired of trying. She doesn't respond. I've forgiven her, but she doesn't seem to —"

"What do you mean, you've forgiven her?" I said. "You're the one who's never around. You're having an affair, aren't you? Isn't that why Mom's so upset?"

"No, I am not," Dad said. "I'm not the one —"

He stopped.

There is a separation between parents and children that shouldn't be breached when the children are young. The parents' adult follies are private. They're disturbing and hard to understand. But eventually the kids wise up, the follies start leaking out, and the parents are revealed in all their flawed humanity. Dad and I were about to cross that boundary for good.

"It isn't me," Dad said. "It's your mother. She's the one who had an affair. With some guy in Ithaca. It ended when we moved. He was married too. He wouldn't leave his wife. That's why she's been so upset."

Mom was having an affair? How did I miss that?

My head reeled.

"What guy?" I said.

Dad shrugged. He looked exhausted. "I don't know. Some loser who works at a costume shop."

Oh my God. Motorbike Mike's? Mom had an affair with Motorbike Mike?

I remembered the mysterious phone call in New York, the man who wasn't Dad. That must have been Mike.

Maybe Mom had secretly planned to meet him in New York. That's why she wanted to go with me so badly. It wasn't meant to be "just us girls" at all.

I felt queasy. I automatically scanned the place for a bathroom in case I needed to throw up. *Next to the closet. Check.*

"You know what?" I said to Dad. "Don't tell me this stuff. Don't tell me any more. I don't want to know."

I drove home and confronted Mom, only instead of begging to be left out of their business, I demanded to know why she hadn't clued me in.

"Dad said you've been having an affair!"

She looked startled. "He told you?"

"Yes, he told me. He said a costume-shop guy. It's not who I think it is, is it?"

"Don't worry, that's over."

"So it *was* him? Motorbike Mike?"

She nodded. I felt like I'd been punched in the stomach. I flopped down on the couch. I couldn't believe I'd thought Dad was the bad guy.

"Honey?"

Mom touched my hair. I knocked her hand away.

"Mom, that is so . . . ick."

Now it was Mom's turn to knock me away. She didn't even have to raise a hand. All it took were a few words and a glance.

"You'll never understand," she said.

"What's going on, anyway?" Anne asked me. "At dinner your father told jokes and acted all cool. But he looked like he hadn't slept in, like, a long time."

"Just a spat," I lied. "Nothing big. Dad's coming home soon. Probably."

"A spat? That's not the feeling I got —"

It was time to change the subject. "Was it fun?" I asked. "The prom and everything?"

"The prom was okay. The after-party basically never ended. Half the class spent the weekend at Harlan's house. His parents were away, and they've already filled the pool —" She looked at me straight in the face for the first time that morning. "Hey, where were you?"

"You just noticed I missed the prom?" I said.

"Well, sure, I noticed that night," Anne said. "After you nearly ruined my silk dress with your squirt gun. Totally juvenile, by the way. But then I forgot, and I just remembered again. Give me a break — I've got the hangover of the century."

"Jonah and I went to Ocean City," I said. "But don't tell your mother. I told my parents I went to the prom. So if anyone asks —" I was just going through the motions. My parents had bigger things to worry about than where I'd spent the weekend.

"Don't worry, I don't tell my mother *anything*. But —" Dismay played across her face. "You and Jonah? Did you — you know —?"

"We slept in the same room, but we didn't —"

"Oh my God! In the same bed?"

Technically, we *had* ended up sleeping *on* the same bed, in our clothes, on top of the covers, sideways and about a foot apart. This was not the juice Anne wanted to hear.

"We had twin beds," I said. "We didn't sleep together. Or kiss, or anything."

"But — why? Why go to the beach with a boy who's not your boyfriend?"

The stupidity of the question, the narrowness of her vision, gave me a headache. "To go to the beach?" I said. "To ride the rides and eat ice cream and play pinball? For fun?"

Anne leaned away from me as if I had bad breath. "I was just curious. You don't have to get mad."

"Jonah and I are friends. I don't understand why nobody gets it."

"Maybe because he hasn't been friends with anyone in about ten years?" Anne said. "So we're all just a little surprised."

The room began to fill. Jonah slipped into his seat. Anne clammed up.

Lockjaw took the podium. "I'm glad to shee you juniorsh and sheniorsh shurvived the prom lasht weekend, if barely. Now that we've got *that* mileshtone under our beltsh, I'm happy to announche that the yearbooksh are almosht ready and should arrive from the printer'sh next week."

Anne glanced past me at Jonah. "How does it look?"

He shrugged. "Like a yearbook."

I came home from school that day to find Mom energetically cleaning the house. She hadn't cleaned in months. I'd kept things livable, but the grime was starting to catch up with us.

"Is somebody coming over?" I asked. "Motorbike Mike, perhaps?"

"Don't be silly," Mom said. "I told you, that's over." She put on some music and danced while she dusted.

"So what's the occasion?" I asked.

"No occasion," she said. "The house just needs cleaning. Haven't you noticed what a sty it is?"

Yes, I'd noticed. Where'd she been all this time?

"So we're not having company?" I said. "No one's coming over?"

"No. And it's nice to know for sure who's going to be home and who's not, for once." She danced around like she used to, bumping and grinding to the beat.

"Mom, have you lost your mind?" I said.

"On the contrary," she said. "I haven't felt this good in ages."

"Did you see Dr. Huang today?" Dr. Huang was her therapist. At that moment I thought she must be a miracle worker.

"Yes, I did. She said that now that everything's out in the open and your dad and I have stopped denying our problems, things can only get better."

"Get better? How?"

"However is better. We don't know yet. We'll have to wait and see. The suspense is part of the exciting mystery of life!"

"I don't like the suspense," I said.

"Don't be such a stiff. Suspense is good. Embrace it!" Mom fluffed a couch cushion and threw it triumphantly back in place. "She also upped my Celexa and refilled my Xanax prescription, in case you were wondering."

I escaped to my room and closed the door. A few hours later Mom called me down for dinner: broiled rockfish, scalloped potatoes, baked carrots, spinach salad, and cupcakes for dessert.

"Where's the roast chicken?" I asked.

"Haven't we had enough chicken for a while?"

It was the best dinner we'd had in a long time. I ate it, completely baffled. Mom had been falling apart all year, and I expected Dad's leaving to blow her to smithereens. But it didn't. Unless becoming supermom was her way of going to pieces. Anything was possible.

Mom continued on her personal road to sanity. Now Dad was losing it. After four days, he was tired of living with his students and wanted to come home. But Mom told him she needed more time and to submit another request next week.

"She's in the wrong, you know," Dad complained when he took me to dinner at the Hopkins Rathskeller Thursday night. "*She* cheated on *me*."

"It's complicated. Can I have a beer?"

Dad looked at the graduate students drinking all around us. "Sorry. I have to set an example. Will root beer do?"

He rambled on about how Mom had wronged him and if she had any heart, she should let him come back. Sure, he left her, but he never meant it to last more than a day or two. Her weirdness was getting to him and he'd needed a breather, that's all. "She's up, she's down, which is it? It's like living on a roller coaster. . . ." I drank my root beer and tuned him out, watching the students play darts. *Next year that will be me*, I thought. *Mom and Dad can stir up all the drama they want; I won't have to know about it. I'll be in New York with Jonah, learning about the real world.*

Then I thought, *No, I won't. I'll be in Ocean City, waitressing at Phillips and taking care of Matthew.*

Which was it? Which was my real future? I didn't know. They both felt equally unreal.

I told Jonah about my new domestic arrangement, and he listened sympathetically. But his mind and heart were focused on Matthew. He burned with a new intensity. All his thoughts were on his reunion with his twin, just days away.

So I focused on Matthew too. I was too confused to think about anything else.

CHAPTER 22

On Saturday, Jonah came to my house to get into costume. I dressed up as Georgia Keane in a blond wig and a frilly dress that Jonah said approximated one he'd seen her wear. Jonah was going to be my friend, young Professor Tannhauser. I gave him a curly brown wig, tinted glasses, a newsboy cap, and layers of sweaters to bulk him up under Dad's tweed jacket.

"I would never wear a cap like this in a million years," Jonah said.

"That's the point," I told him. "Don't forget to speak viz a Cherman eksent."

"Jahwohl, Mein Kewpie Doll," Jonah said. "Now let's go get my brother."

We drove out of town to the country. It was late May, warm, a haze of pollen in the air.

"I wish it were cloudy," Jonah said. "This doesn't feel like kidnapping weather."

"Good beach weather, though," I said.

"First things first."

Twenty minutes later, we rolled through the gates of St. Francis. We skipped the circular drive at the front entrance and pulled the car around to the side door.

"So far our plan's going perfectly, see," Jonah said in a James Cagney voice.

"You're supposed to be German," I said.

"Oh, right."

"Don't talk unless you have to."

We left the car unlocked and walked around to the front entrance. "Hello," I said to the receptionist. "I'm Georgia Keane. I'm here to visit my aunt Candy."

"Oh, hi, Georgia," the receptionist said. "Where's the rest of the family?"

"They're coming later," I said. "They had to stop off and pick up a present for Aunt Candy. Some, um, candy. Aunt Candy loves candy. Obviously."

The receptionist checked her logbook. "Oh, they're already here," she said. "They're back in the dayroom." She squinted at me. "Do you have a twin?"

"Us Keanes all look alike," I said, taking Jonah's hand. "By the way, this is my friend, Professor Tannhauser. Okay, see you later."

"Jahwohl!" Jonah said.

Jonah and I walked down the hall as fast as we could, too scared to look back.

"Do you think she suspects anything?" I whispered.

"Yes," he said. "Let's move."

The dayroom was crowded with patients and visitors and aides, who proudly showed off the patients' latest art-therapy projects. Maybe Matthew would have a blob of clay to show us.

"Do you see him?" Jonah said.

I scanned the room. It was hard to pick out Matthew among all the wheelchairs and helmets.

Jonah tensed up beside me. *Do you see him?*

"No," I said.

"He's not here," Jonah said. He approached one of the aides. "Excuse me. I'm looking for Matthew Tate."

The aide peered at Jonah, who must have looked strange in his tweed cap, glasses, and wig. She opened her mouth, then stopped.

"Where is he?" Jonah's voice cracked. A few visitors glanced our way.

The aide didn't answer, and now she looked nervous. Jonah grabbed her arm.

"Where is my brother?"

"Who are you?" the aide said.

"I'm Jonah Tate. I'm Matthew's brother." The German professor was forgotten.

"You're not supposed to be here," the aide said.

"But I am here," Jonah said. "Where's my brother?"

No one answered him.

"Where's my brother?" Jonah shouted. *"Where's my brother? Where's my brother?"* His voice grew louder and shriller with each repetition, until he was screaming. *"WHERE'S MY BROTHER?"*

"Quiet! Quiet!" the aide said. "Just a minute." She went to a phone on the wall and called someone. Jonah trembled beside me, muttering, "Where is he?" I watched the aide as she spoke, trying to read her body language, but it told me nothing.

When the aide returned, she said, "Dr. Kramer will be right with you."

"I know my father said I'm not allowed to see him," Jonah said. "But my father is wrong. He wants to keep us apart, but I don't know why!"

Dr. Kramer walked in and said, "Jonah, is that you?"

Jonah took off the cap and the wig and the glasses. I took off my wig too. I waited for her to ask why we had disguised ourselves, but she didn't.

"Come with me," Dr. Kramer said. She led us down the hall into an office and shut the door. "Sit down."

Jonah said, "Where's my brother?"

"Jonah, please sit down," Dr. Kramer said.

We sat down. She sat behind the desk, taking cover.

"Your father hasn't spoken to you?"

"About what?"

My stomach clenched. Something bad was coming.

Dr. Kramer licked her lips and took off her glasses. "Jonah, Matthew is dead."

The air thickened, so that everything in the room seemed to slow down.

"What are you talking about?" Jonah said. "Dad didn't say anything —"

"He died two weeks ago," Dr. Kramer said. "An accident. He choked. On some food. We ground up his food for him, but he was having trouble swallowing, and —"

"He choked on food?" Jonah said. "He choked on *food*? How could that happen?"

"It's — I'm afraid it happens to people in your brother's condition fairly often. He may have had a seizure. We were planning to switch him to a feeding tube soon, if things didn't improve, but —"

"How could you let him choke?" Jonah said. "How could you let him die in such a stupid way? Wasn't someone there? Wasn't someone watching him? Who was taking care of him?"

"The aides are responsible for a lot of patients," Dr. Kramer said. "They do the best they can."

Her face looked tight and tired. I wondered how often she had to have these conversations.

"Why didn't my father tell me?" Jonah said.

"I don't know," Dr. Kramer said. "I fully expected he would —"

"That fucking bastard."

Jonah's breath came fast and shallow. I reached for his hand. He turned his face to me, his eyes wide with panic. Two frozen ponds. A boy screamed and pounded on the surface, trapped under the ice. Panicking. Trying to break through. But his screams faded, his fists flailed, and he slipped away into the dark. The boy was gone. Nothing left but the ice, clear and smooth enough to skate on.

Jonah pulled his hand from mine and turned back to Dr. Kramer. "Was there a funeral?"

Dr. Kramer shifted in her chair. "Matthew was cremated, at your father's request. We are still waiting for your father to pick up the remains. I assume he'll arrange some kind of service —"

"No, he won't," Jonah said. "There won't be any service. Matthew already had a funeral, ten years ago. My father will forget he ever had a son. He's tried to forget all these years."

"Jonah, your father made sure that Matthew had the best care possible," Dr. Kramer said. "He spared no expense —"

"It didn't cost him much," Jonah said. "He has plenty of money."

Tears pressed against the back of my eyes. I wanted to cry, but Jonah wasn't crying, and it didn't seem right to cry without him. I didn't know how much longer I could hold out, though. A large tear wriggled out and dripped down my nose. I wiped it away.

"Is there anything else I can do for you, Jonah?" Dr. Kramer said. She wasn't a bad person. She had a hard job. "I'm sorry for your loss. We're very sad about Matthew. We miss him. I'm afraid there's not much more I can tell you."

I stood and helped Jonah to his feet. He was shaking, pale. His legs seemed too weak to hold him.

"One thing. I want Catso."

"Who?"

"Matthew's toy cat. Do you still have him? Or did you burn him up too?"

"We have a box of Matthew's things. I'll see if it's in there." She walked out, leaving us alone in the office.

"Jonah —" I whispered.

"Shh. Don't talk. Shhhh . . ."

He trembled and rocked on his feet. A picture of Jesus hung over the desk. His eyes followed me around the room.

Dr. Kramer returned with the box. "Feel free to take whatever you like."

The box held some clothes, a few pieces of construction paper smeared with fingerpaint, a plastic watch, and Catso. Jonah took Catso and held him under his arm.

"Again, my deepest sympathies." Dr. Kramer led us to the door.

"Is he going to sue you?" Jonah asked. "Did my father at least threaten to sue for malpractice or negligence or something? He's a lawyer, you know."

Dr. Kramer stiffened. "I'm aware of that. He hasn't made any mention of litigation at this time. I'd be surprised if he did, frankly. He knows as well as I do that he couldn't win this case. Not with the condition your brother was in."

"I just thought he might try, for Matthew's sake," Jonah said. "Put up a fight or something, you know?" He shook his head. "Stupid."

Dr. Kramer steered us toward the front hall. "Actually, we parked over this way," I said, nodding at the side door where Gertie sat, waiting to make a quick getaway.

Dr. Kramer looked puzzled but didn't bother to ask. "All right. Goodbye."

We crept down the long, shiny hall like an old couple with arthritis. It took forever to reach the door. An alarm went off when we pushed it open.

"I'll drive," I said. Jonah didn't protest. I helped him into the car. He gripped Catso as if he were afraid the cat would run away.

I parked Gertie in Jonah's driveway, next to his father's Mercedes. Jonah fled the car without a word, still clutching Catso.

"Jonah, wait," I said, but he stalked into the house without looking back. I followed him inside — *just to leave the car keys*, I told myself, but I was afraid for him.

He'd left the front door open. "Jonah?" I called. No one was in the living room or dining room. "Jonah?" No one in the silent kitchen.

I heard a crash overhead, glass shattering, a thud, and Jonah's voice.

I ran upstairs and found Jonah in his father's bedroom, tearing framed pictures off the wall and smashing them on the floor. Mr. Tate stood by the bed in a dress shirt, boxer shorts, and socks, caught in the middle of changing his clothes.

With a sweep of his arm Jonah cleared the top of a dresser. Bottles shattered, change clattered onto the wooden plank floor. He picked up an unbroken bottle of Bay Rhum and smashed it on the dresser, glass showering his feet.

"He's dead! You liar! You're a liar! He's dead AGAIN! Go ahead, lie to me. You've hidden him somewhere else this time. Where did you put him? Tell me where!"

Mr. Tate's face was gray. He caught sight of me lurking in the doorway but said nothing. I knew I shouldn't be there but I couldn't leave Jonah like this.

Jonah grabbed his father by the throat. "You're the one who should be dead! Why aren't you dead? You hideous, fucking old man —"

Mr. Tate struggled. He fell back on the bed. I grabbed Jonah from behind and tried to pull him off. "Jonah, stop!"

"Get off me!" He shoved me away and I smacked against the wall. His voice was hoarse with rage. He let go of his father and screamed long and loud.

Mr. Tate fumbled for his trousers. "Jonah, calm down. I'm taking you to the hospital." Then he added to me, "He should be sedated."

"I'll take him." I wrapped my arms around Jonah, half-hug, half-restraint. He was panting like an animal. "I'll bring him to my house to calm down. If he needs to go to the hospital, I can take him."

"Young lady, this is a family matter. Jonah's not leaving this house with you."

I squeezed Jonah, trying to hold on to him. "We'll get out of here soon," I whispered. "We'll go to New York together and forget all this —"

Jonah turned his head and glared at me — the coldest, hardest look I'd ever seen. "You WANT to forget him. You're glad he's dead. You hated him!" He broke out of my arms. "Well, I hate YOU," he roared in my face. "If the whole human race was annihilated and I could save one person, I wouldn't save ANYONE."

He fled the room. I ran after him. He flew down the stairs, through the kitchen, out the back door, and through the backyard. He hurdled over the stream that bordered the property and disappeared beyond the houses the next street over. "Jonah!" I shouted, but I couldn't catch him. I stopped at the edge of the yard, my toes just dipping into the stream.

Mr. Tate stood outside the back door, still in his socks and boxers, holding his pants in one hand, staring at the neighborhood rooftops, as if his son might somehow be up there, slicing through the sky.

I returned to the house. On his legs and hands, blue veins snaked under paper-thin skin.

"Are you all right?" I asked.

"I'm fine. Go home."

"I'll help you sweep up the glass in your room."

"Go away now, young lady. Go home."

"I'm sure he'll be back later, once he calms down," I said.

"I have no doubt."

I walked slowly away, through the yard, up the driveway, and down the street toward my house. I guess it sounds funny, but I felt sorry for Mr. Tate then. I don't think he knew he was standing outside in his underwear, or cared. It's just one little thing I remember. One little thing that made a sad day sadder.

Jonah slipped into his house after midnight. I knew he'd come back because deep into the night I heard Ghost Boy on the radio.

Herb:
Next caller, you're on the air.

Ghost Boy:
Hello, Herb. This is Ghost Boy.

Herb:
Hello, Ghost Boy. What's on your mind
tonight? I heard your birthday party was quite
a bash.

Ghost Boy:
I, um . . . my brother died. I just wanted to say
that somewhere, publicly, out loud. My
brother died.

Herb:
I'm very sorry to hear that.

Ghost Boy:
We were twins.

Herb:
Oh no.

Ghost Boy:
It's my fault. I killed him.

Herb:
What do you mean?

Ghost Boy:
My brother died for me. To save me.

Herb:
How did he die, Ghost Boy?

Ghost Boy:
There wasn't enough for both of us. When we were babies. Inside our mother. Not enough food or blood or whatever. Only enough to sustain one. So my brother gave his share to me.

Herb:
That doesn't sound like something you could help. It couldn't be your fault.

Ghost Boy:
It is, though. Because I'm living, and he's dead. And I wanted to live. I must have wanted to live pretty badly. I don't know why, but I did. And my brother gave his life to me before he could even think. That's generous. Isn't that generous?

Herb:
It's very generous. Though I'm not quite sure what you're talking about.

[The "time's up" music comes on. Ghost Boy appears not to notice. Herb says nothing.]

Ghost Boy:

I just wanted to say something about him, to shoot his spirit out over the airwaves and see what it will do. Maybe he'll come to one of you and give you something you need. Help you get rid of the blues, or keep the sun from catching you crying. A lot of you believe in ghosts. I've heard you say so. My brother is a ghost now. If he haunts you, you're lucky.

Herb:

[Silence.]

Ghost Boy:

Good night, Herb. Sweet dreams to you all.

NUARY FEBRUARY MARCH APRIL MAY JUNE

CHAPTER 23

The Canton *Yodel* came out the first Monday in June, followed by a signing frenzy. The seniors spent their free periods scribbling in the halls, their friends' yearbooks stacked beside them on the floor.

I found AWAE's yearbook open on a lunch table and peeked at some of the messages. *Black Rock!!! Kissing DW at Deep Creek — OMG!*

TG + AS caught ifd at Boomer's!

The notes seemed to be written in code. My classmates had shared their whole lives with each other. You had to be there, and I wasn't.

Anne Sweeney grabbed my yearbook at Assembly one morning. "Why haven't you asked me to sign?" she bluntly asked, shoving her book onto my lap. She opened my yearbook to her page — each senior had a page of his or her own — and scribbled across her face in silver gel pen.

Bea,

I'm sorry I didn't get to know you better this year. But thanks for being my faculty brat buddy and Jonah buffer — where were you twelve years ago????

I can tell you're a good person. You have such a pretty smile —

you should use it! ☺ Put yourself out there, and you will find more
friends — and guys — than you can handle.
Best of luck next year. I'll miss you!
Kisses xxxooo, Anne
p.s. See you at the pool this summer?

She slapped the book shut. I sat beside her, stumped, her yearbook still open on my lap.

"You haven't written anything yet!" She flipped to my page.
BEATRICE ROSE SZABO bannered across the top in black letters. I'd
skipped the traditional yearbook portrait, filling the entire page with
my Icelandic hairdresser photo — me styling the Barbie head in
Santaland. I limited myself to one quotation, superimposed over the
picture: *THE WRITTEN WORD IS A LIE — Johnny Rotten.* I didn't
know if I believed that, but there it was, baldly stated on my page
in black and white. Guess I had to believe it now.

Jonah's page was next to mine. JONAH MARTIN TATE. A black-
and-white photo of a chubby-cheeked three-year-old was centered
in plain white and framed with a pen-and-ink design of vines and
flowers. There was a quotation under the picture.

Goodbye to them he had to go
— Daniel Johnston, "Casper the Friendly Ghost"

"Why did Jonah put nothing but a baby picture on his page?"
Anne said. "Years from now, how will his children know what he
looked like in high school?" She tapped the page with her pen.
"On the other hand, what are the chances Jonah will ever have
children?"

"He's in some group shots," I said, flipping to the "*Yodel* Staff"
page. There we were, posing in our hats, masks, and funny glasses.
I'd forgotten about that — Jonah's "concept" for the photo. His face

was completely obscured. The caption listed our names, but you couldn't see most of us clearly enough to identify us.

"Maybe the class photo." Anne turned to the large group shot of our class, forty of us perched on the hill outside the Upper School door.

All the seniors were present and accounted for and captioned as usual. But Jonah's face had been cut out of the shot and replaced with a cartoon drawing of Casper.

"Is that supposed to be funny?" Anne said. "He defaced our class picture."

Was there a clear shot of Jonah anywhere in the book? I skimmed through page after page.

"Aw, look." Anne pointed to a photo of a tiny Anne and tiny Jonah eating graham crackers at a small table. "That's us in kindergarten."

Kindergarten, yes, and second grade. But in the entire book there was not a single recent picture of Jonah's face.

"It's almost as if he really *is* a ghost," Anne said. "You know, like he doesn't show up on film."

"But he's not a ghost," I said. "He's not. He's real."

"Okay," Anne said. "Calm down. He's real. Now sign my yearbook."

I kept Anne's yearbook for a while. I needed time to think of something to write.

I read through the signatures· Anne had gathered, the nicknames and in-jokes and memories of pranks and good times. The compliments — "You're so pretty!" "Everyone loves you!" "I'd kill for your eyebrows!" — and promises — "We have have HAVE to keep in touch! Come visit me in Snoozeville Ohio and we'll rip it up!"

What could I write to Anne? What could I say that would mean something? That I wouldn't be embarrassed to read twenty years from now?

I thought about Anne, the kind of person she was. We weren't really friends, but she'd been friendly to me. She'd tried. And in a funny way, I felt related to her. Our parents' friendship — her mother, my father — linked us. And she was going to Cornell, in Ithaca, the town I'd escaped less than a year before.

Dear Anne,

Thanks for noticing me, and for trying to teach me the ways of the Cantonites. Sorry I was such a lousy pupil. I appreciate the effort, though. I really do. Best of luck in college next year. You'll love Ithaca. It gets cold, but it's beautiful.

Beatrice

p.s. Watch out for the gorges.

Anne and I traded yearbooks at lunchtime. "Someone asked to write in your book, so I let him," Anne said. "I didn't think you'd mind."

I flipped through my book until I found the page she meant: WALTER MINTON CARREY.

Walt's page was very traditional, dominated by the classic yearbook portrait, his unruly hair parted, combed, and flattened. His freckly face. His lopsided smile. He looked like a happy person.

Beneath the portrait, two smaller shots: Walt in full Canton lacrosse gear, mid-game, shooting a goal; and Walt on a bike as a ten-year-old with a younger girl who must have been his sister. He quoted Charles Dickens ("It was the best of times, it was the worst of times . . ." — so hokey) and, to my surprise, Emily Dickinson.

Much madness is divinest sense
To a discerning eye;

Much sense the starkest madness.
'T is the majority
In this, as all, prevails.
Assent, and you are sane;
Demur, — you're straightway dangerous,
And handled with a chain.

In the white space, in a boy's messy scrawl, he'd written,

To Beatrice — the cutest girl in school!
I've had a crush on you since the beginning of the year. Maybe
you could tell. (You should have — I asked you to the prom!
Duh!) You seemed like you had other things on your mind. That's
okay. I'm sorry I didn't get a chance to know you better, but the
year's not over yet. There's still time. I'll be around all summer. No
pressure, I just think you're cool.
Walt

I smiled. I felt happy and sad at the same time. I guess I did have
other things on my mind. Why wasn't Walt ever on my mind? I
didn't know. He just wasn't.

Jonah hardly came to school anymore, and when he did, he kept
his distance. He drifted around like a phantom, there but not there.
He cut Assembly every morning. It was the end of the year. No one
teased him or called him a g-g-g-ghost, even though he was more
ghostly than ever. No teacher bothered to call on him. What did it
matter now?

I called to see how he was, but he rarely answered the phone,
and when he did, he was morose and untalkative. I left messages —
Want to go to Carmichael's for a beer? Want to go downtown for a
movie? Want to come over to my house and just sit? — but they

went unanswered. I listened for him on the Night Light Show every night, all night long, but Ghost Boy never phoned in.

One morning I caught him at his locker. I'd decided to ask him to sign my yearbook, even though I knew he'd probably hate the idea. I didn't care; I'd be brave and ask, anyway. If Anne and Walt were going to be in there, I wanted Jonah too, for at least a little sense of what my life at Canton had really been like.

I started to ask him but then the first bell rang. He shut his locker and turned to go.

"Jonah, wait," I said. "Please."

"Sorry. Calculus." He drifted down the hall toward his class. I watched him the whole way, but he never looked back.

So I left my yearbook in front of his locker, with a note. If someone stole it, so be it. The book meant nothing to me without Jonah in it.

Dear Jonah,

I would be honored if you would sign your yearbook page for me. You are the only person at Canton — or anywhere, really — that I care about at all. We've been through a lot together this year, and you are the closest friend (forgive the inadequate word, but we never came up with a substitute) I have ever had. I'm sure you think it's silly but I would be grateful if you would grant me this small token of our friendship.

Love,

B

I checked his locker between every class. My yearbook sat in front of it untouched. Then after lunch I found it resting against my locker. He'd turned my note over and written on the back, *Signed with an X.* I opened the book to Jonah's page. He'd drawn a big, fat, perfect *X* over it, right through his baby face. And that was all.

I came home from school that day to find Mom and Dad in the living room, talking quietly. They stood up when I walked in.

"Bea," Mom said. "We have something to tell you."

Ulp. That's never a good sentence to hear from your parents.

"Yeah?"

"I'm going to get an apartment," Dad said. "Near Hopkins."

I looked at Mom. "We've decided to live apart for a little while," she said. "Just to try it out."

I blinked, stunned. I couldn't believe this was happening. Dad looked sad, but Mom looked composed, calm. She was fully dressed, with shoes, makeup, and everything. Even pearls. After all these months of craziness, now she was normal? Or at least normal-ish? What was going on?

"I got a job," Mom said. "Finally. At the Walters Art Museum." Something about antiquities, slides, permissions, reproduction rights . . . I barely heard her. "So I'll be busy and more independent now."

"That's great," I said without enthusiasm.

Dad came over and hugged me. I wanted to be cold and mean. I wanted to be Robot Girl, but I couldn't. I hugged him back, hard, and tried not to cry.

"We'll have a swinging downtown bachelor pad," he told me. "You'll love it. You can come over any time you want. I'll only be a couple miles down the road. Okay?"

"Okay," I said. What choice did I have? I kept thinking, *Why do you always leave me alone with her?* But maybe she wouldn't be so hard to live with now, without him around.

They prodded me a little more about my feelings on the issue, as if that could change anything, and made more sunny predictions about how fun it would be to have two homes. Then Dad kissed me on the forehead and left.

Mom got brightly to her feet. "Well," she said, and I could almost hear her wiping the dirt from her hands, *now that's over* ... "guess I'll get dinner ready." She clopped into the kitchen in her sandals. I followed her, still dazed. She tugged at the chicken curtains. "These curtains are so ugly. What was I thinking? I'll have to make new ones right away. Blue gingham might be nice."

She opened the refrigerator and got to work on a salad. I watched her for a while. I felt like I was in a dream.

"Mom," I finally said. "Your marriage is ending. Why aren't you falling apart?"

"I don't know." She shrugged. "I'm just not." She washed a head of lettuce. "Maybe all that therapy is finally kicking in."

"Uh-huh." I wasn't convinced that therapy could "kick in" so suddenly.

"Or maybe I feel better having things decided, one way or the other, you know?" she said. "It was hard on me, the way your dad was always kind of halfway here and halfway not."

"Uh-huh."

"I think I was too dependent on him. But after he left, I realized, *Hey, I can live without him. It's not that hard or anything.*"

"Uh-huh."

"Also, Dr. Huang said the antidepressants are working better now. That might have something to do with my good mood."

"You think?" I was skeptical that even drugs could be so effective. Mostly I was just baffled.

"She said that once I feel strong on my own, I might want to let your Dad back in. I won't feel so smothered by him. Maybe."

"I guess that would be good." I really didn't know what to say.

"I think I'll make a soufflé," Mom said. "Would you like that?"

"You know how to make a soufflé?"

"Well, I can try, right?"

She made a cheese soufflé, and it turned out okay. Those antidepressants Dr. Huang gave her were some kind of miracle drug. I considered giving them a try, but I didn't think they'd work for me. I had no cause to be happy. I felt sad with good reason, and it wouldn't be right to mess with that feeling. I thought I ought to just stay sad for a while.

CHAPTER 24

Jonah called me on the telephone the Saturday before graduation. "This afternoon, five o'clock," he said.

I was so excited to hear his voice I could hardly speak. After days and days of ignoring me, here he was on the telephone, inviting me to his house. At last.

"It's a memorial service," Jonah said.

"I'll be there," I said.

Mr. Tate had picked up the urn of ashes and agreed to let Jonah keep it. Jonah decided to bury it in the backyard. It was probably illegal, but he didn't care. Mr. Tate wasn't invited to the service or even told about it.

Since Matthew's death the two of them lived in an icy détente, side by side in the same house, speaking only when necessary. Mr. Tate woke up early, left for the office, worked late, and came home after Jonah was in bed. Sometimes at night, Jonah saw his father pacing in the garden behind the house, his face like stone in the moonlight, hands gripped behind his back, alone with his grim thoughts.

The day of the memorial service was cloudy and muggy. Jonah led me into the dark old house. Oriental carpets covered highly polished floors. The heavy furniture seemed set in place as if by God, immovable, permanent as rock. The rooms were shadowy, yet everything gleamed.

"Want anything before we start?" Jonah asked.

"Do I want anything? Like what?"

"I don't know. A drink or something."

I did want an iced tea, but it didn't feel right to drink iced tea at a memorial service, even though he'd offered.

"No, I'm fine," I said.

"Come on then. Everything's ready."

He led me through the kitchen — a dowdy old kitchen, I now noticed — down the rickety wooden steps and into the backyard.

Near the stream that bordered the property, under a willow tree, a small hole had already been dug. Catso and the Evil Miss Frankenheimer, tiny but fierce, stood guard over the hole. Jonah carried the urn.

We bowed our heads and stared at the hole in silence for a few minutes. Jonah raised the urn over his head. He shook it at the sky, as if shaking a fist at the heavens.

Then he set the urn in the hole.

"I'm sorry for everything, Matthew," he said. "I tried to help you, but it was too late. It probably wouldn't have worked, anyway. It was a stupid idea. Working at a carnival. Running the rides. Baby stuff.

"Beatrice would have helped me, though. She would have loved you too. The two of us — the three of us — together . . ."

He glanced at me in implied apology. He didn't really think I hated Matthew. He hadn't meant those terrible words. I was forgiven for suggesting that life would go on. I forgave him back.

"If we ever meet again, I hereby give you permission to punch me in the face. You'll be able to punch hard, next time I see you. And dance like crazy. And tell a mean joke."

He turned to me. "Beatrice, do you have anything to add?"

I swallowed. It felt like time for a prayer. So I bowed my head and recited a few words from the Canton School hymn. It was the only prayer I really knew.

"I don't know if I remember this song right," I said, but somehow, magically, I did.

For lambs without a shepherd
For fish who rivers roam
For ships without a compass
We pray Thee bring them home.

For all of us are wanderers
Our hearts are full of holes
We pray Thee lead us homeward
Embrace Thy poor lost souls.

"Matthew Tate, you were loved."

"Thank you." Jonah gave me a nod. "Catso and the Evil Miss Frankenheimer will miss you, Matt. I'll take good care of them."

He picked up the shovel. He touched the urn one last time. He covered the hole with dirt.

He rolled a smooth stone over the wound in the ground. Then he picked up Catso and the Evil Miss Frankenheimer and carried them inside. I started to follow.

"I'm sorry, Beatrice. Thank you for coming. But we need to be alone now."

He left me in the yard. The kitchen door slapped shut behind him.

I stared at the door for a while. I guess I was hoping he'd see me and come back out. Finally, I walked around the side of the house to my car and drove downtown.

CHAPTER 25

For graduation, the girls wore long white dresses and the boys wore white dinner jackets with a red carnation pinned to the lapel. Each girl was paired with a boy based on height. I was paired with Harlan Zimmer. He reeked of pot.

"My mom made me take a shower this afternoon, but I refused to wash my hair," Harlan told me as we lined up at the top of the hill, waiting to march down and receive our diplomas.

"Why?" I asked.

"Shampoo is really bad for you," he said. "Besides, why should I graduate with cleaner hair than I usually have? Why should today be any different from a normal school day?"

"Well, you *are* wearing a white dinner jacket," I pointed out.

"Only because they made me," Harlan said. "Lockjaw said he would revoke my diploma if I didn't."

"The dinner jacket is definitely not an issue worth taking a stand on," I said.

"Secretly, I think the jacket's kind of cool," Harlan said. "Like James Bond."

He didn't look like the James Bond type, but you never know about people and their secret identities. In Harlan's mind, he might be a stoner 007.

"Sean Connery talks kind of like Lockjaw," Harlan added. "Ever shink about it?"

Jonah stood a few couples ahead of me in line, paired with AWAE. He hated AWAE on principle, the principle being that an acronym is not a good substitute for a real, proper name. I tried to catch his eye, but he wouldn't look at me.

The Homeland Brass Quintet played the Processional. We marched down the stone steps couple by couple, arm in arm, like a mass wedding. At the foot of the hill, in front of the auditorium, the parents and underclassmen awaited our arrival. We filed into our seats beside the podium and faced the audience.

Lockjaw spoke, then Mr. Meath (we'd voted him Teacher of the Year), then the Commencement Speaker, someone's aunt who was a published poet.

I watched the audience while the aunt read her inspiring yet amusing words. My parents sat together in the third row, as if they'd never split up. Next to Dad sat Caroline and Ed Sweeney. In the last seat of the last row, a man in a black suit and hat sat alone, stiff and grim-faced. Mr. Tate. He had come. Of course he had. His son was graduating from high school.

I peered down the line of seniors at Jonah. He stared straight into the audience, not looking at his father, not looking at anyone. He seemed to be off somewhere far away. We hadn't spoken since Matthew's memorial. I'd hoped that including me in the service meant we could start working our way back to friendship, but he still avoided me. He'd just wanted a witness, I guessed. I didn't know.

I missed him desperately, even though he'd said he hated me, even though his anger — the rampage at his house, the X through his yearbook page, the cruel way he withdrew from everyone — scared me. I didn't care if he wasn't my boyfriend, or even my friend. He was my Jonah. I felt more alone without him now than I'd ever felt before I met him. My life had a hole in it.

The speeches finished and Lockjaw began to call out our names. We stood up one by one, walked to the podium, shook Lockjaw's hand, received our diplomas, and sat down again. That was it. Graduation.

The post-graduation party was held at Anne Sweeney's house. My parents stopped by for a little while. They stayed in the living room, where the small parents' party took place, holding hands as if they were on a date. Maybe Dr. Huang was right: Mom had to drive Dad away before she could start liking him again. Whatever. Their behavior baffled me but it was my graduation — my milestone, not theirs — and I didn't want to think about them.

In the backyard, where the seniors' party sedately raged, I found Jonah standing alone next to the cake.

"I saw your father," I said.

"Yeah."

"Did he say anything to you?"

"He shook my hand and said, 'Well done.' Then he went home."

"Want to get out of here?" I said. "We could go down to Carmichael's and grab a beer."

"No, thanks," Jonah said. "I think I'll just go home."

He turned away from me, but I clutched his arm to stop him.

"Hey," I said. "What about me?"

"What about you?"

I let go of him, feeling awkward.

"I'm sad that Matthew died," I whispered. "But I'm still here. I'm still your friend, just like before."

His expression didn't change. He said nothing. I pressed on.

"Jonah, don't you remember all the things we did this year? The radio? The Night Lights? Your birthday, the ocean and all our plans . . ."

"No," Jonah said.

"We went to the Christmas luncheon together and met Myrna and Larry and Herb. . . . You waited for me on New Year's Eve, out on my porch in the cold for hours. You gave me a boardwalk prom, with a tiara and a corsage and everything. . . ."

His face didn't move. I hardly recognized it. The features were the same but the person behind the skin had changed. My heart cracked, a sharp pain.

"That couldn't have been me," he said.

"It was you," I said. "It was you and me, both of us, together. We can have more happy times. We can spend the rest of our lives together if we want to. . . ." Even as I spoke, I saw the distance growing between us. He was sliding away from me. "Or not, whatever. Just don't tell me it wasn't real." I felt like crying but my whole body was wrung dry. "I miss you. Why won't you let me back in?"

His face remained immobile, but I thought I saw a flicker in his eyes — the icy gray melted to milky blue in a flash, then froze up again.

"Let you back in where?" he said.

Then he walked away, dissolving into the dusk. How you say *Go to Hell* in Ghost. I stood nailed in place. Gradually I became aware of my own breathing, in, out, in, out, and came back to the world.

Someone tapped my shoulder. I turned around.

"Hey! We did it! We're done!"

"Hey, Walt." His timing had never been great.

And, as usual, he didn't seem to notice. "Aren't you excited?" he asked gleefully. "No more school!"

"Well, there's college."

"Sure, but that's different." He must have finally sensed my sour mood, because he cooled the enthusiasm. "What's wrong? Is something up with Jonah?"

"Yeah, I guess so," I said.

"Mind if I ask what?"

"He's just . . . sad," I said.

"He's been sad since the third grade," Walt said. "But he did seem a little happier this year. After you came."

I tried to remember how Jonah seemed when I first met him. Sad wasn't quite right. Vacant was closer. Absent. Was that the same thing as sad?

"Well, he's sad again," I said. "And I don't know how to make him feel better."

"Maybe he needs some time to himself."

I shook my head. "That's all he ever has. Time to himself."

"What about you?" Walt said. "Don't you ever need anything?"

I did. I needed a lot of things. A lot of things that I didn't have and hadn't thought about in a long time.

That night I stayed out until three. A bunch of us sneaked over to the Roland Park Pool, jumped the fence, and went skinny-dipping. Walt drove me home, both of us soaking wet, and I let him kiss me.

Then I went inside, fell onto my bed, and turned on the radio.

Kreplax:

I want to remind everybody that the Twelfth Annual Powwow is this weekend, off Waterview Avenue — just look for the long lines of parked cars. No cops allowed!

Herb:

Are you racing this year?

Kreplax:

I'm racing my supercanoe, the *Time Viking*. It's the boat to beat. Come down to watch the race and say goodbye. After I pick up my Wildflower

Wreath of Victory and a few nitrous balloons for the road, I'll be paddling the *Viking* out of there.

Herb:
Where are you going?

Kreplax:
Back to the future, Herb. You're all welcome to visit me, if you can figure out how to get there. I'll just paddle out over the horizon and *bloop*! I'll be gone.

Herb:
Thanks, Kreplax. Hope you make it this time. Next caller, you're on the air.

Larry:
This song is in honor of the departure of the great time traveler, Kreplax.

[A needle drops on a record. A song plays: the Fifth Dimension's "One Less Bell to Answer."]

Larry:
[singing along] "One less man to pick up after, I should be happy . . ."

The phone rang. It was four-thirty A.M. I turned down the radio, my heart happily speeding. It had to be Jonah.

"Let's run away together," he said.

He was back!

"You mean, to Ocean City?" I said.

"No, I mean for real. Let's run off to someplace far away, someplace we've never been before, a place we know nothing about, where they know nothing about us."

"Okay. I'll start packing."

There was a silence on his end. Then he said, "I've got to get out of here."

"We'll be gone soon. We just have to make it through the summer. We'll drive up to New York together. I have to live in a dorm next year, but after that we can get an apartment. Everything will be different up there —"

"Bea, I'm not going to SVA."

He'd never said . . . but how could he not go?

"I'm not ready for more school right now. I need a year off. To think about stuff."

"No," I said. "You think too much already. You don't need to think about Matthew anymore. Think about yourself. Think about art. You need a distraction."

"Nothing can distract me. That's the trouble."

"Just come to New York with me. You don't have to go to school. You could get a job, something easy, and just hang out. You can live in my dorm room if you want. I'll hide you under the bed —"

"You don't understand. It's too much."

"I'll sneak you food from the cafeteria —"

"That's not what I mean." In the background, his radio echoed mine. "This was a mistake. I shouldn't have called you —"

"No! You snapped out of your trance. I'm so happy you called me."

"It's more than a trance," Jonah said. "The whole world is pressing in on me, like a weight on my chest, slowly pushing me down and down. And there's nothing between me and this weight but my flimsy skin. It's not enough. It won't protect me. It doesn't keep anything out. The outside will keep pressing in until my ribs are crushed, and then my organs, my heart and liver and stomach. . . ."

"Jonah —"

"It hurts, Bea. It really hurts."

The crack in my heart ached, a dull throb, in sympathy.

"I know," I said. "But it can't hurt forever. Eventually you'll feel better, and we'll have fun again."

"It can hurt forever. That's what I'm afraid of."

"Jonah, stop it. I'll take care of you. I'll do whatever you need to make you feel better."

His voice was faint. "I know you would, Bea."

The radio echoed again. *YOU'RE ON THE AIRyou're on the air.* Jonah could be calling from anywhere: from overseas, from Europe or Asia, from Iceland, from far away.

"Want to go to Powwow next Sunday?" I said. "Kreplax's canoe is ready. After he wins, he's going to paddle it into the future. Or something."

"I don't know —"

"It will make us both feel better," I said. "Come on. Take me to Powwow. I've been looking forward to it all year."

"All right, Bea. We'll go to Powwow."

"Pick me up at noon?"

"Yeah."

We hung up. The radio transmitted clearly now, the echo gone.

That week was oppressively muggy for June: ninety every day, overcast, humid. The pinkish-green air promised rain that never came. Moisture hung in the atmosphere, weighing down on us. We were living inside a cloud.

In spite of the heat, the new, perky Mom persisted. She installed air conditioners downstairs and in our bedrooms. The guest room remained stifling, but she didn't use it much anymore. "If we ever have a guest," she said, "they'll just have to suffer."

"Or we could limit guests to wintertime," I said. "No summer guests allowed."

"Good idea," she said. "Want to go to the pool?" At last she had a place to wear her polka-dot bikini. Fun Mom was back. Fun Beatrice, however, was in a coma. I resented Mom. I didn't think she should be enjoying separation from Dad so much. And I still didn't understand what was going on between them. Now *I* was the one who had changed. I didn't depend on Mom anymore. I had Jonah. Sort of.

"You need to find a summer job at some point, kiddo," Dad said. "I'm not rushing you or anything."

"I will," I said, though I'd made no efforts at all to find a job. We were having pasta primavera for dinner at the bachelor pad, a spacious two-bedroom apartment on the top floor of the Broadview, right across from the Hopkins campus. The Broadview was known as a blue-hair building because most of the tenants were old ladies. I liked the bachelor pad — Dad had tried to make it feel modern and less blue-hairy — but I'd yet to spend the night in the room Dad kept for me, though he'd invited me many times. It felt weird, and I still had a reflexive anxiety about leaving Mom alone, even though she didn't seem to mind.

Mom slept over at Dad's a few times, though, leaving me home alone with no qualms at all.

"You want to go to a movie tonight?" Dad asked. "They're showing *Vertigo* on campus."

"Okay," I said.

"Why don't we call your mother and see if she wants to come too?"

I shrugged. I couldn't remember the last time the three of us had gone to a movie together.

"Do you know if she's busy tonight?" Dad asked.

"No idea," I said.

Turned out she had a tai chi class, but she could meet us after the movie for dessert if we wanted. "Great!" Dad said.

I felt like I was dating my own parents.

"Why won't you call Walt back?" Anne asked me. We were standing in line at the pool snack bar, waiting for snowballs. "He really likes you."

"I know —"

"And look at his bod! You can't tell so much when he's wearing clothes, but whoa. He's skinny, but he's *cut*."

Walt did look good in a bathing suit, though he seemed unaware of it.

"I've had a lot on my mind," I said.

That wasn't true. I had very little on my mind. Mostly I just felt limp, lazy, and unmotivated. And anxious. Swimming through clouds. Dad said it was the weather, that we had to get used to it. I didn't see how anyone could ever get used to such sticky air, like a thicket of cobwebs clinging to my skin.

"Bea, he's a really good guy," Anne said. "Not like Garber."

Tom Garber, apparently trying to revisit every old girlfriend before he left for college, had dumped Anne for Carter Blessing, who'd let him feel her up three times in eighth grade.

"I don't hold it against him," Anne said. "Tom's Tom. We're still friends. I'm just saying, Walt's different."

"I'll say hi to him," I said. "I do like him. I just . . . I don't know."

I felt like you could open a door in my hollow, tin chest — just flip it open, easy — and see my heart throbbing, raw and bloody and sore. You could even reach in and squish it if you wanted to. I didn't want anyone getting close enough to open that door and see that mess.

We had reached the front of the line. "Get a cherry snowball," Anne advised. "It turns your lips red. Like lipstick."

"I was going to get a blue one," I said.

"Two cherry snowballs," Anne told the boy behind the counter.

He gave us two paper cones filled with red ice. "Take a bite, then go say hi to Walt," Anne said. "I'm going to bug you all afternoon until you do it."

I took my cherry snowball to Walt's towel. "Want some?" I said.

"Thanks." He spooned out a dripping chunk of ice. I sat down on the grass.

"What are you doing this summer?" I asked.

"Working at the *Sun*. I got an internship on the sports desk."

"That sounds like fun."

"Yeah. How about you?"

"I don't know yet. I'd like to take an internship, but I need to earn some money."

"Me too. I'm mowing lawns on weekends for extra cash."

I nodded.

"How about at night?" he said. "What kind of stuff do you do?"

"Nothing much. Read. Listen to the radio."

"The ball game?"

I laughed. I was so not an Orioles fan. "No, the Night Lights. Just this crazy weird talk show. It comes on late."

"Maybe we could catch a movie one night," he said. "Get out of the heat for a couple of hours."

"Sounds good," I said.

"So I'll call you?"

"Okay."

"Do you promise to come to the phone?"

"If I'm home," I said.

"Will you call me back if you're not home?"

"I will," I said. "I'm sorry I didn't call you back before. It's nothing personal."

"You're on probation until I actually get you on the phone," Walt said.

"That's fair," I said.

"Or you could call me. But maybe that's expecting too much."

"Call me," I said. "I'll be good."

I went back to my lounge chair. Anne sat up on her towel and gave me a thumbs-up sign. My snowball had turned to red water.

"I like that boy Walt," Mom said from her chair.

"I know you do," I said.

"Jonah always struck me as kind of, I don't know, *insubstantial*."

"You're wrong," I said. "He has substance. It just flickers off and on."

"Reminds me of somebody else we both know," Mom said. I think she was talking about Dad but, frankly, it could have been anybody.

CHAPTER 26

The weather broke on Sunday. Thunderstorms had swept through during the night, washing the pinkish-green gunk out of the air. By noon it was clear and sunny, the perfect day for Powwow. I put on my bathing suit under a red thrift-store dress and sat on the front porch, waiting for Gertie to chug around the corner.

Kids rode by on their bikes, ringing their bells. An ice-cream truck squealed past as if it were being chased by the police. Various non-Gertie cars whizzed by, their new engines lacking her heft and character.

But no Gertie. By twelve-thirty, Jonah was officially late.

I went inside and called his house. No answer.

Something wasn't right. Jonah and I were going to Powwow together. We were going to root for Kreplax's *Viking* canoe to win, and drink beer on an industrial beach in the harbor, surrounded by abandoned factories and urban decay and people who thought those things were beautiful. Maybe we'd buy a big balloon full of nitrous oxide and huff it, to see what it felt like. Look at the day! The weather had changed. There would never be a more perfect day for a powwow.

But where was Jonah?

*   *   *

At one o'clock I drove to Jonah's house. Gertie was parked in the driveway. So was Mr. Tate's old gray Mercedes.

I knocked on the front door. No one answered. I checked the driveway again. Somebody had to be home. The Tates weren't in the habit of going out for Sunday walks together.

I knocked once more, but no one came. I walked around to the back. The yard was empty. A little grass had started to grow around Matthew's stone.

I peered through the kitchen door and rapped on the window. I thought I saw something, a shadow, move through the hall past the kitchen. I tried the door. It opened. I stepped inside.

"Hello? Is anyone here?"

The floor creaked somewhere deep inside the house. "Hello? Jonah? Mr. Tate?"

I found him in the living room, sitting in a monstrous leather chair. All alone, hands folded on his lap, staring at his knees.

"Mr. Tate? I'm sorry I walked in, but I was looking for Jonah —"

"Jonah is gone," Mr. Tate said.

"Gone? What do you mean?"

"He's gone. He left. He's disappeared."

I still didn't understand.

"He took a few things and left. No note."

"Have you called the police?" I said.

"He's eighteen. He has every right to do as he pleases."

"But . . . I was supposed to see him today —"

"He's gone for good. He isn't coming back."

I stared at a clutch of family photos on the table. There was a picture of Mr. Tate with a multiracial group of children standing under a banner that said THE CHILDREN'S FUND THANKS YOU! There was a framed certificate from the Episcopal Charities of Baltimore thanking Mr. Tate for their largest gift ever.

I picked up a picture of Jonah, age three, his hair as white as dandelion fluff. I felt a pang and remembered what Jonah had said months earlier about Matthew and the phantom limb, the tugging he'd always feel.

"How do you know?" I said. "How do you know he isn't coming back?"

"I know my son. He's been planning this for a long time."

"Planning this?" I didn't understand. "If he's gone, we'll look for him. I'll look for him."

"There's no point in looking for him."

"We could call the TV stations and the newspapers. Put up posters with his picture on them and . . . and start a Find Jonah website — "

"There are no pictures. He took all the pictures."

"What do you mean?" I was holding a picture of Jonah in my hand.

"Look." Mr. Tate pushed a photo album at me. I turned the heavy cover and flipped through it. There were baby pictures encased in plastic, pictures of Jonah and Matthew as children, pictures of their penny-bright young mother. Then there were no more pictures of their mother, or of Matthew. Or of Jonah. After age eight, there were blank spots in the album where the pictures of Jonah used to be. Mr. Tate was still there, but Jonah aged ten, twelve, sixteen, eighteen . . . all gone.

And in the few family shots, the group portraits taken on birthdays or holidays, there were holes. Little round white holes. Mr. Tate and maybe an aunt or a friend stood next to someone who had no head. A thin, pale, headless boy. A round, empty circle, cut with a scalpel.

He'd cut his face out of every picture. Every picture in the house.

The yearbook, I thought. The baby picture on his page. The hats and funny glasses in the Yearbook Committee shot. And the Casper cartoon in our class photo.

He'd made himself impossible to find.

Mr. Tate was right. Jonah had planned this. But for how long? How long had he been planning to disappear?

When I thought about it later, I realized he'd been planning for at least a year. He volunteered to design the yearbook knowing it was the only way to keep his picture out of it. And then he found out Matthew was alive. Finding Matthew might have derailed Jonah's plan, but only temporarily. Losing Matthew a second time sealed the decision. Everything was in place. All Jonah had to do was fade away.

"I don't know what he thinks he's doing," Mr. Tate said. "He was there when those pictures were taken. Just because he cut his face out doesn't mean he wasn't there. It doesn't change anything."

I clutched at a thread of hope. *Maybe he left for the weekend. He went to Ocean City. He had to get away, but he'll be back. He left a message at my house, and Mom forgot to give it to me. . . .*

"You'd better be going now," Mr. Tate said. His eyes still stared ahead, unseeing. "There's nothing to be done."

I didn't believe it. I ran upstairs to Jonah's room. The Casper mask we'd bought in Ocean City hung from the doorknob. The room was a mess, the drawers and closet open and hemorrhaging clothes and papers, books and records and art supplies. I sat on the rumpled bed and looked around. There was no note. No message for me. No coded clue scrawled on his dresser mirror.

He was really gone.

I walked down the polished stairs, numb. I heard my feet hit the floor but I couldn't feel my weight on them. I had to trust that they were carrying me safely down. One hand gripped the banister — I saw it with my eyes but couldn't feel my palm glide along the wood. I felt nothing but a prickly tingle, my whole body shot full of Novocain.

Mr. Tate still sat in the big leather chair. He hadn't looked at me yet, not once. I felt free to stare at him because he refused to acknowledge me. His hands were shaking. The chair seemed to swallow him up, and I thought about how all alone he was, more alone than anyone I knew. Except for Jonah.

"Can I do anything for you?" I asked.

"No, thank you."

A clock ticked on the wall across the room.

"You may go now," he said.

But I couldn't leave yet. I saw Jonah in his face, and I couldn't leave him.

"Why did you do it?" I asked. "Why did you keep them apart?"

"Jonah was just a boy," Mr. Tate said. "I thought he'd forget."

"But he didn't," I said. "He couldn't."

"No, I suppose he couldn't. But I hoped that he would. I was trying to free him. I was trying to give him the life I would have wanted. Unencumbered. Matthew was a burden on Jonah. It warped him."

"He didn't think Matthew was a burden," I said.

"He was foolish."

"*You* were foolish."

He pressed his feet on the floor as if trying to rock the leather chair, but it wasn't a rocking chair. He pretended it was, anyway, and leaned forward and back, forward and back.

"You were foolish," I said again.

He stopped rocking. "I was foolish too."

I wiggled my fingers and toes. The feeling was spreading back into them, slowly.

"He's trying to hurt you," I said.

"He's trying to hurt us all," Mr. Tate said. "But it's too late. We're already wrecked."

CHAPTER 27

I didn't know what to do with myself. So I painted my room. Black.

"Oh, Bea," Mom said. "What are you doing to your room?"

"Decorating," I said. I climbed the ladder and daubed black paint on the ceiling.

"It's like a cave in here."

"It's eternal night."

She sat on my bed. "Do you feel like talking?"

"No."

"I don't care," Mom said. "I feel like talking."

My hand jerked, and paint dripped on the floor.

"Did Jonah say anything to you? Leave you any kind of explanation? How could he do it?"

She'd been asking this question since the day Jonah disappeared. I gave up trying to answer her. I didn't have an answer, anyway. I just wished she'd stop asking the question. It was like being stabbed in the neck with a safety pin, over and over again.

"Leave me alone," I said.

"No," Mom said. "I can't leave you alone. I won't. Your father won't, either." She reached toward the ladder and touched my bare foot. "You're not going to do that to us, are you, Bea?"

From above she looked as fragile as a leaf. Her bony hand reminded me of Mr. Tate. I climbed down the ladder and sat next to her on the bed.

"You're not going to leave us like Jonah did, with no word, no explanation?" she continued. "You're not going to break our hearts?"

I thought about it for a minute, remembering all those times I thought I saw that look in her eyes begging me to leave. And lots of times I did have an impulse to run away. I imagined boarding a Greyhound bus headed west, to somewhere, to nowhere, I didn't know where or care. Someplace bigger, wider, and more open than anyplace I'd ever lived. And I'd be free somehow . . . to do what I didn't know.

I remembered how, before I met Jonah, I used to dream of being dead. I didn't find that comforting anymore.

I told my mother I'd never do that, never abandon them, and when I heard myself say the words, I knew I meant them.

"Thank you," she said. She got up to leave. I climbed the ladder and started painting again.

"Won't it be depressing?" she said. "All this black?"

"I'm going to add stars," I said. "Glow-in-the-dark stars, all over."

That night, I crawled into bed and turned out the light. The room glowed with tiny stars. I closed my eyes and saw pinpricks of light against my eyelids. I opened them and saw the same thing. I felt like I was floating.

It was twelve-thirty. I turned on my radio and prepared to lose myself in Night Light Land.

Myrna:
Herb, did you see that story in the paper about

the boy who disappeared? Jonah Tate? That's our Ghost Boy!

Herb:
Is it? I thought the description sounded familiar, but there wasn't a picture, so —

Myrna:
The composite the cops drew was terrible. Looks nothing like him. The poor boy. I wonder what's become of dear Robot Girl.

Herb:
Perhaps she's listening. Maybe she'll call in and tell us what happened and how she's doing. I hope she's all right. I hope they both are.

Myrna:
Me too. What a cute couple! Such nice kids. I was looking forward to seeing them at my God Bless Elvis party in August.

Herb:
Maybe they'll be there. Maybe by then everything will be all right.

Myrna:
I sure hope so. If anyone hears any news, please call in.

Herb:

I'll second that. Nighty-night, Myrna. Next
caller, you're on the air.

Larry:

Herb, it's a good night for a Flying Carpet Ride,
don't you think? Moon's out. What do you say?

Herb:

Good idea, Larry. Pile on, everybody. Who's coming with us? Caller?

Myrna:

It's Myrna again. I know I just called but I want to
go out tonight. To look for Ghost Boy.

Herb:

All right. Who else is coming?

Dottie:

This is Dottie. I want to find that boy too.

Herb:

Welcome aboard, Dottie. We have room for one
more.

Caller:

[using high-pitched girl's voice] This is Helen Wheels.
I'd like to go look for that poor, sweet, darling boy.

Herb:

We're not in the mood for jokes tonight, Don.

Helen Wheels:

Who's Don? I told you, my name is Helen. Helen Wheels.

Herb:

If you insist. All right. Here we go. *[Ding-ding!]*

Larry:

The city looks extra beautiful tonight.

Myrna:

I see a skinny blond boy on a boat in the Inner Harbor. On one of those peddle boats!

Dottie:

Are we flying over Annapolis yet? I bet he's sleeping on somebody's sailboat, under a canvas cover.

Herb:

Over the Bay Bridge —

Myrna:

We're up so high now, I can't pick out any people.

Larry:

It's too dark. And we're so far away from the earth.

Helen Wheels:

La la la la la . . . I love flying high like this.

Myrna:
Let's fly low when we get to Ocean City. Runaways like to sleep under the boardwalk.

Larry:
I wish Robot Girl was with us. She could help us find him.

Myrna:
I hope she's okay. Call in and let us know you're all right, okay, honey?

Herb:
We're coming into Ocean City now. It's awfully crowded tonight —

Dottie:
Fly low, like Myrna said. Maybe he's playing skee-ball or miniature golf.

Myrna:
He's not wasting his time with that. He was a good boy. A smart boy. But I don't see him on the boardwalk. I don't think he's here.

Larry:
I don't think we'll find him. Even if he's down there somewhere, we could look right past him.

Herb:
Should we stop and see Morgan?

Myrna:

Herb, I'm just not in the mood.

Dottie:

Me neither.

Helen Wheels:

Me, either. *[Voice changes from high to low]* Don Berman! Don Berman! Don Berman!

Myrna:

Why do you always have to ruin everything, Don Berman?

Don Berman:

Don Berman!

I was crying.

The phone beside my bed gleamed in the light from the window. I stared at it. Watched it. Willed it to ring.

What if I dialed Jonah's number and he answered? Wouldn't that be funny? Maybe I'd dreamed this whole thing. He hadn't gone anywhere. He was still in his bedroom, in his house on the other side of school, listening to the radio like always.

I reached for the phone and dialed his number. I listened to it ring. It rang on and on. I imagined the phone crying out in his empty room.

I didn't count the rings, but it felt like hundreds. Could Mr. Tate hear them echoing through his house? Was I torturing him? Making him scream in frustration, pressing his hands to his ears to block out the noise?

If he wanted to make the ringing stop, all he had to do was pick up.

Maybe he had unplugged Jonah's phone. Maybe he couldn't hear the ringing at all.

I hugged the receiver to my chest and let it ring. *Ring, ring, ring . . .* He wasn't there. He wouldn't answer. *Face it,* I told myself. *Just face it.*

I dropped the receiver in its cradle and turned up the volume on my radio, turned it up loud.

The next morning, someone knocked on the front screen door. Mom was in the kitchen making ratatouille.

"Bea, can you get that?"

I went to the door. It was Walt.

"Hey," he said. The screen blurred his face. "How are you doing?"

"Okay."

"Um, can I come in for a second?"

I glanced back at the kitchen. Steam puffed out of a pot on the stove. "I'll come out."

We sat on the porch swing. "You haven't been to the pool lately," Walt said. "I wanted to see if you were okay."

"Here I am. I'm okay."

"You broke your promise. About returning my calls."

Mom kept telling me Walt had called, and I told myself to call him back. But I couldn't keep that thought in my head. I couldn't keep anything in mind for long. Jonah crowded everything out.

"I know. I'm sorry."

"I don't blame you, though. I mean, stuff came up, right?"

"Right."

"I'm sorry about Jonah."

"Me too."

"I wanted to tell you something. I haven't been able to sleep much. It's funny, because usually I'm asleep before my head hits the pillow. But not lately. So I started listening to that radio show you told me about —"

"The Night Lights?"

"Yeah. I heard them talking about Ghost Boy and Robot Girl, and looking for him on that Flying Carpet thing. And they said Ghost Boy was Jonah. So Robot Girl . . . it's kind of a funny show, isn't it?"

"Yeah."

"I like it, though. The only bad thing is, it keeps me up half the night listening and then I'm tired at work the next day. But I can't stop."

"I'm the same way."

He reached for my hand. His felt warm and dry.

"I'm always looking for him," Walt said. "Isn't that weird? I wasn't even friends with him or anything, really. Not like you. But I still find myself, like when I'm riding the bus down-town, scanning all the faces on the streets, thinking, *Is that him? Is that him?* Do you do that?" He paused. "You must do that."

"I do. I don't want to. I can't help it."

I looked out at the yard, at the street. Someone had tossed a pair of sneakers over the telephone wire. They dangled in the air, abandoned and unreachable. I wondered how long they'd been there.

"Walt," I said. "Let's go downtown tonight. Want to? I know a place you might like."

His smile was a jolt, a jump start. My pulse quickened a bit. Walt was a boy who knew how to be happy.

"I'm up for anything," he said.

I smiled. Up for Anything. I wanted to be Up for Anything.

"I could learn a thing or two from you," I said.

"I could learn a thing or two from you too," Walt said. "I've always thought so."

RY FEBRUARY MARCH APRIL MAY JUNE JULY

CHAPTER 28

I imagine Jonah alone in his room, on his bed, staring at the ceiling. Matthew is dead. Jonah has buried him. School is over. The long hot summer stretches before him like a desert. Nothing to do but go to silly boat races and dusty bookstores. Art school beckons, but Jonah is immune to its call. He doesn't need to go to school to make art. He doesn't want to paint or draw anymore, anyway. Art has lost its meaning. Everything has. He's incomplete, and he can never be whole again.

And so he begins to float, weightless, up toward the ceiling. There's nothing in his family or home, nothing in the whole city of Baltimore, to ground him. A mere girl, one single friend, is not enough to tether him here. How can he stay in that house? Those who love only half of him do not love him at all.

His flesh drops away from his skeleton; his spirit, uncaged from his bones, flies right through the ceiling, through the roof, past the ancient elms and into the sky, the cold ether, where it fades and disappears, lost to the warm, human world forever.

I still listened, hoping.

Kreplax:

I think I know what happened to him. I always got an eerie vibe from him, you know? And now I understand — he was from the future too. Like me, only from a different time thread, even further ahead, deeper into the future than I've been. And he went back. It's the only explanation.

Herb:

I thought you'd left for the future yourself.

Kreplax:

I did, but I came back. I like it here too much. You can't stay away from your own time for long. It warps you. It gets harder and harder to go back. I'm afraid all this time travel is taking a toll on my soul. Once I felt this whoosh, like something flew out of my body. Do you think I lost my soul, Herb?

Herb:

I don't know. Do you feel different?

Kreplax:

Not really.

Herb:

Do you feel . . . evil?

Kreplax:

No, not evil. Just kind of vacuumed-out.

Herb:

I don't know, Kreplax. I don't think you lost your soul.

Kreplax:

I did, Herb. Why don't you ever believe me?

Herb:

[Music] Nighty-night, Kreplax. Next caller, you're on the air.

Caller:

Hello. My name is Casper.

Herb:

Welcome, Casper. First-time caller?

Casper:

I have a message for someone. She knows who she is. I hope she's listening. I want her to know . . . I left something for her. She can find it in a box behind Iceland. She'll understand. I want her to know I'm okay. I'm always thinking about her. I'm sorry if I hurt her. I love her. But I'm never coming back.

Herb:

I hope your friend is listening, Casper, and gets your message.

Casper:

She's a faithful listener. Also, I wanted to tell Kreplax that I believe him. About losing his soul.

And I wanted to ask him: Do you ever get
used to it?

Herb:
Okay, Casper. Nighty-night.

Casper:
Nighty-night.

The sign on the door of Carmichael's Book Shop said they
opened at noon. I got there at five to twelve. The gray, potbellied
man arrived at twelve forty-five.

"I thought you opened at noon," I said.

"It's a target," the man said. He unlocked the door. I went
inside. The musty smell made me sneeze.

"Looking for something in particular?" the man said.

"I know what I'm looking for." I walked to the back and found
Dreaming of Iceland. Stashed behind it was the hidden treasure
Jonah and I had wished for on his birthday — a cigar box wrapped
in newspaper.

I put the Iceland book back, in case Jonah ever wanted to leave
me another message. I slipped the cigar box into my bag. Then I
went to the used record section and picked out a copy of Engelbert
Humperdinck's *A Man Without Love*.

"I'll take this, please." I placed the record on the counter.

The man lit a cigarette. "You waited all morning to buy Engelbert
Humperdinck?"

"I have to have it."

"One dollar."

I paid him and left the store. It was Saturday and the downtown
streets were quiet. The sun blazed on the sidewalk, bleaching color
from everything it touched.

I sat on the bookstore stoop and unwrapped the box. Inside was a toy tiger. Catso. And half of the strip of photos Jonah and I took of ourselves in Ocean City. Two shots, including the last picture, the shot of Jonah without his mask.

I kept two and gave you two, his note said. *You are the only person IN THE UNIVERSE who has a recognizable picture of me now. I expect you to take that responsibility seriously AND NOT ABUSE IT. You know what I mean. Do not give or show this picture to anyone. It is for you alone. If you use this photo to track me down I will never speak to you again.*

I laughed. What difference would that make? He wasn't speaking to me as it was.

I will curse you and you'll be doomed to walk the earth alone, like me. I sent this picture to you, because you are the only person I want to remember me. I'll keep the other half, so I can remember you. I don't need a picture, though. I'll never forget you, Bea.

I'm sorry if I hurt you. It just had to be this way. I can't explain it.

Take good care of Catso. He's yours now. I've got the Evil Miss Frankenheimer with me. Perhaps one day they will sword-fight again. But don't look for me, Bea. I'd only drag you down.

J

LY AUGUST SEPTEMBER OCTOBER

CHAPTER 29

I'm in Poughkeepsie now, in my first semester at Vassar. It's October. When I got here, I checked with SVA to see if a Jonah Tate had registered. I even checked under Matthew Tate, and Casper.

He wasn't there. I was foolish to think he would be.

I miss the Night Lights. All summer long I listened to the show, every single minute of it, curled up with Catso, hoping Jonah would call in again. Maybe he'd disguise his voice. Sometimes, in the first few seconds of a strange call, my pulse would race . . . but I'd soon realize it was only Don Berman.

I never called in again. As long as Ghost Boy was gone, so was Robot Girl.

My parents are having a second wedding at Christmastime, renewing their vows. Fast work, Dr. Huang. The date is on the opposite end of the calendar from their original wedding day in June. Mom thinks that means their marriage will now be the opposite of before, in a good way. After their second honeymoon, Dad will move back in. I hope Mom doesn't go all kablooey again. But it's their marriage, their lives. They can screw them up if they want to, I guess.

Walt goes to Drew, in New Jersey, and sometimes on weekends we meet in the city to prowl the East Village. He's a funny guy. Persistent. Dogged and puppyish, qualities I'm learning to appreciate. He's gradually wearing down my resistance. I keep wishing, reflexively, for a glimpse of the future, so I'll know what to do. But I don't kid myself. I have to feel my way forward blindly. I try not to be afraid. Even if you know what's coming, you're never prepared for how it feels.

I still look for Jonah everywhere.

Sometimes, I think I see him walking down the street. Or I see a car that looks like Gertie. But it's never him. Then I wonder, *Could he look different? Completely different, plastic surgery different?* I wouldn't put it past him. A guy who went to so much trouble to wipe his image off the face of the earth is capable of anything.

That means, almost anyone could be him. The receptionist at the dentist's office. The guy selling Slurpees at the 7-Eleven. The weatherman on the local news. The boy who mows the lawn. The bachelor who moved in next door to my father. The girl in my dorm who says she's from Indiana.

Anybody.

He's probably nowhere near here. Not in New York, not in Baltimore. He's miles away, in Paris, LA, Tokyo, Berlin. . . .

Maybe he's in Iceland, having his hair cut by the happiest person in the world. Hoping to figure out her secret.

I have to stop looking for him. He doesn't want to be found.

Someday, I tell myself, the memories will fade away. Catso will just be a toy. A lock of white hair won't make me jump. I'll stare at the picture of the boy in the Casper mask, struggling to remember why I loved him.

That's how I imagine it, anyway.

ACKNOWLEDGMENTS

I am indebted to many people for their help with this book: first, to my editor, David Levithan, the Maxwell Perkins of Young Adult publishing, as well as the calm center of its frenzied social whirl and one of its finest writers. To my smart, tireless, and beloved agent, Sarah Burnes, who has revived my flagging spirits countless times and is fun to celebrate with too. Also to her associate, Courtney Gatewood, whose early enthusiasm was much appreciated.

To my first readers, Elizabeth Mitchell, Rene Steinke, and Gregory Wilson, for their insight, attention, and tact. To Eric Crawford, M.D., and Willard Standiford, M.D., for advice and information about medicine, hospitals, hospices, and other aspects of care for disabled children. To my old friends Cameron Griffith and Chip Crosby for shining a little light into a shadowy corner of our shared past.

To John Standiford for introducing me to much-mourned Will Taylor's legendary radio program, *Over Fifty Overnight*, and to Ron Rosenbaum and Jennifer Hunt for leading me to my current late-night addiction, *Coast to Coast AM*. And, for their support in innumerable large and small ways, thanks to: Elise Broach, Bennett Madison, Betty Standiford, Jim Standiford, Kathleen Standiford, Will Standiford (he deserves double billing), Greg Wilson (so does he), Darcey Steinke, and Karen Yasinsky.